Prais

I AM GERMANY

"Gripping. Compelling. A boy's love of a girl—and her love of Germany and its centuries-old culture—survive the worst they could imagine. This is a completely absorbing tale of the heroic idealism of a young girl, Anna, set against others' fear and cowardice as her beloved Germany sinks into chaos in the 1930s. Having loved Anna deliriously as a boy, the narrator comes back to Germany in 1989 after the fall of the Berlin Wall to find her chastened by history but still vibrantly alive. Readers of *I Am Germany* will better understand how ordinary Germans dealt with the Nazis' control of their thoughts, beliefs, and actions. A book both disturbing and uplifting, it reveals the power of love and culture to endure despite seemingly insurmountable obstacles."

—Thomas R. Smith, PhD, retired professor of English,
Penn State University

"In this hauntingly beautiful novel, Michael Witt explores the scars that war, violence, and cruelty leave not only on individuals but on the soul of an entire nation. More importantly, he shows how those scars might one day heal. This is an unforgettable story of heartbreak . . . and hope."

—Anita Mumm, editor and publishing consultant,
Mumm's the Word Editorial Services

"Because of Michael Witt's new novel, *I Am Germany*, I had to go see Berlin for myself. Witt shakes awake little-known facets of WWII history through daring and heartfelt storytelling, capturing a forgotten story of German culture and the Nazi euthanasia of children. Between its vivid descriptions and believable, sometimes cantankerous characters, the story gets deeply inside you . . . and doesn't let go."

—Stuart Horwitz, author, award-winning essayist and poet, editor, and founder of Book Architecture

I am Germany

by Michael Witt

ISBN 978-1-64663-775-1

This is a work of fiction. All the characters in this book are fictitious, and any resemblance to actual persons, living or dead, is purely coincidental. The names, incidents, dialogue, and opinions expressed are products of the author's imagination and are not to be construed as real.

Published by

köehlerbooks™

3705 Shore Drive
Virginia Beach, VA 23455
800-435-4811
www.koehlerbooks.com

I AM
GERMANY

Michael Witt

VIRGINIA BEACH
CAPE CHARLES

For the real Rosalie Blume

1

I was sunken in my Laz-Y-Boy recliner that night, haunted by the ghost of Thanksgiving, only two weeks away. My Helen had passed the year before, leaving behind only half of us. This would be the second Thanksgiving in a row I would not wake up to the scent of a roasting turkey being basted by her in that Pilgrim apron. I sank to the bottom when it struck me that this would be only the second Thanksgiving without her in the forty-two years since she and I bought the house. My mending heart broke again. I was back to where I started a year and a half ago on the day I buried Helen.

After she died, I exiled myself from this world, leaving me alive but nowhere. I kept the blinds down in the house and in my life. I stopped going to the dentist and the American Legion. I quit the good habit of watching the nightly news, caring to know nothing about nothing. So I flipped on the television that evening and searched for an old movie, hoping it would take me to a different place.

A scene on NBC finally grabbed me. Having vacationed with Helen in Greece once, I reckoned the scene had been filmed at night in front of the Acropolis in Athens—with thousands of people shouting, pumping their fists, riding up on people's backs. A few wielded sledgehammers. A fire hose was spraying. It seemed mindless, so I had my entertainment for the evening.

But less than a minute later I found myself back in the here and now when I saw another ghost, this one of my forgotten childhood. A word was graffitied on a tall concrete wall: *ACHTUNG!* Having left Nazi Germany for Iowa shortly before the war, at age sixteen, I knew all too well that it meant *"BEWARE!"* Instantly, I felt shame. As a boy in Germany, I had painted that word in red on a Jewish family's front door. All my adult life, though, I have despised that word. There is something almost macabre about it, more so when garbed in red and embellished with an exclamation point.

As I glowered at that appalling word on the TV, it occurred to me that if this had been a Hollywood set, the word probably would have been painted in English. Suddenly I remembered that the massive gateway to the Acropolis was crumbling at the top. So this was no movie. This was no cameo appearance by Tom Brokaw. This was life at its most real. The mammoth structure in the background was the Brandenburg Gate in Berlin. The monstrosity in front of the gate, the Berlin Wall, was being assaulted before my eyes. Hammered, battered, even kicked by people whose souls had been shackled behind it. Certainly, I feared, they were at risk of being shot by the East German police.

But then Mr. Brokaw announced that this was a *celebration*, not some terrible riot. He noted, with a bit more emotion than a famous national news anchor is supposed to show, that the East German government had declared earlier that day that its citizens could walk through any opening in the Wall and into the free West without fear of being arrested or gunned down. A miracle. Mercy at long last granted. It was then that I noticed the policemen were just standing there with their pistols holstered, allowing it all to become history, some even smiling as if these elated people had just brought home the World Cup for the first time in fifty years.

Then I saw something strange, very otherworldly. I'd forgotten how a man's heart can suddenly race to an extraordinary woman the moment he sets eyes on her. A teenaged girl started dancing up on the Wall. She was the spitting image of the girl who lived next door to me in Germany— Anna Himmel, my first love, though she never knew it. The slender figure. The thin nose, seraph lips, and angelic movements. The chin-length blond hair styled in a "bowl" or "skater's" cut. As the girl danced, she cried out something that couldn't be heard over the mass commotion. I'm no expert lip reader, but I swear she shouted, "Remember me after all these years?"

As if breaching a dam, the dancing girl's figure ripped out more memories of my German boyhood in the 1920s and '30s, flooding my mind. And while none of those memories began with Anna Himmel, they all ended with her. She was a singular but peculiar girl, a *sui generis*, literally one of a kind. To me as a boy, Anna had been more than a child-prodigy violinist and the daughter of the owner of Germany's most famous violin company. Much more. She was a human goddess who made a concert debut at age twelve. And in my crazed adolescent mind, she had been a *concept*. I had been so insanely in love with her that I actually thought she was German high art and culture. Not a mere part of that world, inaccessible to me, but the very embodiment of it.

But then the dancing girl vanished, and I could only watch the continued shattering of that damned Wall. It should have been a joyous event, but the shame of who I had been as a German in the pre-war Nazi era shoved aside shimmering thoughts of Anna, pushing me down underwater again. To keep myself from drowning in shame, I held on tight to the present moment: November 9, 1989.

But that only took me back to the dark political history that built the Wall. To how the prevailing war powers met in 1945 at the end of the conflagration in order to manufacture the future. To how they divided up Europe the way children might divide up a pot of candy. How the areas to the east would be dominated by the Communist Soviet Union while those to the west would be free and democratic. Those people dancing and hollering on TV were the children and grandchildren of people who, by pure cosmic chance, lived in the eastern half of Germany at the end of the war. By default, their ancestors became East Germans in 1949 when the two Germanys were officially carved out of the broken fatherland. And in 1961, after more than two million repressed East Germans had escaped to freedom, the Communists all but imprisoned the remaining people by erecting what would be unassumingly called the Berlin Wall. The thing might more truthfully have been named the "Berlin Prison Gate." Those innocent people on TV were exhilarated by a luxury I take as much for granted as the air I breathe—freedom.

I tried to stay in my head, but the crowd seemed to reach through the television screen and pull me into them. I think they wanted me to understand more than what I could plainly see from a third of the way around the globe. They wanted me to know that they mattered. I had never had dreams on their behalf, never dreamed that the Wall could fall during their lifetimes. For me, thinking about East Germans becoming free had always been like thinking about a person walking on Mars someday in the distant future. Or maybe never.

I nailed my floating mind down to my easy chair in America. That's when my stomach knotted. I had just eaten a potentially frightening thought: *Berlin and the two Germanys might be reunited someday soon.* For me, the unification jury was still out. The two sides had been opposite their counterparts for forty years. You mix black with white, the best you can hope for is gray. I watched a young man with a shaved head and a swastika painted on his sweatshirt dance up on the Wall where the girl had danced earlier. Yin and yang, my Asian friends might say—but how could the two ever join? I imagined the skinhead howling the same words the girl had earlier, but with a two-word predicate: "*Achtung*, Germany. Remember me after all these years?"

So, while I was happy for the good people on TV, I was not necessarily happy for the world. Could another Nazi Germany happen again in this modern age? I had been hiding from that very question for more than half a century.

In bed that night, I spiraled lower, unable to sleep, the TV images flooding my consciousness. In the wee hours of the morning before dawn, I arrived at a theory on how I had done what no one ever tries to do—bury memories of a happy childhood. There I was, age sixteen and in the heartland of America for only two months, now out of the reach of what my mother called "growing terror in the fatherland." My parents, both self-celebrated anti-Nazis, had forbidden the speaking of German in our new house. But at the supper table one night, I innocently slipped up without thinking and said to my father, "Mir bitte das salz" (Please pass the salt).

It was a bad mistake, very bad. His blue eyes flashed fiery orange. He was highly educated, always chose his words carefully, was kind by nature, and had never raised his voice or hand to me. He did something I never thought possible, something he would never do again: he struck me in the face, drawing blood from my lip and nose, then screamed in broken English, "Speak German words never more! Never! Be ashamed you live in Germany in past, down to bottom of soul of you! And forget about zat crazy Anna!" I yelped and cowered under the table like an abused puppy.

So, my theory? I am as suspect of armchair psychologists as I am of Monday-morning quarterbacks, but the science of psychology might call it repression. I hid my German youth in the deep underground of my mind for a half century. I loved my father as much as a boy can, wanted him to be proud of me. So I buried my German existence there at that supper table. Down at the bottom of my soul. And worse, I banished all memories of Anna and what she meant to me and perhaps portended for Germany. Those who assume that happy childhoods and first loves are never forgotten are badly mistaken.

The howling wind outside vanished, and an idea overwhelmed me: *I will go to Germany for Christmas.* My second-favorite holiday, Thanksgiving, surely would be a bust, but staying here for Christmas, my very favorite, would be a self-punishment. It would be only the second in forty-two years, I wouldn't sing carols with Helen at the midnight church service, wouldn't give her a present, wouldn't pack the empty goose belly with raisin-and-pecan stuffing, and wouldn't have a long kiss with her under the mistletoe. Being without those joys would be like burying my Helen all over again for two years running. One had been one too many.

Going to Germany for Christmas would allow me not only to leave behind a memory-laden house but also to drift back to my boyhood in the *"land der dichter und denker"* ("land of poets and thinkers"). I had been a light thinker and a heavy doer all my life. I was seventy, and my frame was shrinking, but it is never too late to grow and become a serious thinker.

Of course, at present, now that I'm back to Iowa, I must put those reasons for going at the bottom of the list. I now understand that the predominant reason was to look up Anna. After all, I could have escaped my life for a week much less expensively by going to sunny Florida. The mind is a mysterious thing, a clouded labyrinth. I didn't quite know yet that I wanted to find Anna even if it was the last thing I ever did. I didn't know where she lived or even if she was still alive. It was like throwing a dart at a dartboard a hundred feet away.

***

I flew to West Berlin on December 17 and returned eight days later. What follows is a recounting of the time I spent there, including hearing a story that shook and altered me to the core. And tonight, a year later, as I make preparations to travel around Germany to tell a tragic story, it is still beyond me how a German social worker could take money he's saving for a new car, use it instead to buy birthday presents for his child, and a month later go take a new job throwing poison gas pellets down a shower room vent and then hauling the dead naked bodies to ovens to be burned at a death camp. I refuse to even try to understand it because I'm afraid what I might think. Serious thinking is not always a good thing.

2

oarding the jet in Des Moines should have been a happy, warm
moment, but I was chilled by the past. I sat in my seat, unable
to shake off the thought that this would be my first time in
Germany since the day I boarded the ship bound for New York. In the
gray-lit jet cabin, I envisioned a shiny ocean liner in all its glory in a harbor
in France in 1936, heard engines revving, and felt my young self's hope
that the ship would sink in the middle of the Atlantic like the *Titanic* so
that my mother would drown.

I shuddered and instantly managed to strike that memory of teenage
sociopathy. Then I tried to focus on the present and remember the girl
dancing up on the Wall.

I slept unevenly on the flight to JFK and was woken by a flight
attendant as the plane circled a few miles off the southern tip of
Manhattan. She smiled and said, "You're awake just in time to look down
and see the Statue of Liberty." The dancing girl told me to look down at
nearby Ellis Island instead.

I closed my eyes and saw a teenaged Heinrich Schultheiss being dragged by his mother to the door of the elegant brick building on that small island, his father shuffling in tow with his head down. Once inside, the three stood in a long line, and when it was their turn, Mrs. Schultheiss muzzled her son's mouth with her hand. An indignity to him. She said to the clerk in broken English, "You spell zee boy's name H-E-N-R-Y. His last name be spelled S-C-H-U-L-T-Z."

What was so wrong with a miniature paper umbrella in a rumrunner on a beach in Florida? But it was too late to turn back now. And after a minute, I didn't want to.

The memory of my name change led me to rethink the debacle with my father and the saltshaker. Maybe *Mother* had wanted me to forget Germany altogether when we arrived at Ellis Island a few months before that infamous supper in Iowa. They say that amnesia is caused by trauma. If you were to put a gun to my head and force me to psychoanalyze myself, I'd say that my mother ripping me away from the country and girl I planned to love forever had been almost a physical trauma. I hadn't been thinking right. I think now that my brain made a secret place where the German boy Heinrich could go on living without revealing himself to Henry. My father's violent outburst at the supper table a few months later only forced Heinrich back in the hole; he had already been there.

Visions of the skulls of my German name and boyhood set a mood for the flight from JFK to Berlin. I longed to forget 1989. It had not been a good year. It started without Helen. Then I put my small hardware store into bankruptcy. Bankruptcy is what happens when a national chain store comes to town and sells the same goods at lower prices and the man with the more expensive goods never opens for business at the time advertised because he can't get out of bed for mourning the passing of his wife. There's only one positive thing I can say about the young owners of the Starbucks on Main Street who charge an arm for a cup of coffee: they took over my building lease. I kept relatively sane the same way I managed to right after Helen passed—by practicing the religion of fishing at the river.

As the plane flew into the rising sun, I felt inspired enough to try to erase the past half century so that I could have my boyhood back—and my memories of fishing in Edelberg at the Spree River, of twirling a girl at a school dance, of carousing in nearby Berlin. Then the present bit me. I had to use the john. Walking to the back of the plane on arthritic knees painfully reminded me that it was December 1989. I didn't know then that there were other things time wasn't going to let me forget.

I arrived at the Berlin airport shortly before 6 a.m. local time on December 19, tired but as tightly wound as a boy about to venture out on his first date. When I walked through the airport door and breathed fresh outside air, Germany started. I goofily got down on my sore knees and kissed the ground. I was home. Sort of.

Less than sort of, I would soon discover. On the twelve-mile cab ride to the hotel in West Berlin, I was disappointed. I had been foolish, stupidly not realizing that time doesn't stand still. My tiny hometown of Edelberg is only thirty miles from Berlin, so you can imagine that I spent a good deal of time in the city during my youth. I knew that the man who had played the accordion on city street corners would be long dead, but where were the bratwurst carts, the fresh-produce stands, the newspaper shacks? In short, the city denied its old self.

I had gotten little sleep on the plane, hankering for Anna, so after checking into the hotel, I went to my room and got some shut-eye. I wanted to fall unconscious and wake up a new man on my search for her, unburdened by dark thoughts of an Iron Cross and Ellis Island and the dead old man with the accordion.

After a three-hour nap, I shaved, trying to make my face so smooth and young that I nicked my chin. An unintended consequence of cheating on Helen in my heart.

True, I wanted to see some historical sites, but that could wait. Feeling a bit like a fan hunting down a celebrity, I itched to begin the search for Anna. I went to the concierge, an older woman who greeted me with a warm, professional smile. When I asked in English for an Edelberg phone book, she rubbed her cheek as if I were a rash on her skin.

"Yes, Edelberg," she said in an almost accusatory tone. "Eighty percent or more of it is gone. Kaput. Your American planes bombed it in 1945 near the end of the war." Irritated people love to make the irritator irritated.

"I wasn't one of the pilots. I only want to see your Edelberg phone book. I'm looking for a Himmel."

What an about-face! It was as if I had just handed her twelve roses. She flashed a huge smile and seemed tickled to say, "I had a Himmel violin when I was a girl!"

Here was a shining moment. I smiled back but looked straight through her face to the image of a Himmel violin. The Himmel violin company was more than 200 years old, so whatever relative of Anna—or maybe she herself?—was now running the factory had large shoes to fill. A Himmel was an eminently affordable, mass-produced instrument with quality spilling from its entire body. There were an enormous number of them in "everywhere" German places, and they were owned by an enormous number of "everyone" German people. They were in schools, universities, churches, synagogues, and homes. They were played by all races, colors, and creeds of people, save the tiny percentage of professionals who of course wanted expensive violins like those handcrafted in Italy.

Some wealthy people who only wanted to fondle them with their eyes would put them on stands in their music rooms. And even if you didn't play, you heard them played by your neighbors' children or by amateurs on your village square, etc. Somewhere, someone, at some time in Germany—I doubt anyone knows who, when, or where—named it the "People's Violin." Maybe this gave Hitler the idea to name his mass-produced, inexpensive car the "People's Car"—later named Volkswagen—when it was introduced in 1938. But you can bet that Anna despised the People's Car on principle as much as she cherished her People's Violin. Her Himmel was the only violin she would touch. And how delicately she handled it! She held it as if it were a newborn bird vulnerable to everything in the world.

"Sir?" the concierge said, breaking up my wild daydream about an elderly Anna frantically sprinting away from a Volkswagen Beetle. "Did you hear me?" she asked. "I said I owned a Himmel when I was a girl. But none have been made since the '40s when the factory building was bombed to rubble. There was no one to rebuild it."

I took a deep breath and breathed the question, "What? Say again?"

"The company is gone."

The concierge's words stung me hard. What she had just told me, in so many words, was that Anna Himmel had probably perished in the war. Had she survived, she would have gone to the ends of the earth to have the Himmel factory rebuilt. "The company will last more than a thousand years," she promised us in school.

"But you do not want to go to Edelberg anyway," the concierge warned. "It is small and ugly. And Communist too." She added, as if I were a Berlin neophyte, "Perhaps you would like to go to the Victory Column right here in the city, or the Kaiser Wilhelm Memorial Church, or Museum Island, or the Charlottenburg Palace. Most tourists rave about the palace. It was built around 1700 and was the home of seven generations of Hohenzollern emperors. It is Versailles-like, now filled with classical paintings, tapestries, ornate porcelain, and—"

"Maybe in a few days," I said. "This moment, I only want your Edelberg phone book."

"Certainly." She brought it out, and as I furiously flipped to the *H* section, I tried to protect myself by thinking the worst. I said to myself, *The sudden dashing of an extremely high hope of meeting a woman you once loved with all your soul, on an extremely low chance of actually meeting her, is only a moderate defeat when you're not going to die because of it.*

But there it was, as if by magic: a phone number assigned to an "Anna Himmel." I read it twice, then showed the phone book to the concierge to verify my eyesight. It was true. Anna was alive and still in Edelberg.

The concierge then explained the bus system. The travel restriction lifted as of the day the Wall started to fall on November 9 allowed me to drive or walk freely between West and East Berlin and thus the two Germanys without a special visa. I jumped onto a bus to Edelberg, thirty miles into East Germany. I would be in the presence of Anna Himmel again after fifty years, a sunray of a thought but an intimidating one.

Yet as the bus streamed through the streets of West Berlin, I felt something like bereavement, seeing up close and personal that a good part of my boyhood had been blotted out when Allied bombs pounded the devil out of Berlin in 1944 and '45. The incredible photographs I remembered seeing in magazines following the war were suddenly all too credible. So many buildings that clung to my childhood memories were no more, dematerialized into thin air. I'd expected to find at least a few of the old stores I remembered. But none of them existed, not one. Gone, for instance, was my favorite nook in Berlin, the House of Chocolate, which had beautiful, creaky hardwood floors in need of refinishing and tall ceilings decorated with intricate patterns of wedding-cake-icing plaster. The new one-story building, looking like it dated to the late '40s, now hosted a dry-cleaner.

Then, there it was, on the border of West and East Berlin a few blocks to the east: the massive Brandenburg Gate rising above the modest skyline. I had strolled through it many times growing up. It brought back memories of Anna but also of what it holds: human conflict and the Iron Cross. From that distance, the sculpture at the top of the gate was too small to make out the details, but I knew what every German child has learned for two centuries: that the woman in the chariot on top of the gate is Victoria, the Greek goddess of military victory. She's holding a pole pointing skyward, defending the fatherland against possible attack, and garnishing the top of the pole is a laurel wreath with an Iron Cross in the center.

To avoid the dark thought of the Iron Cross, I turned my mind to Victoria alone, hoping to see Anna in her. When I had been in church preschool, I thought that the woman on top of the gate was a statue of Anna. A few years later, I realized that she and Victoria had absolutely nothing in common—save they were both goddesses. Victoria was a mythical goddess celebrating military victory, whereas Anna was a real-world goddess who despised war. I was not yet ten when my secret title for Anna became "Goddess of Culture," even though I hardly knew what the title meant—I myself was about as cultured as a rock.

The bus was now at the Berlin Wall, the border of West and East Berlin (and thus one of the borders of the two Germanys), fifty yards or so to the west of the gate. Seeing the Wall in person on this sunny day was like seeing a total eclipse of the sun—total darkness that could blind a person looking at it. On the night of November 9, the celebrants had pounded a small opening to make a passage from East to West Berlin. The opening was narrow, so the bus had to slow down and crawl through to East Berlin. I was tempted to put my hand out the bus window and touch the Wall so that I could tell everyone back in Iowa, but I didn't. I was afraid it might bite.

When the bus tires touched East Berlin, I landed on Communist soil for the first time in my life. I had the outrageous thoughts that any grass would look like gray steel wool, that women on the streets would be wearing potato-sack dresses, and that the men would look something like Vladimir Lenin, with bald heads and Van Dyke goatees. Of course, there was none of that. There was only the pounding thought of the Wall left in the bus's dust.

How much can you hate one thing? Let me count the ways. The Wall 1) was an eighty-seven-mile-long, ten-foot-high concrete monster, 2) had more than 250 runs for dogs to hunt down people trying to escape, 3) had 180 sharpshooter towers, 4) had a wide so-called "death strip" where there were no obstacles to rifle fire, and 5) was where at least 138 people were shot dead, suffered fatal accidents, or committed suicide. I blurted involuntarily to the bus driver, "Schnell nach Edelberg!" (Speed it up to Edelberg!).

I was glad that my German speech came back so easily, but I didn't know whether to be more disturbed by the truths of the Wall or by my having kept those truths in that hole in my mind for all those decades. No sight could have been as harrowing, except that of Hitler's underground bunker. I couldn't ward off a glimpse of the bunker site as the bus pressed through East Berlin. It harassed me even though it was nothing but a patch of dead weeds with no marker. I pictured it reaching down to the bowels of the earth and then, after the war, becoming covered up by both innocent dirt and guilty intention. Another set of opposites staring me down. Instinctively I took out a roll of Lifesavers and threw one into my mouth.

From the moment I had climbed on the bus until that moment, I had been bloodying myself. The disappearance of the stores. The looming Wall. The covert bunker. I managed to re-coil my mind warmly around Anna again after the bus passed out of East Berlin and its suburbs and ventured into the colder countryside. I would soon be in my childhood town, so I stopped wondering what had been so wrong with my idea of spending Christmas in Florida.

When the bus was a few miles from Edelberg, I imagined the enchanting town as it was the day I was compelled aboard the ship to America. I felt the almost 2,000 souls, all but a few of them worthy people, who shared life with me there. How had I forgotten about the goodness of my boyhood hometown, the arcadia I had once thought was the most miraculous piece of earth in the world? Was the death of my German name or the saltshaker incident to blame? I closed my eyes and imagined goodness. I pictured a few hundred old cottage-style homes set back along winding, tree-lined streets. Wreathed around their mossy stone foundations were evergreen shrubs frosted with snow and wild-growing perennial gardens. The town square, with the old clocktower, shops, cafes, and churches huddled around it, was defended by a thirty-foot-tall bronze statue of Frederick the Great, the eighteenth-century king of the militaristic German state of Prussia and lover of both war and the arts. For him, there was no contradiction between the two; he was a German's German. Just north of the square, I imagined the medieval spires of Edelberg University rising up through the bushy tree line.

An old woman with a hard-boiled face asked me in German what had me so happy. I told her in English what I was imagining. She shot back, also in English, "You muss be American touriss. You insane if you see zat because it no longer there." I said nothing else, seeing her ripped parka and feeling bad; she looked as if she would die before long.

The ancient bus chugged into town. The old woman in the torn parka caught my eye and pointed outside. Under a dirty-white sun obscured by a pale-gray sky, I saw an old man sitting on his rump and leaning back against a wooden newsstand with a paper bag tipped to his mouth. Another man swayed in a nearby alley while urinating. A third was warming his hands over a fire burning in a rusty fifty-five-gallon drum. That was my first impression of post-war Edelberg.

The fumy old bus was now wending through the narrow streets on its way to the bus station. I finally concluded that the village was virtually the opposite of what it had been when I grew up there: now a four-square-mile Cold War habitat that had been centrally planned into a squared matrix of mostly treeless streets lined with pale-yellow or gray brick buildings. As an American and believer in freedom and democracy, I'm biased, but it seems to me that most post-war structures sprang from the same sterile architectural concept that could only have been conceived by the smartest unfree mind. But the new town was still a living person, as it had been for me back then; today, it simply shrugged at its ugliness.

Even though the bus windows were closed, I heard a faint electro-hum coming from somewhere outside—unless it was the hissing of a snake hiding in the luggage rack. I asked the bus driver what the irritating noise was. He responded in what I call "communized" English: "It iss zee town's power station. Zee after-war Edelberg has 'lectric plant on river to make 'lectricity for Eass Berlin. A few thousand gude peoples lives here to work it. You free peoples call zem 'proletariat.'"

I kept my teary eyes pointed away from the other riders, all of whom seemed content to be arriving. The rebuilt town should have been renamed Lazarus, having risen between 1945 and '47 from the ashes of centuries of German culture. To me, it is now Edelberg only on the signboard at the edge of town.

Feeling I was about to step into a kind of no-man's-land, I inched out of the bus, and my feet were swallowed by Communist soil. I craned my neck around, and what I saw was worse than I had imagined. Nearly everything is gone: most of the old houses and churches, the bait shop, the roller-skating rink, Fredrick the Great, the handsome spires of the university, the scent of fresh breads and krullers in wicker baskets outside the bakery, the sounds of birds stretching out their voices in the tall linden trees lining Luther Way—now called Stalin's Way.

Even the football (soccer) field is gone. These people couldn't make a new football field? A small, empty piece of earth and a little grass seed?

I blurted out, "Is my childhood home gone too?"

The old woman with the ripped parka overheard. She smirked and said, "I unders-sand now. I growed up here too. You not insane after all."

So there is nothing left of old downtown. Or the old village square. Or just about anything I once knew.

The void that hurt the most was the cobbler shop. It had been owned by a grand old man whom I once thought could do no wrong—my grandfather Schultheiss. When I was five he taught me that men don't cry. At six, he taught me how to fish with a worm at the river cove, even bought me my first fishing pole. He would wisely say, "If you feel a tug and only think it's a fish, it's not a fish. But if you feel a tug and know for certain it's a fish, it's a fish." When I was seven, he taught me how to use a hammer the proper way. Between then and the day I joined Hitler Youth, I must have pounded a million nails in a thousand shoe soles.

That was the only day I ever saw Grandpa Schultheiss cry. "You, of all people, Heinrich! Why did you join that nursery for little Nazis? Children are Germany's future! God help the fatherland!" I was offended. I thought he was a weak man for crying. And a hypocrite too. I never went back to his shop. I never spoke to him again.

It was time to stop looking at Lazarus and reminiscing about what he looked like in his prime. It was time to find a public telephone and dial Anna's number. Or almost time, I soon decided. I first needed to figure out what I would say once she answered. I didn't want my lips to freeze like they did when I was at a hardware convention in Los Angeles and passed within feet of Olivia de Havilland on the street.

Procrastinating, I let my feet do the deciding and started south down Stalin Way in the direction of the Spree River.

The electro-hum grew louder and more guttural the closer I got to the river. Finally, there it was, where the Himmel factory had proudly stood: the hydroelectric plant on the bank of the Spree. An intimidating sight, a mammoth, yellow-brick building blocked off by a tall chain-link fence with barbed wire at the top. A pipe protruding from the building spewed orange liquid into the river. Next to the building, an acre of curlicued, glassy poles were yapping all the zaps. The whole complex reminded me of a highly electrified concentration camp. It must be as significant to the typical Edelbergan as the World Trade Center is to the typical New Yorker. I turned around and hobbled in the opposite direction.

A half mile back up Stalin Way, the morning ventured even further outside my control. I turned left where I believed Linden Street had intersected and walked toward where I believed my boyhood home and the Himmels' home would be, about a quarter mile down. I stopped a hundred feet later and closed my eyes. Floating toward me was a vision of twin beige, stucco houses, side by side, with fieldstone foundations, mossy slate roofs, and wavy glass windows with sills holding woven-reed flower baskets. I imagined my bedroom about fifty feet away from Anna's next door, then opened my eyes and walked on.

I froze when both houses said in unison, "We are not here." A garter snake inching along the ground a few feet in front of me seemed to agree. Apparently the two homes, the twins that had held hands, were leveled in the 1945 bombing. Growing in their places now are scraggly post-war trees of species I didn't recognize.

A V in one of the trees twenty feet up is about where my bedroom was—the point in the universe from where I had invaded so many hours of Anna's privacy, spying on her playing violin, reading books, and, I'll admit, undressing. I blurted, loudly enough for the imagined girl to hear, "I'm so very ashamed for spying on you all those years ago. But won't you please play the national anthem for me?"

I felt like a fool now for apologizing out loud to someone who wasn't there.

Yet the phantom girl heard me. She pulled her white dress down over her pretty shoulders and let the hem drop below her gorgeous knees, then vanished into thin air. I could bring her back only with a telephone call to Anna.

3

I abandoned that patch of godless trees and weeds, rushing back toward the center of town to find a phone. The shortest route was the pathway along the Spree River, which meanders through Edelberg. The river ran through my boyhood, too, turbulent in its center and serene in its coves—so much like Anna. Its breath, a winter fog, rose out of it and stopped me in my tracks. I remembered.

My mother told me I could take only one large personal thing with me on the ship to America, which seemed like a cruel edict. I chose the hickory fishing pole given to me one birthday by Grandpa Schultheiss. It certainly wasn't to me what Anna's violin was to her, but her admiration of the river put her inside that pole. I retired it in the '60s, fearing for the continued strength of the wood. It's hanging in my den, one of my favorite keepsakes.

Thank God the mighty Spree River was still bending through Edelberg that December. When I stepped off the bus and realized that most of the buildings are gone, I wondered for a second whether the river had vanished too. Because I once heard Anna say that a river is a living thing. She said that any river will naturally bend and change shape over time, bit by bit, unperceptively, as a human does. Yet the boulder at the river cove shore, the one on which I would sit as a boy and fish until Mother rang the cowbell announcing supper, had not eroded one inch to my eyes. Nor has the cove changed shape, though maybe my judgment was colored by the rose-colored, make-believe glasses I slipped on just then to have that moment.

If the boulder and the cove remained unchanged after I went to America, then why is the once sparkling-blue river water faintly orangish now? Why was it handing me a slightly chemical smell? Why were fish floating dead in it? Why are its banks no longer a place for recreation or kissing in the moonlight but instead only a place to hold up a behemoth electricity machine? How could this little town through which it flows no longer host the A. F. Himmel Violin Company?

And could a person, over time, become like this particular river—a flowing contradiction? I stood gazing at that antithetical river, momentarily forgetting about making the phone call I had been waiting to make since the plane took off in Des Moines.

Then I heard a noise to my right and saw a small boy standing on the boulder, my boulder, skipping stones across the cove. For a moment, he was me. I must have lost my wits, because I heard myself shout in English, "Heinrich, where is your fishing pole and can of worms?" The little kid seemed scared and didn't answer, looking at me the way youth looks at senility. He scampered away like a rabbit hearing a gun go off—and there had been no ringing of a supper bell.

The boy abandoned me to my memory. The darker part of the river where the choppy currents flow became the vision of my childhood, opening the floodgate wider now and letting out more ghosts.

My feet moved in the direction of the river park, where as a boy I had fallen to pieces, finally realizing that I would never kiss Anna. By now in this opposite world of Edelberg, I was not surprised that the old linden and oak trees, the tall, dignified, maternalistic ones under which you could stay dry waiting out a rain shower, are gone. Every countless one. The few leafless saplings shivered in the wind. A hoard of birds, having nowhere to make nests, shotgunned up from the ground.

But at least the park now has the honor of hosting a memorial cemetery, intimately packed with those who perished the night of the Allied bombing in April 1945. There are exactly 986 graves. I counted them. I wanted to know. Each grave is marked by a simple white cross, standing along perfectly straight rows, making the cemetery look like a miniature of the World War II memorial cemetery at Normandy. Of the 986 graves, exactly 223 have no names; those 223 people must have been charred beyond recognition. Of the 1,000 or so other estimated residents in 1945 who are not buried there, about 600 were reported to have survived the bombing; the other 400 or so who are not buried must have been literally blown to bits. There is not one single Star of David marking anyone's grave. We can assume, sadly, angrily, that the few hundred Jews living in town when I left in 1936 had gone elsewhere by 1945, probably each at the point of a gun or the growling jaw of a German shepherd, or both.

I browsed the names as I counted the graves. Families are huddled together. I didn't know everyone personally, but there is not one surname I didn't recognize. Everyone had known, or at least known of, everyone. Every single soul had been somebody. I shivered when I came to the markers for Frau and Herr Himmel because there is no grave for their son, my best friend Bernhard. My head suddenly dropped when I pictured him disappearing in fire vapors and literally becoming nothing but charred dust on that terrible night. My knees gave out and I had to grab onto Herr Himmel's grave marker for support. I became ashamed when my eyes welled—as much as I loved my Helen, I had been rock solid and shed not one tear right before her casket was lowered into the ground.

The little boy at the cove had fled probably in fear, making me think that I should get the hell out of there too. My only goal at that moment was to get ahold of Anna. If there was a reason for me to stay there and keep looking at the graves, it was only to do what Anna's father had intended in 1929 the day the bank foreclosed on the Himmel mansion—

namely, run to the icy river, jump in, swim out until the rapid currents were over my head, and drown.

Hobbling out of the cemetery in the direction of downtown, I suddenly stopped, overtaken by an eerie feeling. I felt someone behind me, staring at me. I turned, and what gazed at me a few hundred feet away was infinitely friendlier than the smoke rising from the power-plant smokestack in the distance. The face. The lip-length skater's-cut hair. It could be no one else but Anna Himmel, a jewel hanging on my earlier daydream.

She looked mystified. "Heinrich Schultheiss?" she shouted. "Sind sies?" (Is that you?).

I shouted back, "Anna Himmel, sind sies?" knowing full well it was her yet not believing my eyes. I came within three feet of her to verify that this was reality. I said in English, "It's me, Henry—I mean Heinrich. Schultz—I mean Schultheiss."

She was an early Christmas present. I reached out my hand to shake hers, but oddly she didn't take it. I had never touched her as a boy either.

"You are a young seventy," I said. In truth, the wrinkles on her cheeks and around her eyes made her look older than seventy. Her small, five-foot-three frame seemed to have shrunken a few inches. Her thin, once-perfect nose had widened a bit. Her once red, full lips were now thinner and barely pink. Her skin was pale, as if she hadn't seen the light of day in ages. I suddenly remembered what time does to physical beauty. But her skater's-cut hair, though silver now, was wonderfully childlike, and she had those complicated Mediterranean-blue eyes she had when she was sixteen, the age when I last saw her.

I loved Helen. I still do. She smiles at me every day from her portrait here in my den. They say it takes about a year after the death of a spouse to finally feel a little normal again. They're wrong. It takes longer. But I must say that the moment I set eyes on Anna that day, I felt something I hadn't felt for more than a half century: a first love all over again. There is no love like one's first. Nothing like it. I instinctively tried to straighten my thinning hair by brushing my fingers through it. I was self-conscious about the shaving nick on my chin, then felt my face turning red. God knew what Anna thought when she saw me faltering on my old legs.

"Wir sprechen Deutsch?" (We speak German?), she asked. She added in communized English, "Or instead should we speak in English?"

"In English, if you don't mind."

"Of course I do not mind. So, Heinrich Schultheiss. After all these years, it is you. Why are you . . ." She stopped, seeming to struggle to locate the right English words. "What are you doing here, Heinrich?" Her shoulders were slightly stooped, but her eyes were as lively as a curious child's.

"I, I came—the fall of the Wall, you know. I got this little inspiration. To come for a visit. I'll be in Berlin. Only for another few days, I mean."

"You are alone, yes?"

"Afraid so. My wife, Helen, she passed last year. Her heart."

"I am so sorry."

"It's okay. We had forty-two solid years, good years."

"I, you, it is . . ." She stopped again, her shoulders pulling inward. She seemed not to know what to say. Things were up to me. I struggled to think. More words had just been exchanged between us than had been spoken during the entire sixteen years we had both lived in that tiny town—seven of which were in houses only fifty feet apart.

After her lips stumbled she said, "You have been walking fast, yes? Your forehead is dripping with perspiration." She handed me her handkerchief, seeming careful not to touch me. *Strange.* I used it to dab the perspiration on my freezing, nervous forehead.

I managed to move my tongue in my dry mouth. "I arrived in Berlin early this morning and took a bus here." I turned to the cemetery on the other side of the woods. "The cemetery," I said. "It moved me, saddened me. I heard about the bombing and knew it must have been terrible, but walking through the cemetery was . . ." I couldn't finish the sentence.

"Yes, Europe has changed slightly since you left in 1936. Edelberg was bombed out of Europe."

Satire? Anna Himmel? I looked back to the cemetery and spoke seriously. "I stopped by your father's and mother's graves. I'm so sorry. I looked for a grave for your brother, and when I saw none, I thought the worst. How were you . . ." It was difficult for me to ask it. "How were you able to . . . survive the bombing?"

"I was not here in Edelberg."

"Oh? Where were you?"

"Forget it," she said quickly.

My glottis froze shut. I had the good sense not to ask the question again. "But look at you," I said. "You made it through the war."

"Yes, I suppose."

"And did you ever marry?"

"Oh no, that never happened."

Common sense told me I should leave that subject alone too. "What ever became of your brother, Bernhard? Is he living?"

Suddenly her face aged another ten years. "No." She shook her head. "Bernhard is—he is dead, killed soldiering in Stalingrad. In the end, he became the brother of— The young man who— Never mind."

I didn't know what stopped her from finishing the sentences. I was left with my shock that he, who never shied from saying how much he despised Hitler's regime, had become a Nazi warrior. Back then I revered Nazism, of course, but despite our differences, he became my best friend because there was something about him, something ethereal and magnetic. My shock quickly leapt to mourning. He was dead, one of five million German soldiers killed in the war.

"Why do you think you never got any letters from Bernhard after 1942?" Anna added.

"Actually, I received no letters from him after late '39, I think it was."

She thought for a few seconds. "I suppose I am not surprised. Did you not hear about him?"

"Hear what?"

Suddenly her eyes darkened. "I am a fool," she said. "Of course you do not know about Bernhard. Most people never knew. It was one of a million things that happened in the war, and it went on way out in the hinterland. We will not talk more of Bernhard. Okay, as you Americans say?" If there had been an open door between us at that moment, she would have slammed it shut.

She shivered and looked at her watch as if she was ready to go. I had found her and didn't want to leave her. "C'mon downtown with me," I offered. "I'll buy you a cup of coffee before I go back to the city." Though having coffee and preferably a dinner with her was part of my plan, I couldn't believe my bravura. It was two o'clock. I happily feigned that I didn't need to get back to Berlin for a few hours. "I'll get the four o'clock bus."

She looked at me as if she had never been asked by a man to have coffee. I finally said, "Anna, you needn't go with me if you don't want to," inflicting on myself the possibility that she didn't want to be with me.

"If you are certain, I will go," she said.

"I'm certain"—though by now I was certain of nothing.

"Then you give me no choice," she said, giving me a small smile as a gift.

The next thing I knew, Anna Himmel and I were walking side by side. Just she and I. "We better go to the bakery," she said. "It is the only place in town that sells coffee not out of a vending machine." I let her lead the way, hobbling along on my arthritic knees. But it was not a disaster, because Anna had a moderate limp too. We noticed each other's gait and were now simpatico. I loved being in East Germany.

My stomach was cartwheeling, though. When time has produced a half century of personal history and thick volumes of world history since you last saw someone you hardly ever spoke to in the first place, what do you say? Especially when the person is someone you secretly loved as much as your own life. For a moment, I was tempted to give out a little laugh and tell her that when I was four, I thought she was a nonhuman angel grown from a cherub. *Or maybe I should turn myself in completely and confess that by the time I was a teenager, I was obsessed with her and thought she was a human goddess.*

Most women, after half a century, would get a kick out of it and laugh, but somehow I pictured her merely drawing a tiny smile, at best, and not laughing at all. She had not been the kind of girl who wanted boys to love her. By the time I decided not to tell her about the angel or the obsession, we had exhausted the subject of the weather and arrived at the bakery.

The bakery is fairly new by East German standards, circa 1960. Inside the front door, we were greeted by no kiss of the sweet scent of a traditional German bakery; there were no deutsche donuts frying in lard. Tarts and krullers were not in oak-and-glass display cases. There were, however, cookies and breads sparsely populating metal racks behind the Formica counter. Anna ordered a black coffee, and I ordered my usual, one with sugar and cream. They were out of sugar but brought me enough skim milk to make my coffee look like mud. It was strong, too strong. I guessed that is how Edelbergans keep their eyes open in their sleepy town.

Anna's hand trembled slightly when she drank, and for the first fifteen minutes we talked a lot about nothing. Finally she moved into something worthwhile by asking what I had done with my life in America.

"My mother alone decided in 1936 that we three should leave the country and go to Iowa. I loathed her for many years after we left. To me, Germany was everything. The new language was a tough thing too. My mother and father hated Nazi Germany so much that they didn't allow me to speak German after we were in America for a month. My father once hit me in the face for speaking German."

"Your nice, shy, peaceful father?"

"Afraid so. Blood was all over. And in the United States, football isn't football. I mean, it isn't soccer. They didn't have soccer in Donsville. I didn't have the body size for American football, so European football was another thing my parents left me out in the cold on."

"University? Yes?"

We were actually having a real conversation, Anna Himmel and I. Ever since that day I chanced across Olivia de Havilland in Los Angeles, I had dreamed of having coffee with her, Miss de Havilland. But sitting across from Anna was nothing like I imagined sitting with any Hollywood starlet would be, take your pick. There was something almost higher than human about Anna, or so I still thought after all those years.

"I got out of high school in '38 and went to Iowa State for three years. Majored in mathematics. I didn't go back for my senior year. I signed up for military service instead. When I got down to the post office to sign up for one of the armed services, I intended to go into the Army, but a guy in that line called me a 'bastard dirty Kraut.' Said something like, 'We got the neutrality law, but if the war hawks in Washington have anything to do with it, we'll be over there killing you bastard dirty Krauts in a year or so.' I signed up for Marines instead, partly because of that idiot but more because rumor had it that the Marines would never need to fight in Europe. I didn't exactly want to fight against an army that had my cousins in it. Besides, this was before Pearl Harbor. There was no war in the Pacific. I thought I could serve in the military without going to war."

"You wanted to avoid killing. Good for you. And what did you do after the war?"

"Came home to Iowa after the Japanese surrendered. We had the GI Bill, but after being in hell halfway around the world, going back to college seemed like child's play. Just couldn't do it. I guess I was a head case. So I borrowed some money and bought a small hardware store right there on Main Street in Donsville. Met my wonderful wife, Helen, at an American Legion dance in '46, got married and bought a house in '47, and still live in the same house. I sold the store earlier this year. Just couldn't concentrate anymore. It was time to give up screws and hammers and lightbulbs. And, frankly, the store went broke."

"So sorry. Children? Yes?"

"Four. Amanda, Betsy, William, and Katherine."

"Grandchildren?"

"Seven. But most everyone avoids me of late. It's my own fault, I guess. Used to take them out for ice cream, to the circus, things like that, but I'm afraid Helen's passing has made me into a grouchy old man. Except for my grandson Billy, they keep their distance. C'est la vie."

"You better work on that. You only have one family and only go around once in this world."

I would have said something if I had known then what I know now.

"And what about hobbies? Do you still love to fish?"

"How do you know I love to fish?"

"Do you not think I saw you heading for the river with your fishing pole a hundred times? And a few times at night when I was spying on you from my bedroom window, I saw you picking up nightcrawler worms off the grass out in your backyard."

Anna Himmel spied on me. "You *spied* on me from your bedroom window?"

"Sometimes when my light was off, I saw you were doing it to *me*. I wanted to make us even. I once saw you in your underwear and I hoped you saw me in mine."

Even? Obviously she didn't know that I had seen her naked a few times. "Yes, I guess we are even. But look, what about you? Do you have extended family in the area?"

"No. I do have cousins in West Germany I never met. I came back to Edelberg in 1947 alone after the town was rebuilt because of the river, and—"

I had asked at the river but now interrupted to ask a second time, "Where were you before then?"

"I told you at the river to forget it. It does not matter."

Doesn't matter? Come on, Anna, give it over. But again, I didn't press my feet down on the eggshells.

"I imagine you made lots of solo violin records over the years."

She looked at me with blank eyes and forced a breathless, nervous laugh. "No, I gave up violin before the war," she said.

I was stupefied. It was the matter-of-fact way she said it, as if a violin were just any old musical instrument that anyone could stop playing at any time. As if her violin had not been her life. As if she were not Anna Himmel. "Oh? Why?"

She looked at me with a stone face. "I would rather not say. It is no big thing."

I was getting tired of her playing coy, but she seemed too delicate to push.

She continued, "I went to work at the new power plant when it opened in 1947. I retired a few months ago." She looked away, coughed, and felt her chest. Her smile returned, though, when she said, "I told you good Schultheiss folks to leave Germany, and thank God you left before the war."

America and my initial hate of it—I didn't want to get into a touchy subject with a practical stranger. She must have seen a certain look on my face.

"I did not mean to upset you, Heinrich." Her words *did* upset me, piquing a bad memory about a certain night a few days before we shipped off to New York. There was something in my nose—Rudy Gendler's imagined breath wafted into my nostrils, went to my mind, and stirred my memories. I slid up to the edge of my chair and couldn't help but spew the role that Rudy had willfully executed in overturning my and my family's lives.

4

S haking from nerves, I hardly needed another cup of coffee. I
couldn't be angry with her for snooping into my mind; I was digging
up lost history on my own. "Do you remember the Gendlers?" I
asked. "The father, Rudolph Gendler?"

"I called him Rudolph the Terrible."

"I see you knew him." My eyes went to the window as it all came
back to me. The Meister Building, only a few blocks from my hotel, the
summer of 1933. I was fourteen.

How do you insult both your wife and son in four short words? By
then, Herr Himmel knew a way. "Take that son of a bitch with you to
sign up," he shouted to me from his backyard. "If that boy knows I want
him to join, he will run away from home."

Earlier that week, I had asked my best confidante, twelve-year-old
Bernhard Himmel, to go with me on Saturday to sign up for a new
organization, one that was reputed to be much more prestigious than
Boy Scouts. He had declined out of hand, saying that he didn't want to be
in any new organization, that he was already happy being in Boy Scouts.

But how could I possibly refuse his father? By then, Herr Himmel was not a man you wanted to cross.

"Come with me, Bernhard," I said to him that Saturday after he opened his front door. "We will take a bus to Berlin, and I will treat you to lunch. Come on."

Bernhard went, saying he hoped we'd go to the penny arcade after lunch. He was both surprised and pissed when we arrived at the Nazi office in the Meister Building. We noticed Rudolph Gendler, a fair-weather friend of my father and the leader of the Berlin branch of this new organization. Bernhard immediately turned to leave, but I grabbed him by the shoulders to make him stay. "We will only be a minute," I said as he squirmed.

I was dazzled that Herr Gendler rode a black horse to this office building every day. Fed it the finest oats. Feeling his own oats, he greeted us without a smile and mussed our godly clouds of blond hair with his knuckles. I was not bothered one bit that he was an elf of a man, not much taller than an average boy on the cusp of his teenage years, or that he fit himself with a Nazi hat that was too small, probably to make himself look taller. It was no concern of mine that he seemed to drink too much alcohol, that his nose was red and riddled with purple veins. Nor that his double chin and cheeks were made of kruller dough. All because his dapper Nazi uniform more than compensated for the diminutive figure underneath. To me, he gave off a lordly vibration.

"If you want to join," Herr Gendler said, "I need to measure your heads before we do anything else."

"We want to join, we do!" I said in my deepening voice as Bernhard wiggled to free himself from my hands.

"I surely do not," Bernhard tweeted in his prepubescent voice.

Herr Gendler said, ignoring Bernhard's protest, "If your heads pass the test and you sign the paper, you two will hear wonderful things at your first meeting next Saturday." He took out his little protractor-like device, and the unwilling Bernhard and I passed the exam with width to spare. There were no other requirements—other than our hair, eye, and skin colors, of course, and our sworn declaration that we had no Jewish or Romani blood and would honor Hitler. For what seemed an eternity, Gendler stood in silence and stared at us expressionlessly, tapping his riding crop in the palm of his hand. By now Bernhard seemed not only disgusted by him but afraid too.

Finally Herr Gendler cracked a small smile and said solemnly, "Perfect. Pure Aryans. True-bloods. Hitler Youth, men, is much, much more prestigious than Boy Scouts. Our motto, 'Blood and Honor,' is sacred, and if you two do the fatherland the honor of joining, you will be fortunate enough to wear the handsome uniform." (Membership wouldn't become mandatory until 1939.) In high spirits, I signed both the oath and Gendler's roster with a silver pen. Bernhard refused to sign either. As we walked back to the bus station, he spat in a voice that seemed to have just stumbled into puberty, "That Nazi is fat, ugly, and seems dumb."

As a condition of remaining in the house, Bernhard was forced to join. As his guardian, his father went to the Meister Building and signed "Bernhard Christian Himmel" to the oath and to the roster. Herr Himmel said that joining would be good for both Bernhard and the fatherland.

I dragged Bernhard with me to our first meeting the following Saturday. He seemed embarrassed to have to wear sock garters to keep his official Hitler Youth knee socks from sliding down his skinny calves, but otherwise he couldn't help but shine in his starched, military-style uniform. I gleamed too, assuming my bedroom mirror was being honest with me.

"Who knows what the Holy Roman Empire was?" Herr Gendler asked our large group of boys, seeming enamored of the way those three words, *Holy Roman Empire*, rolled off his tongue.

"I have heard of it," a nice boy said.

"Well, enlighten us then," Gendler said, using a preacher's sermon tone. But the boy knew nothing other than the empire's name. Gendler then taught us, "We call the Holy Roman Empire the First Reich. It was a loose confederation of states, the largest and most glorious of which was the sun-like Kingdom of Germany. The empire came together and formed like a solar system during the Early Middle Ages. The single most important fact you men are to remember about it is that black-armored knights who defended Germany rode their black horses all the way to the Middle East during the Crusades in the high service of this glorious land. They risked life and limb to eliminate subhumans called Muslims. Questions?"

An eerie silence floated down. Finally, a mesmerized young boy asked, "Were the knights faceless, like I heard?"

Herr Gendler thought a minute, searching the ceiling for an answer. Finally he said, "Yes, as a matter of fact they were."

That's all I recall about that first auspicious meeting. Bernhard was the only boy who was skeptical about the knight story. The rest of us ate it up with relish.

At that time, a sea of new laws were improving my family's lives. Under the new genealogy law of April '33, Gendler could have thrown me out of Hitler Youth by the ears when he discovered a fact about my father that shocked and disturbed me at the time: Father was half, and therefore I am one-quarter, Jewish. Father had recently been accepted into the Nazi Party, but soon after, he stumbled on this potential bane of his new Nazi existence, this huge disqualifying fact inadvertently missed during the original investigation into his party application. He became so fearful that the party would one day learn his secret that he took doctored-up genealogy records in to his supposed friend Herr Gendler at the Meister Building for him to take to party headquarters and place in Father's official Nazi file.

But the paranoid Gendler did his own independent research first and then became angry. Spitting mad. He called Father into the office. I tagged along against Father's wishes.

"You are not only a half Jew, Karl," this fair-weather friend of Father said. "I have discovered that you are a quarter Roma gypsy." Father was dumbfounded, having no idea he had Romani blood. A few months earlier, before joining the party, he wouldn't have cared in the least that he was half Jewish and a quarter Romani, but now, as a card-carrying Nazi, he had *two* biological truths to fret about every day. Sometimes when you try to disprove the truth, you end up doubling it.

"You are my friend, though," Gendler claimed. "So I am going to file your fake records and destroy the real ones and not throw you out of the Nazi Party. Nor will I have your son kicked out of Hitler Youth. Nor will I have you indicted for document fraud against the fatherland. But *achtung*, Karl."

Why did this passionate Nazi shine benevolence on Father and me? Because he was forced to. He had his own skeleton in his closet; he was part Slav, and my father was one of the few who knew it. Slavs were hated by Nazis almost as much they hated gypsies and Jews. So Gendler did something comparatively benign to Father for giving him phony records: he merely whacked him in the face with the butt of his rifle, breaking Father's nose. Father stooped in pain. I shook. As Father and I left, Gendler put his index finger to his chest and then to his lips, pointed his rifle at Father with his other hand, and whispered to us, "Shhh."

Father arrived home dripping blood on the floor.

"Oh my God, Karl, what happened?" my mother cried.

"I am so embarrassed," my father said. "I broke my nose by accident, running into a glass door." I stood there shocked because before he joined the Nazi Party, a more honorable man had never lived. I realized he had just lost his dishonesty virginity, but I was too frightened to speak up.

Father wept in bed that night. My concerned mother asked him what was wrong.

"Go wake up Heinrich," he said. "He already learned some of this today, but I want him to hear the rest." So Mother woke me, and I joined them in their bedroom. "I have been a devout Lutheran all my life," he said, taking hold of his Bible on his nightstand, "and I swear I have not lied to anyone since childhood. But I have been keeping a secret for some months. Gendler told me today that I am not only half Jewish but also a quarter Romani. And Claire, I did not break my nose by running into a door. Herr—"

Before Father could say another word, Mother turned to me and scowled. "Heinrich, you as good as lied to me! I care nothing about your father's genes, but you stood right there, silent, and let your father lie about how he broke his nose!"

Then, to cover up my lie-by-silence, I lied again, saying, "But, Mother, I have no idea *how* Father broke his nose. No idea!"

Immediately I felt sick. Not because of my lies: *What if the kids in school find out I am part Jewish and part gypsy?*

"*Achtung,* Jew boy. *Achtung,* gypsy stink bomb," Derek Gendler, Rudolph's youngest son, warned me on the school playground a week later. I went home from school fearing for my limbs. An hour later, there was Anna, strolling across to my house. She hardly ever spoke to me. Hardly even looked at me. She was slender, with blond hair and blue eyes, and about as Aryan as they came. I opened the door nervously, and she just stood there, silent for the eon of five seconds. I remained conscious, but anxiety leapt up my spine. *Is she going to call me out for what I am, like the other kids in school did?*

She looked nervous too. "All I came over to say, Heinrich," she finally said, "is that you should not be so upset about the rumor. Everything is okay even if it is the truth. Good Jews and good gypsies are just like other good people."

That was all she said. Then she simply smiled, turned, and walked home. But she said it with an aura that made me trust her, believe in her. I couldn't love her all the more for it; I already loved her as much as a person possibly could. She didn't love me, so I needed to be happy just knowing she lived next door. I learned from her that even when you hardly know a person, you need to go out of your way to stop their hurting inside. You need to help them see, and then love, the truth.

***

At the bakery, Anna had ordered a second cup of coffee during my private reminiscences. "Earth to Heinrich," she said. My eyes slipped from the window back to her. "You were going to tell me about the Gendlers?"

"Oh. Yes. One night in the late summer of '36, Rudy Gendler, who was about eighteen, about two years older than you and I, came to our house. He had always been the one white sheep of the family. Didn't care for his younger brother Derek, but Rudy taught me how to dribble a football and play the net. I had always looked up to him.

"He walked in dressed to a T in a sharp, black SS uniform. He had started growing a mustache. And his breath had an adult aroma, like cigarettes and schnapps—I can smell it right now. I was very impressed. He had restless blood. He handed my father a letter, saying self-righteously, 'Read and sign it, Herr Schultheiss. It is a letter from you to your boss, Dean Lerner at Edelberg U.' My father read it and looked shocked. He shouted, 'What is going on here? Someone is forcing me to resign my post at the university? But I am a member of the Nazi Party!'"

"It was the new Rudy," Anna said, lifting her eyebrows in that strange way that made our classmates laugh at her, "so I am not surprised."

"Well, I myself was stunned that someone as goodhearted as Rudy had gotten himself mixed up in my father's firing."

I couldn't believe I remembered it after so many years, let alone was willing to spill it to someone I hardly knew, but I couldn't stop now.

"And then my father shouted, 'And if I don't sign this letter, then I'll be indicted for fraud and treason?' Rudy, the fellow who used to march in the Christmas parade and throw candy canes to children, said in the coldest voice I had ever heard, 'Take your pick, Herr Schultheiss. Sign it or come with me to Berlin. The SS jail there is quite comfortable, and you will be arraigned on an indictment in the morning. The conclusions from your genetics research are simply wrong, and dangerous to the State.' That night, Anna, the late-summer air was steaming, but Rudy's words made me shiver."

"I bet the university person who ordered your father to do the research was a member of the Nazi Party and lied about the research."

"No. It was my *father* who lied. He lied through his teeth for the second time as an adult." I was so angry that I launched what was practically a book:

"See, on orders of the dean, my father had been studying two groups of monkeys, each with slightly different physical characteristics. My father was to determine whether they were two different subspecies or the same one. He found that they were two separate subspecies but reported just the opposite. Back in 1933 or thereabouts, he learned that he had some Jewish blood in him. After that, he worried every day whether he was going to be found out. He was so paranoid, so caught up in the whole Jewish issue, that he had this crazy idea that if he reported the truth in that monkey study, the Nazis would get ahold of it and say it supported their theory that the Jews are a lower subspecies than Aryans. My father ostensibly got fired for lying.

"Father signed the letter. The next morning, he straggled to the university to get his books and clean out his desk. He could only stand there with his hands over his eyes as the dean and a bunch of professors burned his books and the false monkey-study conclusion in a bonfire, all while retaining the truth—the underlying research notes. They glorified the truth. An irony wrapped in a paradox if there ever was one, huh?

"When Father returned home, he didn't speak. He shuffled like a zombie. Eventually, he mumbled something about not caring what happened to him. He could live or die. He could stay in Germany or go to Antarctica. You should have seen the look in my mother's eyes. She gave him a few days to turn around, but he only got worse. So she went straight to the bank, took out all the family savings, and bought bus tickets to France and ship tickets to New York. I had loved my mother as much as a boy can, but suddenly I despised her for ripping me out of the fourth year—and the best year so far, I thought—of the Third Reich. She threw away my keepsakes. My toy Wehrmacht soldiers. My model of the Red Baron's triplane. My model Panzer V tank. My Hitler Youth swastika pin."

Neither Anna nor I spoke for minutes. The silence was high drama. Finally she said, "Your mother should not be blamed entirely for insisting that you all go to America. Maybe I should be blamed too."

"You?"

She hesitated, then said, "Forget I said anything."

I thought, *There she goes being coy again.* She quickly added, probably to get my thoughts off her secrecy, "And you folks fled hardly without saying goodbye to anyone, and leaving most of your things behind."

"Yeah. The Nazis came a few days later and confiscated the house and our belongings. So now, Anna, you should know the reason my mother decided to rush us off to America. The reason was simple: She loved her husband and knew he just wouldn't be able to function in Germany anymore. She loved him deeply, more deeply than her deep love for old Germany. I felt terrible for him as he rocked in his chair like a sad little boy, unable to talk or do anything else. My mother and I packed up the house and said our goodbyes on the telephone to people we could trust. I hated my mother for a long, long time. Years. Hated her with a passion."

By then, I had forced down my bitter coffee and lost track of time. I had missed the four o'clock bus. Which was perfect. It was consistent with my original plan of getting lost in conversation—though it was supposed to have been light and cheerful—and intentionally missing the bus. I wanted to take Anna out for a gourmet dinner.

"Damn," I said. "I'm afraid I've missed the four o'clock bus to the city."

"No problem," Anna said. "You will come to my flat for supper. I made a bread and a pot of lentil soup this morning. I even made cherry tarts. We will finish well before the nine o'clock bus."

"Let me take you out to dinner. Maybe we'll have time to go to your place afterward for coffee." Again, I couldn't believe my daring.

"I am afraid the closest restaurant that serves supper is in the city."

Dinner at her place was far more perfect than my original plan.

5

A younger man could throw a stone from the bakery to Anna's flat, but for us two limpers who had been branded septuagenarians a few months earlier, it took almost forever to walk there. Along the way, I asked how she could stand the constant zaps coming from the hydroelectric plant, getting louder the closer we got to her flat.

"Some people say they do not hear them after a while," she said, "but they have been a constant every day since coming back here forty-some-odd years ago. I am afraid the plant is where the Himmel violin factory was."

"Yes, so I heard."

Puddles grew in her eyes when she said "factory." I didn't touch the subject. We had fatigued the topic of the weather on the walk to the bakery, but it filled the time for the rest of the walk to her flat.

The paint-chipped sign over the entrance to Anna's apartment building tries to act proud—*Die Edelberg Wohnungen* ("The Edelberg Apartments"), it read in gold letters, as if it were *the* place in Edelberg to reside. But to me the building is a microcosm of the town. That thing is a nearly perfect cube—four floors, thirty-two identical flats, eight to a floor, stacked inside a beige-brick box. From the entrance door, you can see the tip of the tall erection of the hydroelectric plant's chimney a half mile away. Just by looking at the huge matrix of mail slots in the small lobby, you can tell it's a place where too many people are packed in for their own good. It'd make a hell of a setting for a low-budget movie about broken souls.

Anna lived in the same studio flat she had occupied since 1947, a twenty-by-twenty alleged human habitat with two windows that let in only enough natural light to allow an artist to paint a midnight moon scene. Male and female bathrooms are down the hall. Her living arrangements, in short, might present a serious risk of a nervous breakdown to any free person who has to live there.

I'm six feet tall yet felt I had to watch my head as I stepped over the threshold. Inside, the one room crowded in on me, everything getting closer and closer as the seconds passed. My panning eyes became a 1940s movie camera, filming black, white, and every shade of gray. Anna's failure to comment on how depressing the place was told me it was second nature to her after all those years. The furnishings all hung together with a certain consistency, though, all of it vintage early Cold War: two chrome-framed kitchen chairs with seats upholstered in light-gray plastic, and a foldout sofa bed and foldout chair covered in the same upholstery. There was a castoff from the 1975 mayor—a combo hi-fi/TV like the Motorola that Helen and I got rid of thirty years ago. Except the top lid and electronic guts were missing. I looked in and saw toiletries and cleaning supplies.

There was no radio in sight, either. The woman had no music. Except maybe for the uncased violin propped in the corner behind the coat tree? The wood of the body was a deep reddish-brown, the most colorful thing in the room. It shimmered with life, even covered with dust and the room's cloudy light. I picked it up, holding it carefully. The neck was a rich onyx black, and on the back of the neck was the once famous "A ƒH" logo stamped in gold leaf, standing for A. F. Himmel. The pins holding the strings at the top of the neck were cream-colored ivory. One of the strings was missing.

"Are you sure you gave up playing violin before the war?" I asked.

She saw me holding the instrument and looked at it with an indifference bordering on disdain, as if it were taking up precious space and should have been paying rent. Yet it was there, out in the open. "Yes, gave it up before the first rifle shot of the war. Arthritis all these years." She tried to authenticate the pain by curling her fingers into a fist and wincing. "I have played it only a few hours since the end of the war."

I was skeptical. "You had arthritis in your *twenties*?"

"Afraid so."

This all made no sense, especially her look of scorn when she faced the violin. "Then why did you even keep the violin?"

"That is enough."

There she roiled again, refusing to tell me what I most wanted to know. I thought, but was too afraid to say, *Arthritis my foot*. It didn't take Sherlock Holmes to figure out she was trying to sell me something like the Brooklyn Bridge. But why would she lie about it? And why had she kept the violin all these years? She had said that she came back to Edelberg with very little money, and it could have fetched a pretty penny. And why did she keep it out sitting uncased, naked in a corner, where it could stare at her? It was obvious from the thick dust that she never played it and didn't want to touch it even with a dust cloth, so why didn't she at least have it in a case?

As she heated the lentil soup, I kept staring at the lonely violin—the one she had played at age twelve for a charmed audience at the famous Schauspielhaus in Berlin—and tried to plumb her reasons for lying. Where had her music gone? Had her soul fled during the war?

While Anna sprinkled spices in the soup, I looked around the room for family photographs, and when I saw none, I realized they would have been destroyed in the 1945 bombing. I imagined a photo of the young Herr Himmel, always dressed on weekdays in a suit and tie and wing-tipped shoes. In the '20s, I worshipped him almost as much as I did my own father. He was a wealthy business executive and a family man.

But what really captured me was his certainty that the Nazis would save Germany. I copied his certainty like an innocent boy copies a man's swear words. It was a gift to me.

Almost all I discovered about Herr Himmel and his family, other than what I observed myself, I learned as a teenager from my mother, Claire, who had heard it from Elise Himmel, his wife.

"Erich was so dapper the day he left for the Great War," my mother told me, "but the day he straggled home to the Himmel mansion in December 1918 after the cease-fire, he was skin and bones and collapsed into Elise's arms." Mother told me the whole story. He lived in trenches and ate slop for two years. The day after he shuffled home, Elise called her pastor to the mansion to marry them, wondering whether she might receive widow benefits if he should die. That night, she lay Erich in bed, then climbed in next to him. Nine months later, the richest son in Edelberg and one of its prettiest daughters celebrated the birth of their first child, a cherub they named Anna. I came a few weeks later.

As Anna stirred the lentil soup, I said, "I really looked up to your father in the '20s. I was at the factory one Saturday with Bernhard and him when he had men take down those female statues at the four corners of the factory roof. I thought he was a real man's man."

Anna spun around from the stove. Her face lost its silent song in a major key, and she said sourly, "He had those four white statues of ancient goddesses hauled to the town dump and replaced with black eagles. It was the first time I hated him."

"I saw the replacement eagles. What was the big deal?"

"You are full of questions when you should be silent. The eagles were specially molded to match the steel eagle at the tip of Victoria's pole atop the Brandenburg Gate. To me, they sneered war. Does that answer your question?"

I know now, a year later, that her bitterness was sixty years old, sixty concentric rings around a dead tree stump. I hadn't known that Anna Himmel knew how to be snide. She resumed stirring the soup in silence with her back to me.

A minute later she did something strange. She rushed to the door and locked it. "Look," she said, "you started it with the eagle story, and now I am dying to tell you the whole story and get it done with. Maybe this time I will finish. For my sanity I will be fast and brief."

Each sentence rushed into the next as though she wanted to finish before she could force herself to begin. "In August of 1940, the man I still called my father put me in a mental hospital in Berlin, and since there were no police authorities to go to except the Gestapo and the SS, I stole money from a nurse's purse and escaped and made it to London to tell the story about my father, but guards would not let me see Churchill at 10 Downing Street, so I was forced to go to Scotland Yard to report that my father was storing Nazi bombs at the factory, and the detective thought I was insane with my mismatched leggings and my unbrushed hair and my wild story, so I got on a bus to keep Bernhard from falling lower since the higher a person goes, the harder he crashes when he falls, and then he read a girl 'Snow White,' and I tried to save the girl and eventually to save Germany from itself. To make a long story short, the B-17s came here in 1945 and destroyed the bombs by bombing Hell out of the factory, and it was terrible that they could not help bombing the whole town because except for factory there was zero of God's opposite in Edelberg. Fifteen hundred people dead. All my fault. There. Done. Now maybe I can serve supper in peace." It took her a long moment to stop panting.

I was dumbfounded by that confusing, racing stream of consciousness. A mental hospital? Storing Nazi bombs at the violin factory? Bernhard "falling down lower" and reading a girl the fairy tale "Snow White"? She had fed me information I couldn't digest. Her words had a sharpness that cut me even though I was unsure what they meant. She looked at the floor as if the rest of the details were down there. I think she wanted to kick them under the rug to save them but hide them, apparently as she had done so many times with other people over the years.

"That's all more than I can process at once," I said. "Look, Anna, start again, slow down, and tell me the details. Calmly and in more measured proportions."

But all she did was stand and keep her mouth zipped and chop garlic
cloves for the soup. She chopped forever. The knife hissed. There was
nothing for me to say. In the long silence, I turned my thoughts back to
Herr Himmel. As I've said, all my memories of my German childhood
end with Anna. Since she was one of the proverbial apples that fell from
her father's tree, might my memories of him help me understand the
smorgasbord of confusion that Anna had just dished out?

Who was Herr Himmel, who *really*, aside from Anna's obvious
prejudice? I entered my own stream of consciousness.

***

For her first nine years, Anna lived like a princess in that rambling
Himmel mansion, built up on a hill on Teutonic Way in the late 1870s
by her great-great-grandfather, violin maker Jerold Himmel. Fashioned
after an old château in the German wine country, money trees grew from
seeds of privilege in its sprawling yard, and Erich was likewise fed the
fruit from his earliest years. He was pampered as a boy but as a teenager
styled himself a proud patriot.

"Until he enlisted in the Wehrmacht at age sixteen in 1916," Elise told
Mother, "he had never smelled human blood or eaten sow liver." Growing
up in Edelberg, the "rich kid," Erich Himmel, and my father, the "poor
kid," Karl Schultheiss, hardly acknowledged one another even though
Edelberg had only a couple thousand residents and the two were only a
year apart in school. Before the war, they had just one thing in common:
they were both young German males with no whiskers yet.

One day, as Anna's and my belly buttons were still healing from snipped
umbilical cords, the two crossed radically different paths downtown. "You
are a new father too, no, Schultheiss? And you served in the infantry in the
Great War as I did?" When Father nodded, the intrepid Erich announced,
"Then we have in common what matters most. Next Monday you are
coming with me to Berlin."

"Me?"

"Do you see anyone standing next to you?"

Father told me all about that day. He was only too happy to ride to Berlin in Erich's Mercedes-Benz and have his beefsteak lunch in an expensive restaurant paid for by Erich.

"This proposed treaty is a pile of horseshit," the German nationalist said to Father in the car to begin his rant. "The only moral thing about it is that it would formalize the cease-fire and end the official state of war. France, England, Russia, the US, those bastard Allies. They want to take away our military in the treaty. And the money they want from us! It would bankrupt our nation." (Though the exact figure is unknown, Germany probably paid in reparations to the Allies the equivalent of about $15 billion in 1919 US dollars plus handing over tons and tons of coal and other commodities.)

"If these treaty terms are the best our new Weimar government can dig up from its sewer," Erich continued in the restaurant, "then to hell with every goddamned one of them. Them and our radical new system of government. People actually *voting* for leaders, one person, one vote, even if a person does not know where his own ass is. And three branches of government—a president, a legislature, and the courts? It is pathetic. Give me back the system of kings that worked so well for centuries. Give me a philosopher-emperor, a superman sultan. They did not call King Frederick 'the Great' for nothing. For Christ sake, the man was an artist and a poet."

Almost frightened by that fustian tirade, Father was no longer quite so happy that he'd gone with Erich. But they say there are no free lunches, and after wolfing down the thick cow steak and drinking his own carafe of red Rhine wine, he was persuaded by Herr Himmel that being a "good German" meant marching through the streets of Berlin with hundreds of others to shit on the proposed treaty.

Alas, their and everyone else's blood, sweat, and tears meant nothing. In November 1919, Anna's and my second month of life, a burning Herr Himmel drove down to our house and sputtered, while whacking a newspaper in his hand, "The Treaty of Versailles has been signed! Wait and see, Schultheiss! Our country will go to a hell worse than the war itself!"

He was right. He sniped to his wife a week later, "Our army has been slashed with the sword of the Allies and is no longer able to defend our borders. Our beautiful Rhineland to the west is now occupied by bastard Allied-troop trespassers. Our treasury is being raped. The treaty is wreaking Armageddon upon the fatherland and therefore upon my family's violin company!"

Even Erich, his father, Mars, and the Himmel money were powerless to stop a star from imploding. Erich now despised democracy more than ever. "I have no choice, Schultheiss," he said to Father. "I still have my soul. I am going to boost it back up into the violin company again, the family jewel. If for nothing else, for little Anna's sake."

Anna's brother, Bernhard, burst into world in 1921. "First a girl and now a boy!" Herr Himmel cried. "Yin and yang!" He paused to think. "Or are they yang and yin?"

In either event, according to my mother, Herr Himmel was a model father. "Karl, you should take lessons from Erich. He allows his live-in nursemaid to change the babies' diapers, but he insists that only he should give them their bottles, and . . ."

I'll bet my father stopped listening.

Before Anna could tie her shoes, Herr Himmel took her to the violin factory one Saturday for the first time. As a baby, she had never touched the eighteen-caret gold rattle in her crib or the heavy silver spoon on her highchair tray. But that day when she ran her hand along a spruce soundboard at the factory, her eyes twinkled and she tweeted, "It is as soft as a rabbit!" A few seconds later—or so the story goes—her father could only laugh out the words, "Anna, darling, calm down! You have wet your pants." Later at home, he said to Elise, "I cannot define it, but when Anna touched that soundboard, there was something about her eyes, her soul."

The parents, in short, did not apprehend what Anna would come to mean to Germany in later years. In fact, I don't think that anyone yet recognized her higher, second identity.

Herr Himmel loved reading his children bedtime stories from

Grimms' Fairy Tales by the German brothers Jakob and Wilhelm Grimm. "Whenever Erich reads them 'Snow White,'" Elise told my mother, "he always repeats the finale three times. You know, the part about the dwarfs handing Snow White's coffin to the prince? Which knocked out the piece of poison apple from her mouth and brought her back to life so they could marry and live in the castle happily ever after?" Of course, tiny Bernhard couldn't comprehend the words, yet he was mesmerized by the tone and cadence of his father's poetic voice.

But little Anna eschewed Snow White. Elise told Mother, "Anna whined, 'The lady in the garden ate a bad apple, and that was naughty.' See, Anna confused Snow White for Eve of the Genesis story."

At that budding age, three, Anna was too busy for fairy tales and fables anyway. The curious little girl was preoccupied by the gift her father had endowed her with at birth, the greatest offering he could conceive of to commemorate her entrance into this world: a Himmel violin. Bernhard was still too young to bow the strings of his own Himmel, but Elise said that Anna could not let hers rest. She even slept with it.

She revealed such musical promise that her father, a competent violinist himself, started giving her lessons. She was born with perfect pitch, and to prove it, he started by playing her the simplest scale—the C scale—and taught her "Do, Re, Mi, Fa, So, La, Ti, Do." After that, he would often start a lesson by playing the C scale and stop, say, on F, the fourth note. "Anna, is that 'Fa' or 'So'?" She would glow as she gave the correct answer every time. His deep desire to raise cultured children was every bit equal to his immense appetite for making fine violins, and in Anna's case, this tutelage was as easy as sleeping.

But this was Germany in November 1922. Herr Himmel became compelled to pause in indulging his children with his artistic self. His political activism, born of the aftermath of the war, came out again like a starving bear waking from hibernation—and the reparation payments Germany was paying to the Allies were his prey. He swaggered over to our place one day and gnarred an earful to Father. I overheard.

"Calm down," Father said to the man who thought the world started and ended at the borders of Germany.

"Calm down nothing, Schultheiss!" Erich roared back. "Germany just defaulted under the treaty for the first time, and now French and Belgian troops have their fat asses parked at our best factories and mines out west in the Ruhr River Valley. Before you can count to ten, foreign soldiers will have their asses here in the east. *Achtung*! My company! My mansion! Both of them are who I am. I am Erich Christian Himmel the Second, after all."

"Your company and house? What about your family?"

"Well, them too."

"And what is this business about Erich the Second?"

A few years earlier, Herr Himmel had stumbled on what he now considered a serendipity, not having given it much thought at the time. He discovered from family genealogy records that the fourteenth-century Prussian military regiment of a Himmel forefather named Erich had pushed Jewish settlements eastward out of the Holy Roman Empire. More than a few Prussians back then laid the bubonic plague, which killed probably half the population of Europe, at the feet of the Jews.

My father repeated, "Who is this Erich the Second?"

Herr Himmel proudly explained about the ancestor, then said, "Look, Karl, I want you to come with me to the Ruhr. The mealymouthed Weimar do-nothings are sitting back on their own fat asses and letting those bastard foreign troops have their way. I am trying to raise a private militia. Are you in?"

Father replied, "Do you think you might better worry about your family and your business? What does Elise say?"

"I did not tell her. What does she know about such things? Besides, she does whatever I say. And we are talking about the greatest country in history, Schultheiss. My business, my house. They will both be nothing if Germany becomes nothing."

"And not your family too? But in any event, Germany might become *nothing*, Erich? I assume you are exaggerating to get your point across."

"I am not exaggerating a bit! Schultheiss, our country gave the planet centuries of inventions and culture after the genius Gutenberg kicked off the Age of Enlightenment with his printing press. And Martin Luther practically invented the modern German language with his translation of the Bible. The beauty of our language! And so forth through the centuries. I will be damned if I am going to just sit on *my* ass and watch everything become nothing."

"Our language is not so beautiful. But in any case, England and France have given much to the world too. And the Americans. And Japan."

"Ha! The Brits, French, and Americans attacked us in the war. And now they are absconding with our treasury!"

"And Japan? Erich, you are avoiding my point. What—"

"Look, Schultheiss," Herr Himmel cut Father off, "I do not have time for nonsense. Are you coming with me to the Ruhr or are you not?"

Father became quiet. He had always played follow-the-leader with rich-boy Erich Himmel. I could tell Father was chomping on it. Finally he said, "Count me out, Erich. Claire would kill me. I have a family and cannot get arrested and possibly even executed. I am going to stay right here and work on getting my high school degree."

Herr Himmel had a tantrum, ending by wailing, "I have no more time to fuck around with a bad German!"

So the riled-up family man, unable to find even a single conscript for his "militia," drove alone all the way to the Ruhr in the west with his army rifle and a rucksack of food. He hid up in a tree and took shots at the French troops, seriously wounding one before being apprehended by German police. "Elise was angrier than a German shepherd punched in the mouth," Mother said. "But she thanked God that the German judge was a soldier in the war too, because he only gave Erich ten months in the clink."

With her father in prison and her mother about as musical as a deaf dog, Anna taught herself new violin skills by trial and error. She had no passion for dolls or jump ropes or hopscotch or little-girl tea parties. Her only enthusiasm was practicing her Himmel.

In November of '23, with only a few weeks left on his prison sentence, Herr Himmel read about the so-called Beer Hall Putsch, a botched attempt by a group of thugs to overthrow the Bavarian government. He was stunned when he read what one of the thugs was spieling—that Jews had somehow started the Great War, had profited hugely from it, and, in the end, had been responsible for selling the country into misery in the Versailles Treaty.

If I wanted to, I could go out on a limb and say that if this one particular thug had been shot dead with other rabblerousers, upwards of forty or fifty million fewer Europeans would have died between September 1, 1939, and May 2, 1945. A tiny accidental event can take down a continent.

With nothing to do in prison except slump on his cot, Erich scrutinized the thug's message. Erich slowly turned ninety degrees. The thug might not be a thug after all. He wrote to Elise, "I am not certain that what this man with the Charlie Chaplain mustache says is true, but if it is, then the Jews may just as well have embezzled Germany's reparation money and shat on my violin company and mansion."

What a difference a few weeks can make. Erich got out of prison in December of '23 with the nasty accusations against the Jews now a virtual certainty in his mind. He had just rotated the full 180.

Anna had turned four a few months earlier. They say there's not a more important year in the development of the human brain. I found something in her that I had never seen in another child my age. Except I, unlike her father, was ignorant enough at that wee age to think that I could define it.

And I did define it. I first heard her play at the Lutheran church preschool that year, watching her perform a simple piece on her comparatively huge violin. Before she started, she announced that it would be "a song wrote by Amadeus Mozart Wolfgang," mixing up the correct order of the first, middle, and last names. As she bowed the strings, she sang, a tad off-key, "Twinkle, twinkle, little star, how I wonder what you are . . ."

Even then, she was able to give her violin vocal chords, to make it sing. In her light-blue eyes were the purity of grace and the immaculate innocence of an infant. I had no idea who Mozart was, but from the rapture of the music and her angelic voice, my little brain defined her as an angel grown from a cherub. She was not merely *like* an angel. She was a real, nonhuman one. I was so nonsensical that I didn't think her body was a type that needed to go to the bathroom.

Within a matter of months, the angel told us church preschoolers, "The song about the twinkling little stars is for little children. So I will learn myself the new song about the country I love." Though I didn't realize it at the time, she was referring to "Song of Germany," taken from a melody written by the Germanic-Austrian composer Franz Joseph Haydn in the 1790s. It had become the melody for the new national anthem two years earlier, in 1922. She told her mother, "It makes me shake sweet all over." Her proud mother said to mine, "My little girl dreamed up a very strange idea about herself. It took her weeks and weeks to put together the little puzzle pieces in her brain, but at last she said, 'I learned it is the song of Germany. And my violin plays the song. So my violin is Germany. And I play my violin. So *I* am Germany.'"

Anna was all of four when she became, in her mind, Germany itself. She was the fatherland. A thought if there ever was one! She cried out, wetting herself again, "When Father comes home tonight, I will play the song for him! I will show him what I am!"

Reading about the Beer Hall Putsch, especially the organizer's alleged "truths" about the Jews and the corresponding slippage of Germany into mediocrity and despondency, probably made Herr Himmel a deeper thinker. He must have thought the world of his little girl for having learned the national anthem on her violin, and he must have gloried in her even more for clinging to a complicated, if silly, conviction about being the fatherland. "I made her what she is," he boasted as if he were God Himself. "It is good."

But in the mire of the times, the musical instrument business was not good and was becoming worse. There were few good jobs in Edelberg or elsewhere. Who but a small handful of Germans could afford to part with scarce money to buy a violin? And what little money people had was almost worthless. A loaf of bread that cost one mark in 1919 now cost a wheelbarrow full of marks. If you had enough wheelbarrows full to buy a Himmel violin in those bleak days, you had more than enough money to buy a mansion in Beverly Hills.

The Himmel family ate no more steak except in their memories. "Pass the wieners and sauerkraut" must have been the sum and substance of their conversation at that long dining room table in that huge dining room.

The year turned to 1925. Anna and I were six. I had never seen her so excited in school, so enamored of her father. She cried, "He read a whole book in one day!" though she didn't yet know anything about the author. Volume I of Hitler's *Mein Kampf* ("My Struggle") was published earlier that year, filled with hundreds of pages of anti-Semitic and other venom disguised as enlightenment. Elise said to Mother, "Erich actually believes the author's claim that the Jews are dooming the entire country. Therefore I guess I must too. Erich says there is something about the writer that inspires him. Claire, do you know that the author happens to be the same young war veteran who was awarded the Iron Cross and organized the Beer Hall Putsch? Brave man. Principled."

Herr Himmel forgave and forgot Father's "un-German cowardice" for not having gone with him to the Ruhr. He drove to our place just to hype the famous book. Father asked him, "But what about Hitler's failure as a painter? He just gave up and walked away from it. A person would have to question his character."

"You talk about *character*? Really! They were probably all Bolsheviks in the art school that rejected his application."

"I heard he is somewhat weird. They say he could not even paint real people. Had no feeling for human beings."

"At least he painted real things. Have you seen some of this unreal abstract shit that schooled artists come out with these days? Art for children. The fact that Hitler wanted to be a painter proves the deepness of his soul." Then Herr Himmel launched this long-winded accolade: "And if a poor boy who was often beaten into unconsciousness by a father whose hand was as quick as his temper can go on to win an Iron

Cross for bravery in a war and even publish his own popular book after almost pulling off an overthrow of the do-nothing Weimar government, well, then anyone in Germany can be *anything*."

"Erich, do you think that a boy's getting badly beaten by his father over and over again might make the boy more likely to hand out the same kind of brutality when he grows up?"

"I repeat: you know nothing, Schultheiss."

Himmel violin sales were still in the toilet due to an economy that was ill, and little better than fatally so. But Herr Himmel, passionately inspired by Adolf Hitler's deific vision in *Mein Kampf* to rebuild Germany's greatness, now redoubled (if possible) his passion to once again raise the A. F. Himmel Violin Company to greatness. Given his obsession with Hitler's life story and what he considered the spark of Hitler's genius, he came close despite the distressing economic times. By 1927, larger numbers of players, with Hitler's indirect help, were buying Himmel violins again.

What was Herr Himmel's secret at the factory other than Hitler's vision of what makes a man great? Simple: He started cutting corners in the manufacturing process, probably making his ancestor violin makers roll over in their graves. Perhaps most daringly, for the top piece of the instrument, the soundboard, he substituted a harder and less expensive wood, maple, for the softer and costlier spruce. With a different wood stain, most buyers never knew the difference. The target customers—the average players in the masses—were unsuspecting in this and so many other things; they didn't know that spruce vibrates better and thus makes a richer tone.

Herr Himmel said in an interview by a very skeptical music critic from one of the Berlin newspapers, "I have reengineered the instrument and made it much better than the badly outdated one made since the company's founding in 1745. Yet I sell it at the same price as the discontinued model." The critic's skepticism vanished. For that Sunday's paper, the critic wrote a feature article about "that amazing next generation of Himmel violin." Erich Himmel knew how to sell. Except for the particular nouns, he could have been Hitler talking about his future plans for the nation.

So Germany was being fooled by Herr Himmel. But wait a minute. Wasn't nine-year-old Anna Germany? *She* certainly wasn't fooled! *She* could discern the difference in tone. She told us in school that the new model was "junk." She talked like the unpopular spectacle that she had become and, probably without intending it, sounded like an undergrown professor, a precocious egghead, drawing the roll of many young eyes.

"What mushy tone it has," she tried to explain to us. "The best violin of all time goes up in smoke. I am *so* mad!"

When Herr Himmel saw that he could not pull the wool over Anna's ears, he just steeled his heart even more. He said to Elise, "Pfff! Anna says that I am *cheating* in making my improved violin. Adolf Hitler is the proof that I am *not*. We are both artists. And after all, he is an *Austrian* who tried to replace a corrupt German government yet was not put before a firing squad. He was not even deported. Instead, they shortened his prison sentence and then *celebrated* him and his brilliant book. I can only conclude that it is just plain silly and childish for Anna to think she is actually the fatherland. What narcissism! What conceited gibberish!"

A year earlier, at eight, Anna had triumphed by giving her first public recital at the tiny Edelberg Theater, which had thrilled her father. But now he was jealous of her—his own daughter. He refused to give her more lessons. "I will show *her*," he grumbled to my father. "I will make lots of money with my reengineered violin and then the newspapers will write even more about me." The fever of his jealousy now spiked off the chart.

Alas, the American stock market crashed in late '29, starting the heavy thunder and lightning of the worldwide Great Depression. Herr Himmel lost his entire portfolio of speculative German, American, and British stocks and failed to sell enough of his re-schemed violins to pay for the costly upkeep of the mansion. In December 1929, he wept when it finally struck him that he would need to put a price on his priceless castle and sell it. Fell to his knees and cried like a baby. That grand home was not only a bastion of comfort. It was not only an Eden where he played tennis on a clay court, swam in a backyard pool, and ate gourmet dinners prepared by a uniformed maid. It was the legacy of his great-grandfather, Jerold, the master violin maker. Upon Erich's death, it and the company were to pass to Bernhard, and then from Bernhard to his eldest son, right on down the family tree. It was part of the Himmel soul. Erich "the Second," a social wine drinker, now acquired a taste for hard liquor.

"No regular person could afford our giant house," seven-year-old Bernhard told me his father had said, "but a Jewish man sure could. The Jew had money coming out his nose, which is why my father said the Jew had a huge nose and stole our house. On the last day we were there, my father swigged a whole bottle of schnapps and stumbled off to the river. I chased after him. My mother called the police, and they had to swim all the way out to the fast currents to save him."

The Edelberg police saved Herr Himmel's body but of course could do nothing about his hurting soul. It must have already fled by the time he tried committing suicide at the river. The soulless alcoholic barely decided to stay alive. Elise had to oversee the sale of the mansion and the packing. She used the sale proceeds to pay the delinquent real estate taxes and, with the paltry remainder, to buy the family a comparatively tiny house on Linden Street. Forcibly ejected from the mansion, Herr Himmel so despised himself that he continued plummeting.

His fall was worse than that of other Germans of the day because he was tethered to an angel, a being like no other German. Anna started life as an apple of his eye and of his tree, but now he turned to the darkness as she turned to the light.

But the world, as it has always done, kept revolving. The light eventually, of necessity, turned to darkness. It was a celestial law.

6

Meek Anna took her fury out on the bread that night, hacking the entire loaf into slices with a meat knife though there were only the two of us. When finished, she snarled at the wide knife blade, took a deep breath, calmly sat on the sofa, and started talking about something slightly more civilized. "If you go through enough bags in the grocery store, you can find lentils without dead insects in the bag, and—"

I interrupted her dissertation about communistic insects. Did she really expect me to forget her half-baked story about her father's storing Nazi bombs and her brother's "falling"? "Anna, what did you mean when you said that nasty thing about Bernhard, his fall?"

"I see. You are going back to that story again. If I must, I must."

Tonight, a year later in my comfortable den with the benefit of hindsight, I think she actually wanted to be asked questions, to continue the story, to finish and finally say to her umpteenth listener what she had never said before.

"If I must," she repeated. "So, Bernhard was a good boy, the best brother, the only one in the family who took time to understand me. When he turned seven or eight, he started going to the factory with my father on Saturdays to sand wood, glue parts together, stamp the logo on, and so forth. The company was to be his someday. Bernhard went higher in 1931, when he was ten. There was one night when I played the national anthem for my father, and the angry man whipped me with a belt not once but twice. You were there, as I remember. Bernhard went even higher in '32. There was a certain night about a week or two before the presidential election. He climbed so high he almost could not breathe."

I did, in fact, remember both nights. A few months after we moved to Linden Street in 1931, I was next door at the Himmels' house one night, playing checkers with Bernhard, who was quickly becoming my new best friend. World War II was still eight years away, but this was the night when a silent skirmish of opposites materialized into a war in the small Himmel house, a house that made Herr Himmel miserable because it couldn't hold a candle to the mansion.

"Play the national anthem for me, Anna girl," the depressed, half-drunken Herr Himmel ordered.

There was no hesitation on her part. She grabbed her violin and played the anthem. It was replete with squeals and sounded awful, obviously intentionally. When she finished, her hands were shaking with fright, yet she screamed, "There! How did *that* sound?"

Anna lived in a time when it was not possible for a child to speak to a parent that way; the day when children's tongues were loosened was still three and a half decades away. She had thus far achieved the impossible only in music. I had never heard such a poison scream come from such pretty lips or such terrible shrieks from a gorgeous instrument.

"Honor thy father, girl!" screamed her father, once a believer but now an atheist.

Anna's response was even more shocking: "Those first words of the anthem, 'Germany above all in the world,' are so, so, so *ugly* when they are sung by you!"

She ran to the bookshelf and grabbed a certain book, then leapt up the stairs into her room, slamming the door behind her. As a blossoming Nazi, Herr Himmel exalted the anthem and was hardly going to allow such insolent conduct. He flew upstairs, burst through Anna's door, and whipped her on the back with his belt. Then he walked back down, straightened his tie, and self-administered the anthem by whistling it.

The teary but obedient Frau Himmel slipped up to Anna's room and whispered through the door, "I am so dreadfully sorry, dear, but I can do nothing or will get whipped myself."

I stopped respecting Herr Himmel forever at that moment. I now hated him. As for Bernhard, he screamed to his father, "If you touch my sister again, I will punch you hard!" Then Bernhard was beaten himself.

I'll never forget the title of the book Anna yanked off the shelf before leaping to her bedroom because a half hour later, Bernhard and I shuddered when we heard her scream a single word from the top of the stairs. "Hideous!" she shrieked, undeterred by the whipping. Immediately we saw and heard the book thwacking down the stairs. It was entitled *The Decline of the West*, written near the end of World War I by the German philosopher Oswald Spengler. Someone, most likely Anna's father, had underlined a few passages and circled the word *barbarism* in red ink.

The theory of the underlined passages, boiled down, is that civilizations go through a process of birth, growth, and death before recycling to a new, more enlightened epoch, and that just before entering the new dawn, there is a necessary period of "barbarism." I was not so terribly bothered by it, but Bernhard thought the passages sounded macabre—and I'm sure that the eerie echo of the book thumping down the stairwell didn't help.

After Anna hurled the book down the stairs, Herr Himmel took off his belt again, ran upstairs—now stumbling from drunkenness, trying to take two steps at a time—and whipped her on her back again, this time tearing her dress. She shrieked. Now I not only hated him. I wanted him dead. Bernhard advanced on his father with clenched fists and halted only when his father pulled out a pistol.

This was precisely when Anna became more than a casual book

reader. She began inhaling books. "In their pages," the unpopular Anna tried to teach us at recess in school a few weeks later, "wonderful and terrible events or thoughts are written." The birth of the weal that the Nazis called the Second Reich—the 1871 unification of German-speaking states (except Austria) into a single German nation, to be dominated by Prussia—had opened a door to her great-great-grandfather, Jerold, to expand the suddenly inadequate factory, build his dream mansion, and put more flesh on his home library. Anna continued at recess, "And my great-great-grandpa called his new books the 'great Germanic books.' I have plugged my brain into some."

"Oh yeah?" a boy said. "Like what kind of books, Fraulein Smarty-Pants?"

"Like everything German. They are too hard for me now, but I will read every single one someday." And then, probably without intending to, I'm afraid she sounded like a miniature and conceited librarian. She said priggishly, "Like story and poem books by Goethe and Schiller. Like religion books by Eckhart. Oh, and philosophy books by men like Kant. And life stories of music writers like Herr Schumann and Herr Shubert. My great-great-grandfather Jerold said that a man shows he is a good German by discussing the great books, not by being in the smelly Wehrmacht. And I believe him. So *there*, you Nazi."

No one laughed this time. Instead, everyone except me were so put off that their eyes rolled.

Jerold's reverence for the great books, and his abhorrence of militarism and state authoritarianism, were well known to his descendants. Anna and Bernhard read many of the books, temporarily escaping their lives with their father. Years earlier, before Erich went off to war, he read many himself. The problem with Erich was that when he came home in 1918, he slowly and unperceptively, like a creeping disease, started loving Germany too much. So much that he turned his mind upside down over the years without suspecting he was overturning his soul. As he watched the nation gradually Nazify, he slowly came to think that reading the great books was for thinkers, not doers. He came to want to be a doer, one like the organizer of the Beer Hall Putsch. Maybe he became the unintended consequence of too much love of country?

In late 1931, not long after Anna's innocent show-off-and-tell incident in our class, she made her Berlin violin debut at age twelve at the famous old Schauspielhaus. Said one boy a few weeks later, drawing whoops of laughter from too many others, "Her majesty is stinking up the country on her national concert tour."

It hurt me. She returned home with her music coach a week later and became not only a virtual outcast at school but even more of a persona non grata with her father. Virtually parentless, she had little choice but to cloister alone in her bedroom more than ever. There, she practiced violin endlessly and devoured the dense books that Jerold had cherished the most.

"The books are way over her head," Bernhard told me, "but she wants to read them because of that great old man. He was like a god to her. She goes to our Lutheran minister after school for help understanding the hard parts. Reverend Landis."

With help from Landis, she read, reread, then finally understood some of the most difficult books in Jerold's collection (except that even Landis had trouble with von Schiller's *On the Aesthetic Education of a Man*). Among the books she added to the collection—portentously, in retrospect—was *The Castle*, an unfinished novel by the German author Franz Kafka about a man's futile attempt to deal with village bureaucrats operating out of a castle. My spying bedroom eyes, seeing the light in her face, imagined that after reading the same book again and again, she could grasp all or most of its complex thoughts.

"She hates, just *hates*, that Spengler book," Bernhard said. "But she keeps reading it over and over. She said a queer thing, that to know what you love, you must first know what you hate. And she does a funny thing. After she is finished with a book, she puts it back in the living-room bookshelf *upside down*. Every time. I wonder why."

"Maybe," I said, "it is to force your brutal, anal father to turn them right side up? To force him to touch them again after all those years of forgetting them? And maybe when he touches one, he will read it?'"

Anna overheard from her bedroom. Apparently she clung to a glimmer of hope that her heartless father was still of the human race. "Brilliant, Heinrich," she said from the top of the stairs. "Maybe my father will browse through a few books and cry for having whipped me. I feel desperate for him to read a few, come to his senses, and bring back the original Himmel violin. And to give up recruiting men to join the Nazi Party. And to take the wickedness out of the wicked joy in his voice when he sings those first beautiful words of the anthem, 'Germany above all the world.'"

Those were the emotional diseases, the afflictions of the mind, that Anna's father was inflicting on himself, and therefore on her, as of the November 1932 presidential election. Everyone was talking about the upcoming vote. Every city, hamlet, and farm was afflicted with the same thing: a mania for Germany to be great again. It was a crucial moment, although ten years would pass before a great but downtrodden people needed to worry about a man in America named Franklin Roosevelt, who would be elected to his first term as president of the US just two days after the German election of November '32. Anna couldn't understand— she didn't seem to have the right kind of brain to comprehend—how a foreign-born, uncultured, undereducated, ex-convict, racist (her words, not mine) could possibly become a serious contender for the German presidency. I myself used kinder words to describe Hitler, but while politics can ruin love, divine love is invulnerable to everything.

Germany had lived through painful but comparatively sunny years that it called its Golden Twenties, just as America had enjoyed its Roaring Twenties. But Germany was now being bloodied by the worldwide Great Depression, triggered by the alleged greed of American capitalists at the end of that decade of self-indulgence. Politics, the economy, and most of life for the vast majority of Germans once again roiled in confusion and turmoil. Although there was a long list of candidates in the November '32 election, it turned into essentially a two-man race: Paul von Hindenburg, the aged incumbent, versus Adolf Hitler, the upstart contender.

I had never heard my father call my mother a nasty name or listened to them argue—*really* argue—until one night about a week before the election. "Hindenburg is an infuriating, pathetic, power-grabbing incumbent," my father started in. "He is a Weimar man, and look where it has gotten us. The Depression. Anemia of the spirit. He is so old that he is brain dead. Adolf is in his early forties, fresh blood, a genius."

"Hindenburg is a wise eighty-four," my mother quipped back. "Hitler is green, has never held public office, is anti-parliament, anti-democracy, anti-people."

"You call democracy 'wise' when even lazy idiots have the right to vote, the privilege to choose our country's path? This 'wise' old bum, this former head of the Wehrmacht who lost the war for us, had no idea how to choose military strategy during the war. Therefore only a dope would think he knows how to run a whole nation. Adolf is a brilliant public speaker, knows what is what."

"He looks like a madman when he speaks! And by the way, *Karl*, Germany lost the war because it should have. It was the war-mongering politicians' fault, those men who wanted Europe to be dominated by Germany."

Father blew a fuse at that point. "You are worse than a dope, Claire! You are an ass! It is passion that you see when Adolf speaks in public!" I had never heard him call her a name, much less two. For the first time ever, Mother slept downstairs on the sofa that night.

A few days before the election, Elise and Erich hosted an intimate political soiree for up-and-comers in town, including my parents. Erich had been nursing his despair over his floundering nation and company by campaigning for the visionary and best-selling author who surely would fix the country's and therefore Erich's business's woes and then go on to accomplish more than had ever been imagined by Western civilization. I still despised Herr Himmel. He had become who he had been slowly becoming for years: a manic-depressive, violent, hard alcoholic.

I watched him that night before the first guests arrived. After downing another schnapps, his eyes filled with tears when he looked at the painting of the mansion on the wall and at the original Himmel violin on the music stand. He said to both, as if they had ears, "I will jump off the end of the earth if Hindenburg wins." Then his eyes filled with fire when he turned to Anna, Bernhard, and me, telling us to "run along and get scarce."

The three of us scampered upstairs. Anna had a look in her eyes. I had never seen her so cocksure. "Come, boys," she whispered. "We are going to sit on the upstairs landing and listen in." By that year, she was finished being a human angel and was now a higher thing—a human goddess. I was nervous sitting there with her.

My parents and maybe thirty other people were there, most seeming half crazy with worry about the fate of Germany. I was stunned that Herr Himmel let in Frau and Herr Kretsky, an honorable Jewish couple, because they arrived after he turned away a Communist couple. I was even more shocked that he swallowed his aversion to Jews and let Herr Kretsky kick off the affair by getting up and saying a few words in support of President Hindenburg. Maybe there was a method to Herr Himmel's madness. He knew that Kretsky was a Hindenburg man, and he probably believed that many people in the room were secret anti-Semites and would, for that reason alone, reject Kretsky's political views.

Kretsky started by praising the man for having commanded the Imperial German Army during the Great War, then went on and gave a lackluster talk. But he rallied a bit at the end:

"Hindenburg is very wise. He has an excellent economic plan and shall lift us out of the Depression. He is a thinker, an egalitarian. Hitler is an unthinking racist. To be blunt, his face is dripping with the blood of oppression. So I urge you all to stay the course and vote for the great military commander."

Herr Himmel then strode like a peacock to the front of the group, cleared his throat, and began speaking. He started out giving a reasoned, measured speech, getting angry and raising his voice only once or twice:

"And Hindenburg? He is just too old, too yesterday. He has been sitting in the president's chair so long that frankly his bum has gotten fat as our wallets have gotten skinny. And talk about a face dripping with blood! Hindenburg's is dripping with the blood of tens of thousands of dead German soldiers who trusted him to bring them home safely from the Great War. And I think the old man's brain is leaking oil. He has no clue how to fix our ungodly high unemployment and inflation rates. Do you men want to lose your jobs—those of you who are still employed, that is? Can you afford a new car? And I myself had to—"

He paused and blinked back tears. "My company is going in the toilet, and I had to sell my mansion. Do you people want a better job, a better house? If not, then go ahead and vote for the fat old man. But let me tell you, only Herr Hitler gives a good damn about good people like you! He knows that *you*, the middle class, are the backbone of Germany."

He paused to wipe the perspiration from his brow and to moisten his throat with a gulp of water. Then he became even more spirited. He raised his voice a decibel and talked about the Nazis' twenty-five-point political platform:

"Herr Hitler is all about the middle class and the less fortunate. He believes Germany can actually *spend* its way out of the Depression by raising money from bonds and then spending it by hiring unemployed people to build public works like new schools and roads. What a brilliant idea! And I bet you did not know that Herr Hitler actually wants to do away with real estate taxes so that you, the common people, can have more money in your pockets. He wants to revamp the education system so your children can get better jobs. He wants free university for children of our poorer townsfolk and wants increased welfare for your parents and grandparents."

I saw Anna roll her gorgeous eyes and spit foam on her seraph lips. She looked anxious, agitated, disgusted, even *ugly* for a moment—I guess it was possible. Herr Himmel continued by fondling the heart of the twenty-five-point platform, his voice growing, his hands now gesturing like Hitler himself while giving a speech:

"And Herr Hitler is sick and tired of Germany being told by the Allied countries—the dictators of the Versailles Treaty terms—that our nation has no right to a *real* army. He wants to increase military spending.

He wants to increase spending on national health and physical fitness. And do not be fooled by the rumors you may have heard, because in truth, the Nazi Party is for *total religious freedom*. The leaders of the party have even stated in writing, in the platform, that they would sacrifice their own lives for the sake of carrying out the platform. My God, what more you could ask for?"

Frau and Herr Kretsky—he was wearing a yarmulke over top of his steaming ears—got up and fled out the door. Then Anna startled me and everyone else. She stood up at the top of the dark stairwell like a rosebud rising and opening in the morning sun and said in her usual calm voice, "Father, everything you have said about the Nazi platform is true." But then instantly, in a fell swoop, she shocked everyone by doing something a German teenager was not capable of in those days. She—*she*, this thirteen-year-old girl who now was not only seen but also heard— went lower, from the bloom to the stem, shouting out thorns aimed at her father's head: "But it is what you did *not* say about the demon platform that *really* matters!"

Her iron-fisted German father looked almost traumatized. Frau Himmel looked like she wanted to die. She still loved him. She knew how to love. All Germans did. Their prehistoric ancestors had learned how to at some point, and each generation taught the next. I think she remained quiet and, despite her husband's loss of love for family, loved her husband for expressing love for Germany in the best way she thought he knew how. Even Bernhard, seeing his father pour out his strange heart to his guests, seemed to have a kernel of love left for his father. Bernhard must have wondered at that moment why his sister was going berserk.

Anna rushed down the stairs, ran to her father, and shouted, "Father, why not tell these good people the *rest* of the Nazi Party platform!"

"Shut up and go to your room!" the Nazi father shot back, looking as if he wanted her dead. That was a bad mistake on his part. Very bad. Except for that one night she had intentionally abused the national anthem on her violin, Anna had always been more or less an obedient daughter, but at that moment, at that place, something changed. She squalled,

"*You* shut up, *Herr Himmel*, because it is *my* turn to speak now!"

She rendered her Nazi father speechless, his wide-open lips unable to close. The couples in the room looked afraid for her. She had read the complete twenty-five-point Nazi Party platform and at that moment was compelled, by what she was, to expose what he had willfully ignored in it. I cringed when she cried out, "Father, you know as well as I that the *good* things in the Nazi platform would only apply to *citizens*! And only people who have so-called 'German blood' would be considered citizens! The Jews, the Slavs, and the other people the Nazis detest would not be *citizens*!"

Momentarily she became a bottle of antiseptic that kept refilling to the brim no matter how much she poured out on him. "And the platform says death to all usurers! That is the same as saying, 'Death to all Jewish bankers!' And, and, and *you*, Father, you talk about religious freedom? Well, *that* would only apply to people of the '*German race*,' not to minorities! Jews and others would be expelled from the country! My God, Father, be a man! Be a human!"

Her words were filled with hate for the man she called Father, but there is no word for her intonation. I had never heard anything so scathing come out of a human being. Maybe she wasn't human.

***

Turning the stove on high to bring the lentil soup to a boil, Anna started to tell me about that night at her parents' house in November 1932. I reminded her that I had been there and would never forget it. She said, "Then you know that when Bernhard heard my father beating me that night, he rushed out of his room, pulled my father off of me, and punched my father in the face, screaming that if he ever beat me again, he would kill him."

"I didn't know. I must have gone home by then."

Having mentioned her brother's daring, Anna suddenly seemed to want to tell more about his eventual fall. She couldn't shake Bernhard off her skin.

"And in 1934, a few years after that momentous election," she said, "Bernhard made my father fume at the factory. Something about my brother's wanting to take down some plaques about dead Himmel soldiers. My father had finally had enough of my brother. You are aware that the man threw Bernhard in a military academy for two years after the plaque infamy."

"He was my best friend. How could I forget?"

That night was the first time I drew a connection between Bernhard's hate of the military, Anna's bewildering complexities, and the military history of the Himmels. The history of the violin company had been on public display in the factory lobby in a series of plaques overflowing with information about the military lives of generations of Himmels. Anna's mere mention of the plaques took me back to a conversation that Bernhard and I had around 1934, when he was about thirteen, or a year after we joined Hitler Youth. It was vintage Bernhard. He was becoming his own man and growing to despise everything about his father.

"I am the dummkopf lout who put up that plaque about Conan Himmel," Bernhard said, his blue eyes graying. "I was seven or eight. Conan Himmel was dreamed up by me from my book about Conan the Barbarian, a made-up man that walked the earth killing people and wrecking things way before Jesus was born. I wrote in crayon on the plaque that Conan Himmel made violins at the Himmel factory. Last year, I got so mad at myself for being such a phony that I wanted to rip it down and burn it."

Bernhard turned his teary eyes away. "I wanted to take down some other plaques too, even though they are all probably true—they are about Himmel soldiers that lived way before the company was even made! Count the Himmel soldiers on the plaques, Heinrich. Six, over four hundred years. Everyone from one soldier called Erich the First who was in an army that chased Jewish camps way to the east in the 1300s to another called Hektor who they say beat and did the dirty thing to a girl in the 1600s."

Then Bernhard shined a spotlight on his and Anna's most precious hero, Alfred Himmel. "It is so strange that one family can have opposite people. We Himmels have Erich the First and Hektor, two peas in a pod, and then we have Alfred, who turned out to be the reverse of them. My sister would not be the person she is if it was not for Alfred and the violin company he started. And he never would have quit the army and started the company if he did not build that very first violin. And he would not have done *that* if he did not happen to be walking by the St. Thomas Lutheran Church in Leipzig one Sunday morning around 1744. There he was, in spiffy Prussian Army clothes in Leipzig on a secret army job. He said that he was wowed by the sound of the violins coming from inside the church and walked in to hear the rest of the piece. The little orchestra was playing 'Jesu, Joy of Man's Desiring.' The little choir was singing it too."

Bernhard was still a falsetto at that age. He sang the first stanza of the cantata, his high voice sounding queer to me: "Jesu' joy of man's desiring; Holy wisdom, love most bright; Drawn by Thee, our souls aspiring; Soar to uncreated light."

As he sang, I swear that the occlusions in his grayed irises re-jeweled to every shade of blue. "I bet everything I own that Alfred was wowed by the whole thing—the music, the Gothic prettiness of the church, the ghost of Martin Luther, who once preached there a few hundred years earlier. But mostly, he said that he was wowed by the chief of the little choir, a man with a curly gray wig, a chubby man that was called Johann Sebastian Bach. Music is magic. It can turn a tough army man into good. War into peace."

Being a teenager who revered the old Prussian military, I could only be skeptical, so I asked Bernhard how he knew all this.

"I snooped an old box in the attic and found a letter that Alfred wrote to his wife around 1745. Everything was in there. After my father got mad and whacked me in the head for wanting to take down the Conan plaque, I wanted to add Alfred's letter to the history row. Then my son of a bitch father got madder and hit me in the head again. His Alfred plaque talked big about Alfred's army honors, all right, but said not one thing about Alfred after he stopped being in the army and started the company. Except my father wrote in pen at the bottom of the plaque, *Alfred founded this violin company in 1745*. That was it. Seven words. Over and out."

Bernhard winced when he repeated his father's inert inscription. By then, I think his love for his father was so small you had to use a thick magnifying glass to see it.

Bernhard instantly rehoisted himself, though. He went on to throw more light and explain that by the time of the German-state unification in 1871, Alfred's great-something-grandson Jerold had thirteen employees at the company. By the end of 1879, Jerold had his new mansion, his factory, and was making the People's Violin hand over fist.

"And by 1929, when Anna was ten, our grandfather Mars Himmel was head of the company. He took her in his arms one day and said, 'You are finally old enough for me to tell you. You probably did not know that Martin Luther was far from perfect. He was a good example of the whole German character, loving music and the arts but also being boisterous, autocratic, and prejudiced—he disliked Jews. But, Anna, you are different. You have the good without the bad.' He looked at her as if speaking his final words and said, 'You are German culture.' Her eyes lit. She took him at his word. Why? Because she had the same thought when she was a little girl, and a grand old man was now validating it. The kids at school thought she was stuck-up when she said such things. She was ignored by everyone. You probably saw it yourself. She became a loner. But she practiced her violin in her room all the more because of it. Day and night. A fanatic."

***

Staying at the stove, the lentil soup now boiling and spitting on her arms, Anna spat, "Damn you, soup! Damn you, Bernhard! Father beat you up over the plaques, and then you transformed into a brute just like Hektor Himmel—or worse."

Bernhard? A brute? That was just too much after too many hours. I didn't believe it. The warmth I remembered he had for music during that boyhood conversation about Alfred, coupled with the fact that Anna quit playing violin before the war, led me to wonder whether he, not she, had been the musical star of the family. Was Anna jealous of her brother? Was she therefore lying by calling him a "brute . . . or worse" without any supporting detail?

Such a transformation in him no longer seemed highly improbable. It seemed impossible. Had she lived so long in a Communist country championing such a fraudulent claim about human nature—that people by nature have no individualistic desires and want to live as a collective under an autocrat—that she herself had become a fraud?

7

After handing me that last charred morsel about Bernhard, paradoxically Anna's hands were shivering and she angrily warmed them by putting them almost in the flames of the fire. "Ouch!" she cried. Although I was hungry, oddly she turned the soup burner all the way off, then returned to the sofa. She rushed to change subjects before my tongue could untie and ask questions about Bernhard's alleged and inexplicable "falling." She quickly said, "I cannot afford to think about Bernhard right now, so maybe we can talk about something nicer. Like your mother. I have a confession to make."

"A confession?"

"Yes. On that day in August of '36, after your father was fired from the university, I heard about it at school, then sneaked out and ran to your house. You, of course, remained blissfully ignorant in school. I rushed in your house and told your mother that the firing of your father was only the tip of the iceberg. I insisted to your mother, *insisted*, that she take you three to the United States, said that there is a state called Iowa in a place called the heartland and that many Germans had settled there over the years. Amana and Donsville for instance, I said. Immediately your mother ran to the bank, emptied out the family savings, and bought three bus tickets to Normandy and three ship tickets to New York."

"You told her to take my father and me and flee?"

"I did. Of course I did. That was what I was."

I thought it might be another lie. "All these years I thought that it was Mother's decision alone to go to America."

"But you yourself know that in 1933, three years before your father got himself into that bind and was fired, I told her to take you three to the US or Canada. You were standing right there, in my backyard."

Suddenly I recalled what had happened that day in 1933.

***

My mother went to take a pie next door to the Himmels that day. I tagged along, never giving up an opportunity to see my muse. Anna was bundled up on her back in her backyard, staring at the sky. When she heard our footsteps, she jumped up and said audaciously, "Frau Schultheiss, you should take your family and flee Germany. Go to America, maybe California, or to Canada.'"

Looking perplexed, my mother said, "Anna, why would you say such a thing?"

"Because it is something I feel. I think I even feel it in my violin playing. Hindenburg won the election, and the fool just made Hitler the second most powerful person in the country, the chancellor. Certain things are going to start happening."

Mother certainly did not respect Hitler, but she was not too concerned about him either. She thought Anna might be joking about fleeing. Mother said with a small smile, poking a little fun, "And when are you Himmels packing up to resettle in a castle in the south of France?"

But Anna was deadly serious. "Father would never take his family and leave this country. And Mother? She does whatever that man says. And even if my mother, that man, and Bernhard *did* leave, I would never abandon Germany. *Never."*

Mother couldn't seem to fathom what to say next in this very strange conversation. After a few long seconds, she said, "Anna, if *you* would never leave, why do you think *we* would ever want to leave?"

"There is a difference, one that cannot be measured. You folks are able to leave. I am not. It would be impossible. I am, well, sort of Germany itself."

This was about the most bizarre conversation I'd ever heard. It was bizarre for Anna to tell us to flee a place she so desperately loved, a land where her ancestors had lived probably since at least medieval times. It was more bizarre for her to say that she could feel it in her violin playing. The weirder thing to my mother (but not to starry-eyed me, of course) was Anna's self-important declaration that she was "well, sort of Germany itself"—a proposition my mother thought Anna had cast away as a child.

The weirdest thing to me was the indescribable look in Anna's eyes as she spoke. There are no words.

I think my mother wanted to walk inside Anna's obviously troubled mind to see what kind of demon was stalking there. Probably feeling sorry that the girl had no adult to discuss her troubles with, Mother said, "Why not come over for tea sometime and we can talk?"

Anna perked up, looking as if she wanted our family to adopt her. "Really?" she said.

"Really."

"Then you bet I will."

I had buried in my mind but could never forget that this was around the time I heard from my bedroom window what I had thought inconceivable: a squeak in Anna's violin playing. A tiny one, but something that to me contradicted the laws of possibility. Just two years earlier, in 1931, when this prodigy had done us common folks in Edelberg proud by making her national debut in Berlin, she became for most of us a collective dream-coming-true about the revitalization of Germany. She was revered even by our town's small number of Jews and other minorities whose exclusion from what they called our Aryan culture gave them every reason to despise a girl with blond hair, blue eyes, and the Prussian military in her father's ancestry. But shortly after the November '32 election, that first squeak came down like lightning tearing into the earth.

I think that to Anna, the squeak was a failing, almost a criminal offense, and the start of some kind of devilry in Germany. Within ten minutes of my hearing that violin-fingering fault, apparently she finally had the stuff to venture to our house for her first conversation with Mother. She ran over.

At that time, Anna somehow had been getting her hands on underground newspapers and reading about the little-known derelictions of the Nazi regime. When she came over to our house that first time, I think she felt let out of a cage and like a muzzle had been taken off. She seemed thrilled to be immersed in a realm her parents denied her— discussing politics with an adult. I could hardly believe that she was sitting at my kitchen table, discussing complicated social issues I knew nothing about, and telling Mother what she would do if she were in charge of the world.

By their second meeting over tea, my mother dared to allow Anna's prophecy about storm clouds getting darker over Germany to root in the underbelly of her own mind. Mother actually started toying with the idea of our going to America.

"It is despicable," Anna said, "that President Hindenburg made that demon the chancellor, second in power to himself. So what does the demon do then? He has the Reichstag burned down and blames it on a Communist. And he murders freedom of association and freedom of the press for the Jewish people!"

"It is terrible," my mother said, "but on the other hand, the demon's—I mean Chancellor Hitler's—new deficit-spending ideas will work wonders. For example, his idea to complete the Autobahn." With that, Anna put her head down and slunk home.

But she didn't put herself back into the cage or put the muzzle back on. She came over again in April, more upset and disordered. "The demon has ordered the whole country to boycott Jewish businesses," she said even before she shut the door. "And how about his new law that gives loans and other benefits only to Aryan couples who promise to marry and have children?"

"I know, I know," my mother said. "It is not very good. They should do the same for others. What is good for the goose is good for the gander." But that's when Mother shut up. See, the economy had woken up, giving her more money in her pocketbook. Anna immediately dashed home, looking dejected.

But she wasn't ready to give up on Mother. She came back yet again a month later, almost unable to control herself, constantly interrupting Mother. "How about more Nazi burnings of so-called anti-Germanic books?" Anna fired. "And the banning of all political parties except the Nazi Party? And forced sterilization of certain people?"

"Anna, everything you are talking about is just horrible. But this awfulness will stop soon. It *has* to. It cannot go on forever."

Then Anna's ire jumped almost as high as it had been that night of the political duel between her and her father at her house. "You, Frau Schultheiss, are as gullible as a newborn!" To Anna, I think the Nazi species of evil was something like the arrowroot weed, which was capable of growing a foot a night, edible, and used as a folk medicine. For her, the weed stretched from border to border. She stormed home this time, looking as defeated as I imagined her father had on the day he returned from the Great War.

She never came back.

A few months later my mother was out in the garden when Anna yelled to her from across the way, "What about this phony referendum rubber-stamping the demon's buildup of the army and navy? He is peeing on the Versailles Treaty. And his takeover of an airplane company so he can build military planes?"

Looking perplexed, Mother walked over to her. "Anna, I was completely in the dark about the airplane company." Anna knew every detail of that corporate thievery and enlightened Mother. Later that day, in the house, Mother said to me, "Anna makes such good points, but I think I love Germany too much to leave. And, Heinrich, your father is happy here." Mother still lacked all the emotional equipment needed to uproot our family and flee.

Then came September 1933 and Anna's fit at school. She now considered most of the other students rambunctious and childish; school was a place where her world collided with theirs. The teacher called on her and asked her to tell us about any current event she had read about in a newspaper. Anna shot up and hollered, half crazed but using professorial words, "I'll tell you something! This man they call the Führer just created the Reich Culture Chamber to control film, music, theater, news, books, fine arts, et cetera! There is an expression, 'Art for art's sake.' It is what made our culture great for centuries, but now, the expression is poison. German culture now exists only for spreading the Aryanization of everything!"

Anna darted out of our classroom in tears as the rest of us—all but me, it seemed—started to laugh. The teacher, dressed in a skirt made popular by Eva Braun, just shook her head and let it go.

That night, from my bedroom window, I heard more conspicuous squeaks and saw more tears drop down her cheeks. High-pitched baby shrieks, really. Over the next months, her violin playing kept sinking underwater, one fathom at a time. Tonal belches. Fingering faults. Slightly mistuned strings. Her playing was bending down to a gloomy place. In retrospect, it seemed to parallel the downward slide of Germany. The impresario in Berlin stopped booking her for recitals. In school, she looked depressed, always staring out the window, never talking. At home, she was always hunkered in her room, in her bed with the covers pulled up to her chin, always reading a book or trying to fix the squeals coming out her Himmel. She looked ill. I wondered if she was dying of something.

But Mother was just fine at that time. About most things, that is. And 1934 came.

"Karl, did you read the paper today?" she asked him one day. "The government has passed new laws protecting the environment and wildlife. Oh, and I went to one of those new traveling movie theaters today. Very innovative. And women can now get free screenings for breast cancer. And you know what else? German scientists, probably from the generous budget given to them from our Führer, have discovered that cigarette smoking causes lung disease. You should quit."

But Mother was becoming disturbed by a few other things. For instance, the so-called Night of the Long Knives in the early summer of 1934. "I just heard about it, Karl. It stabbed close to my own heart, because my cousin Tomas was one of the men killed. Murdered. A whole group of Brownshirt policemen, poor Tomas included, were rounded up and shot. And now, the only police forces are the Gestapo and the Sshutzstaffel."

Mother tried to snooker herself into believing that the murderous rampage by Hitler's men was like a tornado, just one cursed event that the laws of chance dictated would never happen again. Yet strangely, a week later when I secretly rummaged for money in her purse, I was shocked to find a Luger and a few bullets for self-defense.

Then, Mother said something totally unexpected at my Lutheran confirmation party at our house a few weeks later. The affair started out uplifting. Made me feel closer to God. Since my grandpa Schultheiss had let me down badly with his hatred of Hitler Youth, my mother's father, my grandpa Lutl, was now the grandfather who could do no wrong. A widower, he came to the party alone. Though Mother knew how much he cherished Germany, she (or the wine she had been drinking?) made the bad mistake of spilling out to him, "It has crossed my mind that things are starting to get a little too dangerous in a few places. Do not think that I have not at least *thought* about leaving Germany."

Looking surprised, Grandpa Lutl said, "Leave? You mean to a Germanic place like Austria or Switzerland?"

"No, Father. You see, there is this girl next door. She is a little high strung and off-putting, but last year she reminded me of this and that. I think about Tomas a lot. The girl said we should go to America or Canada. I am thinking maybe America, but am just wondering is all."

Grandpa's jaw dropped off his face at merely hearing the word

America. I thought the proud old German, who loved his country as much as he loved his daughter, was going to have a conniption. He shrieked, "That girl next door must be crazy! America? Why would anyone want to go *there*? Those people and their cousins, the Brits! They invaded our country less than two decades ago!"

"Wait, wait, wait," Mother interrupted. "First, Germany was the aggressor in that war. Second, I never said we are actually *going* to America. I only said we are wondering."

"Aggressor? Poppycock! Why would you even *think* for one second about running away?" He then screamed out things I believed to be true about America. "Why in hell would anyone want to leave Germany and go to a third-rate country with a bunch of ragtime and cowboy singers? Scott Joplin. Woody Guthrie. Compared to our great cabaret singers and entertainers like Marlene Dietrich."

"Dietrich went off to America, Father."

"Well, forget I said her. Why in God's name would anyone want to live in a place with Communists and gangsters? Al Capone and machine guns in the streets. Men murder each other in America for something as little as the pocket change to buy a whiskey drink! And the Depression the greedy Americans started still goes on and on and on!"

My grandpa Lutl loved Mother desperately. He had taught her as a child how to love a person desperately and how to love her country more. But now I see that the nature of his love for her was like the nature of Germany as a whole back then: the higher it went, the harder it crashed and burned when it fell. He loved his daughter so fiercely that after the party—even though she had not yet decided to go *anywhere*—he stopped talking to her. After we finally went to America in 1936, he refused to return any of her letters. We never heard from him again even though he lived another twenty years.

"My own father will not open the door of his house to me," Mother complained the following week. "He is a proud, stubborn, ornery, ignorant old German, just like all his friends. But I love him as much as I love Germany. I could never leave this country and abandon him."

Not even the referendum of August 1934 just weeks after Hindenburg died, by which Hitler made himself the absolute dictator and supreme Führer, gave Mother the fortitude to want to leave the country that she, Father, and I loved so much. It's a bad cliché that love can conquer all, yet there's some truth in it. She despised Hitler, but her obsessive love for her fatherland gave her optimism about the country's future.

"Later this year or certainly next," she said to me out of Father's earshot, "the truth will sneak out and then bloom all over the country. People will realize what a maniacal scoundrel Hitler is and will throw him in prison *forever* this time around. After all, the Renaissance put an end to all that was barbaric about the ancient civilizations. It is too long after the Renaissance to even imagine that something like the ancient Romans feeding Christians to lions could ever happen again. Not in the twentieth-century world. And *especially* not in a country so high up the scale of civilization as Germany."

I didn't care about any lions, but I did want to see my saliva on her face for spitting such a bratty rant on my government.

I recall an ugly conversation at our dinner table the following year, 1935, after the national flag was redesigned to show a swastika in a center white circle surrounded by red. Father remarked, "Did you two see the sharp new flag that Herr Himmel is flying on his front porch? He burned that old one, that rascal."

"I like the new flag," I said, "but it must drive Bernhard and Anna crazy."

"It is disturbing, even eerie," Mother said. "That swastika against a blood-red background. Just horrible. Blessed be the old flag."

Father laughed at the scorn written all over Mother's face.

"You think it is funny?" Mother said to him. "Rudolph Gendler? Your broken nose for dummying your genealogy records? Need I remind you?"

But Father was certain that Herr Gendler, the part-Slav whose entire life was Nazism and who was happy to have recruited him to the Nazi Party, would protect the secret of his Jewish and Romani genes. A liar usually hates another liar, but not in this case. Father now was worried not one whit that he could be touched by Hitler's Nuremburg Laws, which denied Jews, Romani, Blacks, and other minorities their natural human rights. In advocating for the redesigned flag, Father bypassed Mother's brain and went for her heart:

"Claire, remember that neighbor who finally kicked your dog to death for barking too loud night after night? Well, under Hitler's new animal-protection law, the son of a bitch would be in a work camp like Dachau right now. For God's sake, Claire, the Führer wants pets to be treated as good as people! The least you can do is like his new flag."

That shut Mother up tight. She had loved that dog. Her silence was a voluntarily surrender of ground she had initially won. A week later, I was pleased that we had our own new flag flying from our front porch.

"Heil Hitler," Father said, gazing at it after hanging it. I was torn, though, because later that day I barely endured seeing Anna weeping at her bedroom window. She moved her head from side to side, eyeing the two men's flags, as powerless to take them down and burn them as she was to arrest the squeals growing louder in her violin playing.

Then, in September of '36, a comedy presented itself to Mother. She fell into a fit of laughter when she read a piece in a Berlin newspaper reprinted from an article that had appeared in Britain's *Daily Express* paper. It was penned by a fellow named David Lloyd George, who, during the Great War, had been the prime minister of Germany's bitter enemy, the United Kingdom. At first, Mother thought that the former British head of the government was trying his hand at comedy.

He wrote—I kid you not—that Adolf Hitler was "the George Washington of his country." (The Brits by then had the utmost respect for the father of the United States.) He scrawled that the great leader had filled his people with "hope and confidence" and bestowed them with "a renewed sense of determination." He was "a born leader of men." Mother laughed hysterically, "Lloyd George is a senile buffoon. What he says is so wildly exaggerated and obviously wrong that no one in Germany will take it seriously."

She was wrong. Dead wrong. Father cut out the article and framed it for his den. Many in the masses thought that the former prime minister's fawning was the world's political certification of Hitler's righteousness. When Mother realized how the nation was reacting to the article, she started to turn toward the light. *Anna,* she likely thought, *must see something. George Washington? Really? Really! Good Lord!*

***

Anna had let the soup go cold, returning it to where it had been when we walked into the flat, when only innocence was in the room. We didn't return to innocent times, though. Anna said, "I hope you are not hungry yet because I am anxious to return to your father's firing from the university. I feel I can tell you now."

She started, "I am sure you remember that Joseph Vogel was the editor in chief of the *Edelberg Voice.* He and your father used to fish together at the Spree. Your mother would go to garden shows with Frau Vogel. Around September of '36, about a month after you three went to America, Vogel wrote a stinging editorial defending your father's research at the university."

I didn't realize then that this was a gross understatement. I now know just how gracious the editorial was. It rushed to Father's defense while omitting the lie he had told in his research conclusion:

> . . . *One can only assume that Herr Schultheiss' so-called resignation from the university, unfortunately, has more to do with his suddenly-revealed Jewish blood than with the quality of his research. Certainly I cannot let pass that within just weeks after he left and went to the land of liberty, America, Edelberg University's sub-department of animal studies within the Biology Department broke away and styled itself the Department of Racial Studies, which I dare say, at risk of summoning Herr Goebbels' wrath, we should name the "Demonology Pit" for short.*
> *Unless we believe that time has literally bent itself into reverse and we are once again in the Dark Ages, then we should pray that the wholesale firing*

of some of our nation's finest academicians and the burning of some of
our great books—and the even greater thuggery happening elsewhere in
Germany—is owing to a freak of nature which shall shrivel and die of
hunger before too long, and certainly before building a permanent home in
this great nation . . .

Disturbed, Anna went on, "So at Oktoberfest in '36, I saw Herr Vogel
in a beer tent with a large handful of people. He is sitting there, nursing
a beer and minding his own business, when your grandfather Lutl—you
say he could do no wrong—gets up on a table with his beer stein and
acts crazy. He starts shouting something like, 'My daughter went off to
America with that pudding-headed Jew husband of hers who got fired
for lying in his research.'"

"Grandpa Lutl said *that*? It's almost impossible to believe."

She stared at me. "It was awful. Disgusting. Nobody thought it was
funny at first. But after ten seconds, a man laughs. And when *he* laughs,
another man laughs. After a minute, it is like a chain reaction. It is follow-
the-leader, and then almost all the people in the tent except Herr Vogel
are laughing. Rudy Gendler is there too, laughing and all spiffed up in
his SS getup, but he is looking around and watching who is doing this or
that. Eventually Herr Vogel, all alone in his disgust, sees Rudy. Vogel slips
his crucifix and chain under his shirt and does not appear so disgusted
anymore. A minute later, even *he* laughs. At first it is an uncomfortable
laugh, but then it is not. He is the last to join in, but he does it and he
ends up roaring laughter and ordering another beer."

Anna looked at the ceiling and shook her head as if she couldn't
believe her own words. She continued, "It was monkey see, monkey do.
Well, Herr Vogel was no monkey. He was a human man. He was a good
and decent and thinking man."

Anna should have added that the instant Vogel started laughing, he
stopped being a thinking man with a mind of his own. Hitler once said,
"What good fortune for governments that the people do not think."

Vogel, at the moment of his laughter, became one of millions of the Führer's darlings. Thinking is the profoundest attribute that separates man from lower animals.

Now, I certainly don't mind if people think that I'm part Jew or part Romani, but as Anna finished the Vogel story, I shuddered thinking about Herr Gendler unthinkingly calling me a "pure Aryan" and a "perfect Nordic German" that day I signed up for Hitler Youth. I was no pure blood; I had Jewish and Romani genes. Even being called German makes me uneasy now. I think about that certain Rorschach test—the drawing that could be either a candlestick or two human profiles staring at each other face-to-face, take your pick. All my adult life before visiting Germany, I had been the simple harmless candlestick, but sitting in Anna's flat, hearing about the Vogel incident, I started feeling like the two people facing each other, staring into each other's eyes, a divided self—or, to put it in musical terms, a disharmonious fugue, a dissonant collision of point and counterpoint—split between my Germanness and my humanness.

But I digress yet again. It is Bernhard we should be talking about. So, did he split and then become a single thing? Did he become like Vogel times a billion? That night in her flat after the Vogel story, I started to think that maybe, just maybe, Anna had been at least partially right about her brother.

"Soon after you all fled to America," Anna continued, "Bernhard came home from military school and refused to stay down on his knees. He got up on his feet. He sees Jesse Owens win four gold medals in the '36 Berlin Olympics and, a minute after Mr. Owens bows to receive the fourth, says he thinks he wants to run high school track. But when the demon refuses to shake Mr. Owens' hand, Bernhard is outraged and decides definitely that he will learn track.

"Yes, my father wants him to be an athlete, but certainly not like Jesse Owens. Instead, that man, if that is what he or it can be called, wants skinny Bernhard to learn to box like Max Schmeling and whip a Black kid, any Black kid, just like Schmeling knocked out that Black man Joe Louis. The man puts on the gloves and knocks out the kid, Bernhard, so now the man makes the kid lift weights to be a better boxer. My brother's excellent grades in school are tumbling as his arms and chest are getting larger. Hitler would have been proud of him."

"He was always quite studious," I noted. "He knew his wildflowers, his algebra, his European geography, almost to a fault. Always questioning. I'll never forget he once asked me, 'If God made everything, where did *He* come from?'"

Then Anna said something that baffled me. "Nothing comes from nothing, Heinrich. Everything starts with something, usually something small. My father ended up willfully breaking his own son's nose. It all started small, with a German Reichsthaler five coin, that one with the Potsdam Military Church on one side and an eagle and two swastikas on the other. My father had one, and he shined it up with metal polish until it looked newer than one fresh from the mint. 'It is like a rabbit's foot, a lucky charm,' the man said with paternalism dripping from his voice as he placed it into Bernhard's hand. Then he growled, 'And never let me catch you without it!' Bernhard looked at it and gagged."

"Heinrich, you know the church, yes? Just outside Berlin, built a few hundred years ago for soldiers?"

I remembered that glorious church, all right. Back in 1933, the new chancellor, Hitler, used it as a forum to make an alliance with the unwitting old President Hindenburg, a satanic agreement that eventually gave the Nazi Party total legislative power in the nation. A coin was struck to commemorate it. In 1937 I received this letter from Bernhard:

27 July 1937

Dear Heinrich, or Henry I guess,

. . . .

And that super-shiny coin, that "lucky charm" my father made me take. What a superstitious dope he is! Why did he break my nose? Simple. I refused to carry that damn coin.

And I will tell you another thing. That man who calls himself my father forced me to go with him all the way to Munich to see something called the Degenerate Art Exhibit by the Nazis. He said I needed more of the right kind of education, the kind you do not get in school. The exhibit had mostly modern and abstract paintings by famous Jews, all things that the Nazis want the public to know are unacceptable. My asshole father said the artists should be shot. I would sure like to know what is so terrible about those paintings!

. . . .

Bye for now.
Your best friend always,

Bernhard

"It was 1937," I said to Anna. "Your father was a brute by then. Even evil."

"Father was raised a serious Lutheran, but most Nazis despised traditional Christianity. So the demon became my father's new Jesus Christ, and *Mein Kampf* became his new bible. Bernhard was my father's hope for the future. He made Bernhard stop taking violin lessons from me, and when he found out that Bernhard and I had been defying his orders, he went crazy and smashed Bernhard's violin over his knee. The boy's Himmel! Made back in the old days, before my father cheapened the process. When Bernhard heard his violin getting shattered, he ran out of the house in tears and did not come home for two days."

I glanced at the violin propped in the corner of Anna's flat and imagined its spruce soundboard smashed to pieces. Then I stared at it. I imagined the statue of Victoria, when I thought it was Anna, smashed to pieces. Then I imagined Anna herself—the "Goddess of Culture"—smashed into smaller pieces. Herr Himmel became worse than insane.

"And that was that," Anna said. "My father started life as a normal person in the crowd—a rich one, but otherwise normal—and then became *ab*normal over the years with his Nazi religion. But now he was normal again in the crowd. Being the old abnormal was the new normal, and he despised his only son for being the new abnormal."

Anna labored to stand up and throw three more logs on the fire—forget the soup. Obviously she expected her story to end no time soon. She continued, "And then on precisely 15 March 1938—I remember the exact date because it was the Ides of March—my father made Bernhard have something like a birthday celebration at our house after dinner. A birthday party even though it was no one's birthday. Bernhard despised Hitler Youth more than ever by then, but my father had told him he would be kicked out of the house if he quit, so he had to go ahead and hold this 'party.' Twenty or so other boys from Hitler Youth wore their uniforms, and all except Bernhard put on silly paper Wehrmacht helmets and blew into those whoop-dee-dings you blow into that make a loud quacking noise. Mother made me serve chocolate Lugers.

"The party was to celebrate Hitler's march into Vienna earlier that day to a cheering crowd of tens of thousands. Austria had just been born into the Third Reich. The so-called Anschluss. The news on the radio said that Viennese girls and women were throwing roses at him as he paraded through the streets, standing up in a military vehicle, waving like Julius Caesar in a horse-drawn chariot. It all sounded disgusting to me. The Austrian people had been waiting a long time for that day. Most of their ancestors were angry back in 1871 when the Second Reich was born and Austria was the only big German-speaking state not invited into the new nation-state of Germany.

"Rudy Gendler was a leader of local Hitler Youth and was at our house that night, and I could tell he was livid at the way the day had gone. He—"

"I'd think that Rudy would have been ecstatic about Austria coming into the Reich."

"He was pleased, super happy, about *that*, but he had wanted at least a little shooting, wanted at least one German soldier to go to a glorious death. By then, he seemed to respect death. He was not in the Wehrmacht, yet had taken the Hitler soldier's oath promising to be willing to die for the Führer. The Austrians were so overjoyed seeing the demon's army sweeping in that not a single shot needed to be fired. Rudy was disgusted that no one had died. That bastard made those boys stand at rapt attention, wipe the chocolate from their mouths, and take the soldier's oath. When Rudy got furious with Bernhard for refusing, my brother ran out of the house. He was still gone when my father got home an hour later, so Father beat my mother for letting Bernhard run out."

Here are parts of another letter I received from Bernhard a short time later:

17 November 1938

Dear Henry,

How are you? You are lucky to be far away in America. . . .
As of March, there is no escaping the Reich by moving to Austria. Austria is now part of the Reich, apparently loving every minute of it. But that is old news.
Things have gotten awful for minorities in town. Kids are slowly disappearing from school. The new laws say that Jews cannot own businesses or go to the movies or the library or even drive cars! They made Dr. Cohen shut down his office. A policeman beat a little Jewess for doing nothing but touching the flag in the village square, and now no one has seen her in a week!
Why the barbaric violence? Barbarism! I cannot figure it out. This Hitler has turned into a madman. If he were here right now, my father would kiss his ass. Then I would strangle both of them with my bare hands. God! Bye for now.

Your best friend always,

Bernhard

"Then came an even worse year, 1939," Anna said. "The war started on the first of September, and it seemed to me as if Hitler and I were the only ones who knew it was coming. Right before the war started, I cried so much in my bedroom. My violin playing had already gone bit by bit to God's opposite for reasons that were beyond me. Screeches, getting louder all the time. Those terrible screeches and shrieks!

"There was a second thing that made me cry as much. It was the demon's warped notion of lebensraum, the crazy and dangerous idea that you need more 'open space' for the millions of future people of the thousand-year empire. Where do you start finding more open space? Well, of course you start with the weakest country on your border—not to mention the one with the most Jews that could serve as Reich slaves. Poland. Hitler makes phony pleas for peace, but is he going to get down on his knees and play-act that he is begging for peace? Hardly! He thinks he is some kind of secular Jesus Christ. Did Christ get down on his knees and beg for his life at his trial in front of Pontius Pilate? No! So the demon stages an invasion of Germany by Poland on September 1, and Germany rises to victory in just days. In other words, Germany falls lower."

Anna looked terrified of what she was about to say, like a scared criminal under a bright confession light. "That is when it happens. Even though I know somehow that war is coming, when news of it comes over the radio, something happens inside me. I stare at my horrified face in the mirror, and what I see is not me. The girl in the mirror runs outside and screams so loud that a neighbor calls my father home from the factory. The girl is shaking and she thinks her brain is dying. He leads the girl by the hand to the car and drives her to a hospital in Berlin, then puts the girl in the ward for crazy people. He tries to hide his smile when he kisses the girl—I would come to realize she was me—on the lips."

At that moment, Anna once again looked to the ceiling, where angels might be this time, but her eyes seemed only to get tangled in some nonexistent thing. When she finally freed herself, she just stared through the ceiling as if she couldn't talk on, as if she were a heart not knowing whether to take another beat.

The police can glue wires on you and plug you into a machine to see if you're telling the whole story when all they really need to do is study your eyes. Eyes cannot hide the truth. Anna's kaleidoscopic eyes of multiple blues I remembered loving as a child were now cold gray stones. Something in the apartment chilled me, and ice was all about her now, freezing her into a perfectly unsolvable puzzle. I had never heard such a bizarre tone of voice before, not from her or anyone else. I think she had gotten herself deeper and deeper into the story over the years.

"So, you wanted to go find your 'falling' brother, prop him up, and bring him back home" might have been the most logical way for me to respond. But how could I be logical at a moment like that? I no longer had a right to assume that the story of Bernhard, the alleged "brute . . . or worse," was just a little thing. The more I tried to define this indefinable woman, the more distant my mind carried me from her. Any further imagining around her perimeter, trying to spy inside, would have been a fool's errand because there were no doors or windows at all.

Or maybe there was no great mystery to be discovered after all. Maybe she was just a lovely, old, crazy lady. There are tons of them in this world, and every one of them has a right to be what they are. *Maybe*, I thought, *my striving to figure her out is a waste of time.* So maybe Anna Himmel had sealed herself up under wax in a preserves jar and lacked the wherewithal to pierce the seal and leak out the details of a terrible story about her brother from half a century earlier.

Here's the very last letter I received from Bernhard:

13 October 1939

Dear Henry,

Well, the war came a few weeks ago, the one that Hitler said would never come. He blames it all on Poland. What a liar! With such a scoundrel for our leader, I guess Germany is not so great after all. Because how could millions of people let him get away not only with lies but also with murder?

There is something awful to tell about me. My bastard father said to forget about finishing high school even though I have less than a year to go! There is a special training program about to start in the SS that will take me higher than any school ever could.

But higher than what? He refused to answer me. He simply got me in, and that was that. No time to waste, he said. I did not even need to take a test. I start my training in Berlin in a few weeks. 8 weeks of it. In the worst way, I do not want to go. I will not graduate from high school and go to university anytime soon!

And you should see Anna these days. It is sad. Very sad. Almost makes me want to cry. For some reason no one but God understands, she has lost almost all of her music ability. It is like the same kind of thing has happened to Germany. She looks funny in the eyes and says strange things. Last month, my father put her in a mental hospital and came home all happy. Like an animal, a laughing hyena!

I am fed up. Bye for now but not forever, for sure.

Your best friend always,

Bernhard

"Your father came home as a laughing hyena. Anna, what did you have back then? Depression?" She didn't respond. I pressed. "That's it; you were very, very depressed like other good people were. You were extremely sad about what was happening in Germany."

"Ha! I wish that is all it had been. I was no longer me, but even worse than before. When the psychiatrist in the hospital told me there was a war going on, I would say something like, 'You are silly, Doctor. The war is all done. It was the war to end all wars and ended more than two decades ago.' Then the psychiatrist would say something like, 'Maybe, dear, dusting off your violin over there in the corner and playing it a little will help you remember there is a new war going on right now.' I could see no violin in the corner, Heinrich. I had lost my grip because I was seeking beauty that was nowhere. I remember the psychiatrist saying, 'Anna, your mother told me that you once thought you were the country of Germany.' I replied, 'Who is Anna? And what is Germany?' You see, Heinrich, you see?"

"Oh" was all I could think to say.

"If only I had been here in Edelberg to save Bernhard from himself instead of not existing."

I insisted, "A person can't be her brother's keeper, as they say." I dismissed her remark about "not existing" as nothing but rote melodrama.

"At least *I* could be his keeper. It is *me* we are talking about. I was inside Bernhard, deep down, and I could have saved him from himself. But I was gone elsewhere. I was the definition of 'elsewhere,' and when Bernhard finished eight weeks of Nazi brainwashing, he was—"

"Brainwashing?"

"You heard me. He was the son of Germany's largest, oldest, and most famous violin company, and the SS wanted him for the sake of appearances. By the time they were finished remaking him, he was a lower form of human being. Or maybe he was no longer a human. He fell from choirboy to monster. There is no word for it. I settled on one I found in an English thesaurus. *Transmogrification.* Guess how the transmogrified Bernhard celebrated his graduation from training? By digging up some of his old buddies from Hitler Youth and burning down Edelberg's only synagogue.

"Over the next weeks, he put on the business suit the SS had purchased for him, put on a paper Wehrmacht helmet from the *Anschluss* party, climbed into his treehouse, and downed a bottle of champagne for every country that had fallen—France, Norway, Denmark, the Netherlands, Luxembourg, Belgium. Before climbing down, he blew into a whoop-dee-ding from the party. In his bedroom he once said a hundred 'Heil Hitlers' because the demon now had his own personal Eiffel Tower and Louvre, and—"

"Please stop now," I had to interrupt. "He was my best friend, and I'd just as soon leave it that way. Don't—"

"And there I was, in a hospital bed, throwing bits of oatmeal on the wall, not knowing who Anna Himmel or what Germany were."

"Stop, Anna. I can see how upset it's making you."

She stopped and stared at the pot of cold soup. Secretly I wanted to remember in the future only what I wanted to remember from the past—that Bernhard was a kind, decent kid. I figured her story was finished anyway, didn't think it could get much worse.

But since I'm no seer, I could not have known yet what later I would not want to hear. I had no idea that even in Anna's present imagination, she couldn't whiten the dark clouds she had seen coming back then. Those clouds were indestructible, then and that night.

8

"I'm a little hungry," I said to break the silence. Actually, I felt starved. It was around 8 p.m. Her eyebrows shot up, and she looked at her watch, so lost in the story that she seemed not to know it was well past dinnertime.

"Gosh, so sorry. I forgot," she said. She finally served the soup and bread and sat down with me at the table. After I finished a second bowl, I asked her for the time. My Timex had stopped. She looked at her watch and said I had plenty of time to make the nine o'clock bus. I got up to leave ten minutes later and thanked her for sharing an obviously painful story. Maybe, I said, we could exchange letters after I got back to the States. But when I glanced at the clock on her bureau, I saw it was already a minute or two past nine and breathed a bit of fire out my nose. She brought her watch close to her eyes and squinted, feigning eye trouble (I realize only now). Her watch read 9:03.

She had trapped me there by both hook and crook, had played me like a fiddle. I flipped over and actually *wanted* to leave and go get a room at the inn. Suddenly I felt like I did at my high school reunion earlier that year when I didn't feel sad saying goodbye to old friends I knew I would never see again.

I put on my coat and scarf and said how nice it had been seeing her, et cetera, but when I reached to unlock the door to leave, she rushed over and fenced me in. Apparently the simple act of reaching for the lock was a psychological encroachment, an implicit warning that now she might never have even a half-willing listener to tell the rest of her story to.

She steered me back to the couch and said, "I am so embarrassed for lying about the time, but I did not want you to leave. I need to tell you that terrible thing about Bernhard. Please take off your coat and sit down."

Reluctantly, I stayed. I began to detect something both covering her up and pressing her down like a suit of armor, almost obligating her not to shed the past. Apparently the armor had always been too heavy to take off. I would not know until later that night that the worst of the story had not yet begun. Maybe she had never realized with other people in the past that the best way to start a walk across an entire country is not to dwell on the hardships that will be encountered along the way but simply to take the first step.

She made a fire and kept it burning through the night, but I swear the air in the room grew colder as the rest of the story wore on. If storytelling is supposed to entertain the listener, then this was no mere story. No one would ever listen through to the darkest part. By the time she finally stopped talking, I would know that she had been waiting half a century to find someone who would stay open to her. She had lived with it so that it wouldn't die, had kept remembering it so it wouldn't be forgotten, even if forgetting would give her the gift of time's inherent power to heal.

She took a deep breath, and at long last the words came, pouring in vast volumes; imagine Niagara Falls backed up for fifty years, then instantly let go. Every word was my continuing education on what Germany had become a half century earlier:

"So, the lowest point in Bernhard's life, which now to the rebuilt him was the highest point—and it would get even lower, meaning higher as far as he was concerned—came in August of 1940 after I was in treatment in the mental hospital for a year. He came there for a visit. For one reason only, I would learn: to drop the mimeograph of a document on the floor. He dropped it accidentally on purpose, so to say. He wanted me to know its contents. How could a deadly serious SS agent drop by accident a document that is printed on official Nazi stationery with the swastika logo and the words *TOP SECRET* stamped in red on it? He wanted me to join him because of what I was."

She stopped, closed her eyes, and shook her head as if ready to stop after barely continuing. "Well?" I said at last, thinking what I thought before—that she simply lacked the courage to finish.

"I should not have waited for him to leave the hospital before reading it. When I finally saw the words, lightning struck me and knocked me down. But then somehow I got back up, and suddenly I could see my violin in the corner. Suddenly I knew that lebensraum was a real thing and that there was a war going on and that Germany was a European country called the 'land of poets and thinkers.' That was when I stole the money from the nurse, went to Scotland Yard to turn in my father for agreeing to store Nazi bombs at the violin factory, and then went into the woods to search for Bernhard. Deep into the woods.

"The Nazi who put it in writing was a fool. Not just because he was creating written proof, but because he and his cohorts now would have to deal with the woman I had just become again—Anna Himmel. The document screamed at the top, *Instructions When Picking Up A Person.* They gave Bernhard a new People's Car as a trapping. I remember the document as if it were staring at me here and now, trying to singe my eyes. It said Bernhard was always to wear a dark civilian suit, white shirt, and colorful necktie in the presence of a parent. He—"

"A parent? Were children involved?"

"My word yes. Bernhard was to pick up children in his car. Disabled children. Little people who had the nerve to be born blind, deaf, or unable to speak. Or who were crazy enough to be missing a limb. Or who were selfish enough to be mongoloid—or what we call Down syndrome people today. Or who were audacious enough to have epilepsy, Huntington's disease, schizophrenia, or even manic depression. The instructions said that Bernhard was to shake a father's hand firmly and a mother's hand gently and to always be clean shaven—which he did not need to worry about, since he was still in late puberty and had no whiskers.

"At all times, he was to use his official public title: clerk, Reich Chancellery Ministry of Health. Before leaving the residence, the child was to be told they were going to a 'special place' and would be back home 'soon.' All parents were to be told that they would be periodically updated about the child's treatments and progress, and that by order of the Führer himself, absolutely no visits were permitted the first week. The child was to be walked hand in hand to the car and never to be put in the straps until the car was at least one mile from the house. Any behavior problems in the car were to be treated swiftly with a dose of Luminal.

"After reading it, I was still burning from the lightning and shaking in disbelief."

Though a lump of incredulity was caught in my own throat, I finally started to think that she might be telling the truth about Bernhard. I slammed my fist into the sofa, as if that could stop me from overhearing such a terrible story. "God, Anna."

"'God' is right. I went to see a representative of God. I jumped out of the hospital bed, hopped in a dress, grabbed my violin and money purse, and threw myself on the first bus to Edelberg. I ran to the Lutheran church to see Reverend Landis, the minister who helped me understand difficult books. I spilled all over him what I feared about the children, including that they were to be murdered. He curled his lip and said it could not possibly be true. He was concerned only with how I had escaped the hospital, then said, 'And even if you are right, Anna, which I highly doubt, there is no way a good boy like Bernhard would ever get mixed up in killing children. And besides, what in the devil do you expect *me* to do? If I call the government and it is *not* true, then I look like a fool. If I call and it *is* true, then I know a secret and need to be taken to prison. Or worse. And even if it *is* true, these are the same men who make Jews wear a Star of David, which is nothing but a symbol, a harmless thing. The patch is actually for the Jews' own protection.'

"I said, 'No it is not! It is to mark them!' Landis did not like that. Not one bit. I said, 'Then let me call the British or American ambassadors in Berlin.' That brought back his humor. He laughed and said those two embassies were shut down tight. I persisted, 'Then let me call the White House.' He—"

"The White House? An assistant to the president?"

"The president himself. Roosevelt. Landis got an even bigger laugh out of that one, but when he saw I was serious, he said, 'Long distance across the Atlantic? Absolutely not. Besides, the Americans have no dog in the fight. They have a neutrality law.' Landis was now all out of good grace. He shook his head and said sarcastically, 'Call the pope in Rome if you are so concerned.'

"So that is exactly what I did. Since Landis was so exasperated, I rushed out of the church to call the pope on a pay phone. And that—"

I interrupted. "Slow down, Anna, slow down. You mean *the* pope? The one in the Vatican?" I shouldn't have cut her off because it made her talk faster and louder.

"Is there any other pope? Pope Pius the Twelfth. I thought, *Maybe he will believe me like he believes in God.* Maybe God would visit his body on earth and shine the holiest light on everything that the small handful of evil men wanted to do to children. But to the Vatican operator I was just a naïve, crazy girl. I did not realize it would be impossible to speak to the pope himself. The lowly operator said, 'Sorry, dear, you seem impatient but ever so sweet. Sweetie, have you not heard of the *Reichskonkodat*, the treaty between the Vatican and Germany requiring bishops to give an oath to the Reich? Why not talk to your local clergyman?' I slammed down the phone. My clergyman? Landis? Good grief!

"Heinrich, it was a cruel thing, my being a powerless girl so far ahead of the truth of the imminent murder of innocent children, of knowledge that was not yet common. I thought that by the time all these high public bigwigs finally figured out what I already knew about the children, they would be too busy trying to save the whole world to be of any help. I felt terrorized by the truth, bullied to the point of understanding that the job

of saving the children was my new calling and mine alone. Most bullies on
the earth cannot be crushed except by a might greater than themselves, if
I may say so myself. What I had to do next was as clear as an abbey bell
and as large as Germany. I would need to find the miscreants, starting
with Bernhard in the woods, and stop them all by myself."

With that, Anna stopped. I think she needed a break to regroup. She
walked to the plate of homemade cherry tarts to serve them but stopped
dead in her tracks only feet away and stared. They were oozing red. She
turned up her nose at the tarts and didn't serve them. Then, apparently
she still feared that I might leave, as so many other listeners had done in
the past. She ran to the door again and blocked it. She continued:

"Those bombs at the violin factory were stacked from floor to ceiling,
row after row. When I told the detective at Scotland Yard, I knew I was
putting almost two thousand people in Edelberg at risk, but I closed
my eyes and played Nostradamus. I envisioned a great battle in a forest
like the Ardennes Forest someday, and I knew that those bombs could
wipe out many more thousands of Allied soldiers fighting fascism. After
Scotland Yard, I kept my eye on the ball. The ball was now Bernhard's
tail. So I went straight down, down to the place called out in that Nazi
document, a place called Hartheim.

"I had barely enough stolen money left to take the all-day bus ride to
the Third Reich city of Linz, Austria, near the secret Hartheim euthanasia
facility. You hear about the six million or more Jews, the two million or so
refugees, and the one million or so Romani who were murdered during the
war. You may have even heard about the two hundred thousand or more
mentally or physically disabled people who were murdered by what the
Nazis whitewashed with the sterile words *mercy euthanasia*. But you never
hear about the murdered children."

She stopped, her face falling into her hands. After a minute, her face
crawled out and she proved how imperishable she was. "History seems to
have forgotten the children. You never hear about the five or ten thousand
of them—who is counting?—who were 'mercy' murdered. A tiny number
compared to people murdered at, say, Auschwitz, no?"

Black satire dripped from her cracking voice. She lunged to the bookshelf and yanked out a scrapbook, then suddenly looked like she despised herself for having made it. She thrust it into my hands. It was labeled *Aktion T4*, which I know now became the name for Hitler's secret euthanasia program, part of his eugenics enterprise. At first, I wondered why in the world she had put it together, but holding it and feeling its gravity and reading a small part of it finally left no doubt that everything in her story was true.

The scrapbook overflowed with newspaper and magazine articles she had collected after the war, now flaking and yellowed by time. She flipped to a page where she had pasted an article from *A New People*, the monthly magazine of the Bureau for Race Politics of the Nazi Party. It showed a photograph of a young boy sitting in a chair, his eyes seeming to look off into space but revealing, unmistakably, that he was very much alive and content. *He* was hardly yellowed or flaking by time; he was a living ghost and didn't know that invisible blood was running down his face. Standing behind the boy was a nurse smiling lovingly and resting her hands on the boy's shoulders. Below the photo was this warning to the German people: *60,000 Reichsmarks is what this boy suffering from mongolism will cost the People's Community during his lifetime. Fellow German, that is your money too!*

The satire in Anna's voice swelled, becoming almost absurd. "Hartheim was one of six killing factories to carry out the demon's new order to 'disinfect' Germany of 'vermin,' a place where mentally and physically disabled children and adults who were 'subhuman' were murdered and burned. Why, Heinrich, would I expect you to know it even today, a half century later, living way out in innocent farm country, in Donsville, Iowa? What do you worry about in Iowa?" She didn't wait for an answer. "Iowa, the heartland, where you grow corn and the worst things you worry about are tornados and droughts."

Instantly my height was reduced by half. I lost my cool for a second. "Anna, *I* didn't kill those children."

"Well, of course you did not, Heinrich. You and all other Americans were settled and safe in a far-off place, but I was right here at the start of humankind's worst storm. Good Germans were still thinking, *Elsewhere could never come* here. But elsewhere *had* come here. Most everyone did *not* know about the children and other citizens who would be euthanized. But Anna Himmel sure knew. She, I, could save them and eventually the whole nation."

There didn't seem to be the English words to express what she was feeling. Were there words in any language for it?

"Being on that all-day bus ride to Austria gave me time to think. I thought, *There are not a billion of me. There is only one of me, and I do not have an army at my command, like the demon does. To fight a war in this world, a person must have the weapons of this world.* So I gave myself one tiny goal to start with—to save one child's life, one person otherwise destined to grow up and enjoy the sunshine of old age. A Nazi would have said that my goal was evil, that the saving of one person would end up costing all that money. Bernhard was only eighteen but had a promising new career as a money-saver. To him, his new job was as important as being a corporate treasurer watchdogging a company. His mind was rewired to think that those children had no business growing up and having children of their own because then someone would have the unpleasant job of killing the offspring so that there would be no one left to cost 60,000 Reichsmarks more.

"So, why did my brother pick this unique career in pediatrics? It all started shortly after the other men in the training program in Berlin beat him up for crying, for desperately wanting to finish high school. It all began small, with a letter Hitler received right before he started the war, a letter from the parents of a deformed little boy—child K, he was called—who was costing the parents oodles of money they could no longer afford. The demon must have thought, *What a brilliant idea! What patriotic parents! They are willing to put their own flesh and blood to sleep forever for the good of the People's Community! Blood and honor!* That one letter incited a brainstorm in the demon that ended with his secret order to start a mercy-killing, money-saving program."

It all kept rushing and rushing, pouring out of Anna so heavily that my facial expression of disgust never had a chance to go away:

"Heinrich, I can just imagine the voice of the headmaster of the program briefing Bernhard and the other mercy-killing virgins in Berlin after getting an earful from the Führer."

Anna jumped off the couch and strutted around, treading a path in the rug and burdened by her flailing arms. She probably felt suffocated by a group of secular gods—doctors, including Hitler's personal physician, Dr. Karl Brandt. My lower lip just hung there.

"I can hear him saying, 'Men, this is all a simple matter of cause and effect. To wipe out malaria in the world, the mosquitos must be eliminated first. This great nation is filled with people who are rotten because they have dangerous genes that threaten to destroy our burgeoning empire, one that will surpass all others in history. To wipe out the danger, we must eliminate the rot. We shall do this always with dignity and grace. With painless carbon monoxide gas and cremation. And if any of you chose this program because you get some kind of pleasure out of hurting people, then you should get up and leave right now! Go back to your lower-paying jobs. The prevention of—'"

"Anna, calm down. You are—"

"'The prevention of suffering in unborn generations in our thousand-year People's Community is written between the lines of the Hippocratic oath we doctors take. We have passed a new law requiring every doctor in this Reich to report problem-gene children to us. We shall make a list of those children, and Bernhard Himmel, you shall be the children specialist. You, Herr Himmel, shall go out in your car, collect them, and drive them to the Hartheim Castle. It shall be your new religion, and—'"

"Wait, Anna. Hartheim is a castle? This killing took place in a *castle*, as in princes, moats, drawbridges, and fairy tales?"

She looked at me with agony screwed into her face. "Yes, a real castle. A place where people are supposed to live happily ever after. The poor innocent castle still exists," she said with revulsion. "I would have gone there on my hands and knees if I'd had to. It is in the small, Upper Austria village of Alkoven, about nine miles from Linz and close to the German border. No one knows exactly when the first section came to be, but it was sometime in the ninth century. The family name Hartheim first appears in the twelfth-century public records. In the 1690s, a wealthy landowner named Aspen expanded the castle to its present state—a grand four-story, four-wing behemoth. Four corner towers. A fifth, higher tower. Tens of thousands of square feet. A lovely courtyard in the center. A place for a fairy tale in the real world. And white. All white. Nothing but white."

"I'm afraid I picture old European romantic chivalry."

"Exactly. In 1799, one of the Starhemberg princes bought it."

"For his family castle."

"No. Nothing of the sort. The Starhemberg family had—and still have—their own, much larger palace in nearby Eferding. The prince probably bought the castle as a playground, maybe a place to hold hunting parties. Many in the family were Austrian politicians. Some were field marshals in the army."

"You can't mean a royal family dynasty."

"I certainly do, but only for about a century. In 1898, Prince Camillo Starhemberg did the good deed of donating the castle to the Upper Austria State Welfare Society. Then it became a psychiatric facility mainly for children, under the care of an order of nuns. But it was holy only until 1940, two years after Germany grabbed Austria to expand the Reich. In 1940 the castle was seized by the Nazis, taking it from the top of a mountain to sinking from the face of the earth. Still a behemoth, but suddenly a Leviathan. No longer a castle for friendly royal princes but a place for the Prince of Darkness."

The knot in my gut twisted so tight that it became Gordian.

After a few minutes of dead silence, I read more of the scrapbook silently. Five minutes later, I thought myself an informed and clever satirist. A moment of levity seemed not all bad. I said, "Excuse my obscenity, but the German government must have thought it looked perfect for its aims: a majestic castle reaching into the heavens when secretly it was an erection poking down to Hell and spilling its seed on German culture along the way."

Anna cracked a deformed smile and mocked, "Oh, do you really think? Because if so, you are not being obscene but only kind." She allowed me to swim in that glop for a few seconds, then said, "The holy healers, the nuns, were kicked out of the castle by the seats of their habits. Public ways to the castle were blocked and major renovations were ordered. With the nuns no longer able to speak for it, it was no longer promoted as a home for the mentally handicapped. Its thieves now boasted that it was a home for the 'feebleminded, imbecilic, idiotic, and cretinous.' Do you know what a plaque near the front door said, Heinrich?"

"Of course I don't know."

She grabbed the scrapbook from me, flipped to a certain page, read, and said, "The plaque spat out a short string of words that said it all: 'Whoever is not healthy and worthy in body and soul is not permitted to immortalize his ailments in the body of his child.'"

Those words pressed through my skin and into my bones yet gave her only fortification: "And the first 'unworthy' people to arrive? They poured in by bus in May of 1940." Anna was now flapping her arms like an injured but energetic bird. "Smoke and hair began drifting through the village. Villagers thought it could only possibly be that a pack of wolves or a sloth of bears were sleuthing someone's garbage pail, all shot dead, too many to remove, so set afire right there. Some people lost their appetites. One man collapsed into unconsciousness from the stench. When humans realized it was human hair, some fell to their knees."

Skeptical, I yanked the scrapbook out of her hands. "Anna, where did you get all these articles and stuff? I thought the mass burning of human bodies only happened in concentration camps—and well after 1940."

"Schultheiss! It is all right there in the scrapbook. As true as the Holocaust that started three years later. A village rumor started that human bodies were being burned at the castle. The town elders, patsies for the Nazis, held a public meeting before an uprising could spark. The citizens were told that whoever spread 'absurd rumors of burning bodies' would be hauled off to a work camp. The mealymouthed leaders lied and said that the foul odor was for the good of the war effort, that the castle was manufacturing fuel for submarines."

"Fuel for naval submarines?"

"Heinrich, Heinrich, they were not manufacturing fuel of any kind. Thirty thousand piles of ash—men, women, and children—were manufactured there by the time all was said and done."

Just minutes earlier, I hadn't known the castle existed, much less that it was the situs of a gene cleansing, a genocide of thousands and thousands of people who had the natural right to live happily ever after. And I had known much less that it all went down as early as 1940. "Never had the slightest idea," I could only say.

"Do you know the disgustingly pretty word they substituted for the word *murder*?"

"Not a clue."

Anna had been shouting the truth, but suddenly she seemed to use all her energy not to be heard. "The answer is *redemption*. Those who were 'unworthy' and given 'mercy' were not murdered. Not really. They were all 'redeemed,' said a former employee after the war."

I tasted blood, must have bitten my lip. Her jugular was pulsing. "Let's go for a walk, Anna. Outside. Some fresh air."

Her eyes narrowed. "Oh no you don't! Don't do this to me! For the first time ever, I have come too far to stop now. I can hear one of the Berlin training doctors instructing Bernhard, 'Afterwards, when you drive back to the parents' house to deliver the ashes in the urn, if a parent asks about the cause of death or why the body had to be cremated without first obtaining the parents' consent, you are to tell them something very specific. And this is important. You are to say that their child died suddenly of tuberculosis and was professionally cremated on a rush because it is a contagious disease, that the germs needed to be destroyed quickly before they could spread to other patients."

Instinctively I covered my ears with my hands.

"Heinrich, you cannot bear to hear about it even a half century later. You should go see the castle for yourself. The grounds are beautiful. They have a nice little memorial there. You can see the big rooms where the doctors and nurses lived, the same rooms where good princes once slept. You can see the poison-gas shower. You can run your fingertips along one of the ovens. You can see a sample urn once delivered to the next of kin to betoken the murdered person's bravery. You can even go to the beautiful blue Danube River nearby and see where they dumped the extra ash that could not fit in the urns."

I wanted to stop her not only for my sake but also for hers, to keep the past from both of us and protect our souls, but her soul kept seeking the past with a vengeance. "You can even see Bernhard's bedroom. By then, he was a mutation resistant to all strains of humanness."

It was as if she wanted to magically put me there at the castle on the day she was there—August 26, 1940. For a moment, I spiraled back to that day, thinking, *This is not your problem, Anna. You should be back at the hospital, getting your mind cured and reengaging with your music. You are wasting your time because even if you get Bernhard out of there, they will just find another driver.* But then I realized that if she had been wasting her time back then, Europe had needed a thousand more of her so that at least a few hundred could break through the door and save people. Or two thousand more of her. Or ten. Or more.

She lunged to the bookshelf again and pulled out a book. Her furious fingers fanned the pages fast, instantly pulling out a black-and-white sketch of a girl who looked to be about seven. Anna searched the sketch longingly for more than a minute, then held it out to me. "I drew this shortly after the war."

This seemed like an abrupt change of subject, a sudden escape to a happy moment. The sketch looked like Anna when she was small, especially the pretty eyes, the small round mouth, and the skater's-cut hair. "It's a great drawing of you when you were a small girl," I said.

"It is not me."

"Come on, it's got to be you."

"It is Rosalie. Rosalie Blume, the first child I tried to save at the castle. My plan was to save all the people there, and then all over the Reich, and the Reich itself from crumbling into dust." When Anna glanced at the

sketch again, she seemed to change into something else. The noises in
the room amplified—the ice particles brushing against the windows, the
water dripping from the faucet, the blood pulsing in my ears. Under that
clamor, she mumbled these words, oddly in German:

"Stop Bernhard, the reincarnated Conan the Barbarian, in the woods.
The Inn of the Woods. Martin Bergman, cultured man, philosophy at the
university. Him and the Mahler *Kindertotenlieder* songs. Going to the castle.
A ride in Conan's car to pick up Rosalie. The Oswald Spengler and Hans
Günther stories. Snow White story. Back to the castle. Trying to shoot
Bernhard the Barbarian. Losing my innocence. Seeing Rosalie strapped
down on a gurney. Chasing after her with lead feet."

After that vague, virtually meaningless dive into the subterrain, I was
certain only that the pain in her eyes seemed bottomless, a hurt to a depth
that hurt me. I wondered whether she wished that she had never been
born—in the flesh, that is. She looked around as if wondering where
she was, as if there wasn't any magic to going someplace else; she had
accomplished it easily. I wanted to be with her at the same place, but when
I looked around the room, I was still in her apartment. She was there only
in body. Watching her second self at that moment was like watching a bird
fly away and get smaller and smaller until it disappeared.

Those last sentences were a pile of puzzle pieces that had spilled
out of her skin. I scanned her face to see if she was ready to spill the
missing links, but they must have been too heavy. With lifeless eyes, her
top eyelids lowered to half-staff and then fluttered shut. She collapsed
back on the sofa and passed out from sheer exhaustion, curling into the
fetal position with her teeth still clenched. The curtain was down. That's
all the theater I would get.

I had just plunged into the deepest gorge in her sea of sorrow and
had no inkling how to get back up to the light. Worse, in coming to
her apartment and poking into Bernhard and the castle, I felt like an
interloper, an intruder who had interrupted something that had been
going along imperfectly but well enough—her life.

I was afraid for her because she was curled up as motionless as a woman on an autopsy table. I took her pulse and it was normal. So I sat there waiting for her to awaken. Unanswered questions pounded me. Had the bullet hit Bernhard? Had she been successful in saving Rosalie? Had she saved others? There was no picture on a puzzle box to guide me. Was there even a final picture? Were there more pieces still suppressed inside her?

I laid a blanket over her and let her sleep. Seeing the disturbance on her face, I had a second thought: How could I wake her? How could I try to jimmy her memory and ask her to root out the other details, to re-travel through a gangland when it had been tearing her apart? Worse, what if she gave up the untold facts and it drove her even lower? She looked so helpless, so vulnerable, sleeping there. I chose not to wake her but couldn't leave her. The time was close to 1 a.m. I just sat there, unable to close my eyes, watching her.

Some hours later, the electro-hum outside seemed to get louder. She was still asleep. Her expression was deeply ambivalent but had become strangely gorgeous, as arcane as anything I'd ever seen, covered with the first white streamers of morning light sliding through the blinds. I took her pulse again, and, satisfied that she was okay, I tucked the blanket in tighter and wrote her a note saying I would call her later.

Before I left for the bus station, I grabbed the scrapbook from the floor. I wanted to read more of it in the privacy of my hotel room. I also took a book from her bookcase, one that shocked me that she would have—*Wings in the Night,* a collection of stories about the fantasy character Conan the Barbarian, the fictional outlaw and warrior who roamed the earth prior to the rise of the ancient civilizations. Right before passing out, Anna had called Bernhard "the reincarnated Conan." Maybe the book would provide clues to why my best friend—the young man whose boyhood hero had been Alfred Himmel—apparently had turned himself completely over and become Alfred's opposite.

Oh, what Bernhard's brain had become in such a short time! The transmogrification, to steal Anna's fancy word, sounded so gross and monstrous that it couldn't have been an accident. It couldn't have been that Bernhard had been the victim of something like a train wreck, hit his head, and instantly became a psychopath. I looked at the Conan book's colorful cover jacket and whispered, "Why, Bernhard? What changed your brain during your eight weeks of training? Was it the wonderful food that Anna mentioned—the beef Wiener schnitzel, muenster cheese, and apple strudel, all you could eat? Was it the Leni Riefenstahl propaganda films? Was it your father's '*Achtung!*—his cruel warning that if you quit the SS training and came home, he would kick you out and make you live on the streets? Or was it your cowering mother just standing there, afraid to speak?"

But Bernhard's ghost remained hidden and silent, refusing to come out and answer my questions.

While those things might have provided him motives to remain in the training, I wouldn't dream that any of them could have made a young man like *him* go completely berserk. Whatever it was, it must have scrubbed his brain with a metal-bristle brush.

Determined to solve the puzzle, I walked briskly to the bus station to take the first bus back to my hotel in West Berlin to shower, shave, and get some sleep. I felt that I was stretching closer to an answer to my grandson Billy's question.

Anna never did serve the cherry tarts. Before I left her flat, I threw them out to the animals so she wouldn't have to look at them.

9

On the walk to the Edelberg bus station, all I could think about was the freezing wind and Florida. But once I arrived inside, having iced worse inside Anna's unfinished story, I started to see the world differently.

I was no longer my American-heartland self. I was hardened, a different man. I was therefore not disgusted seeing two teenaged skinheads outside chasing a harmless and well-fed cat, obviously someone's pet, hunting it down like a couple of bald cavemen. When it ran off and the skinheads came inside, one of them lit a cigarette and took a swig from a bottle in a paper bag. The other said, "Give me some, fuck-nose." When the fuck-nose refused, his confederate punched him in the face, drawing blood and screams. A violent fistfight ensued.

Witnessing that barbaric scene did not make me sick. In my strange altered state, I thought it was hilarious. And it wasn't because they were skinheads. I could only be sick about the upside-downing of a historic castle by a tiny group of detestable men. I couldn't get that death house out of my mind. Try not thinking about an elephant right now.

After the bus arrived in West Berlin, I was walking to my hotel when that past upside-downing incited me to take a cab to the place where it all began in 1939: the chancellery building at Tiergartenstrasse 4, the Aktion T4 nerve center during the war. My shower, shave, and sleep at the hotel could wait for me to first come face-to-face with it and stare it down. Or at least try to stand up to it.

The cab driver told me that this section of the city sports a public park that in the sixteenth century was a private playground for the hunting of wild animals by the elector of Brandenburg. I knew that *tiergarten* in German means "animal garden," and after the cabby told the story, I thought about the pronunciation of the address of the nerve center: "tear-garden-strassa 4." I closed my eyes and had a daymare about old Germany getting teary over a menagerie of innocent animals gunned down by a fat politician. Then, with my eyes still closed, my jury debating reunification suddenly came to a verdict. They walked back in the courtroom, dried my tears for the divided city and country, and the foreperson, suddenly becoming me, announced a verdict in favor of reunification. Such was the peculiar way my mind was strung that morning.

To escape the recurring image of animals shot and maimed, I did the second-worst thing possible, the worst being to shoot myself. I fled into the scrapbook. I saw an article that referred to the Aktion T4 executive building at Tiergartenstrasse 4 as a "villa." I naively imagined a pink or yellow Mediterranean-style building. But that turned out to be hopeless optimism because I flipped the scrapbook page and saw a photograph of the building from the war era, a four-story sandstone-block monstrosity whose façade was splotched with swirls of black soot.

The cab stopped and the driver said, "This is where you want to be, my friend." I jumped out without thinking or looking. As the cab sped away, I began thinking that the driver had taken me to the wrong place, because I turned in a circle and couldn't find a building matching the scrapbook photo. The scene was dominated instead by an ultra-modern, giant, tent-like structure with a unique yellow color. I asked a passerby what it was.

"It is the music hall," she said. "The Berlin Philharmonic Orchestra performs there." For a schizoid moment, I blamed Anna for not being there to show me the way.

I stopped a passing man to ask where the Aktion T4 building was. Before I could finish the question, he grumped back in Germanized English, "I am on my vay to verk. Do I look like touriss center?" Just then, a kind young women, obviously having heard the man's nasty remark, stopped and asked if she might help. Trying to be very careful with my words this time, I asked her, "Where is the building where the Aktion T4 euthanasia program headquarters was during World War Two?"

"Where?" she asked. I repeated myself. After thinking, she said, "So sorry, I guess I have no idea." I asked four more people. No one knew until I asked another woman who looked to be in her eighties.

"The building was right where you are standing," she said with suddenly sullen eyes, "but it is long gone, thank God." Turns out the cab driver brought me to the right place after all. He knew his history. The old woman knew hers too. I was furious that the building was not still standing as a testament to evil.

No imagined convergence of two polar opposites like a music hall and a place where unjust death was secretly planned could be so grotesque and fantastic, or survive a fiction editor's pen. The endless stretch of the two poles of that contradiction iced me again, momentarily paralyzing me until a group of seven young adult tourists approached me. With the music hall serving as a handsome cultural icon in the background, one of them silently motioned me to take their photograph.

Businessmen, delivery boys, women out Christmas shopping—all kinds of busy people—passed behind me on the sidewalk, everyone walking briskly as though buoyed up by the upcoming holidays and the bright prospects for a united city and country. Apparently I was the only person on that brimming street who had the audacity to step back into the past and spend a few minutes striving to feel what it must have been like to live among a people whose history was rooted not in human suffering but in outliving it. In other words, apparently I was the only person around who had time to take a photo.

I snapped the picture, and the happy young tourists were ready to move on. Before giving over the camera, I said to the group in my best German, "Du scheinst vergessen zu haben" (You seem to have forgotten). One fellow said, "No speak German. We Americans." I chuckled and said to them in my Midwestern strum, "You people seem to have forgotten."

I admit it was an odd thing to say. The man looked at me strangely and asked, "Forgotten what?"

I replied, "Aktion T4. Murder and cremation?"

They all looked at me as if I were certifiably insane and then moved on. Anger crashed over me like a breaking ocean wave. I became even more irate at myself when I realized that only a day earlier, I would have been as blissfully ignorant as they.

Maybe I needed sleep, but my sensibilities were anything but normal now. There was so much to be angry about: the innocent animals shot to death centuries ago, the vanished "villa" that had been the creator of houses of horror, the nasty male Berliner who refused to be a gentleman, the five Berliners who didn't know their history, the dead mercy-murder doctors, the poison-gas stopcock twisters, and my former best friend, Bernhard Himmel. I had drifted in my mind to a dark place in an earlier time.

That's when Anna's voice came down loud and clear, repeating something she had said before passing out on the sofa: "You should go see the castle firsthand for yourself." She now added, "I dare you to go witness the unimaginable."

That last word cracked me wide open: *unimaginable*. It was at that moment, still hearing the echoes of those American tourists' footsteps walking away, that someone, or something, made a decision for me: I needed to try to imagine the unimaginable, to think the unthinkable, to step into the teeth of Anna's journey to the castle and find the ending to her story.

But she had given me much less than even a CliffsNotes version. The only way I could finish the puzzle would be to find the missing pieces myself. I would need to retrace her steps through the woods and to the castle without her and fill in the shadowy spaces between the lines of her last sentences by using my own modest powers of deduction. Whatever I could not solidly deduce as a man of math and science, I would need to quarry from my imagination from the clues she had given me.

And it turned out that I ventured well beyond my normal imagination.

10

As hyperactive as a boy on his way to a playground for the first time in his life, I didn't detour back to the hotel to shave and pack a bag but instead immediately set out for the Hartheim Castle. The castle is in Alkoven, Austria, which is a village about twenty miles south of the German border. Since there is no bus service directly there, I had to take a 400-mile bus trip to Linz, about nine miles from Alkoven. It drizzled rain, which my changing mind interpreted as tears from Heaven, and to avoid the gloom, I used the time to catch up on sleep, hoping to have dreams of fishing on a sunny day. I would need to be well rested and at the top of my game when I got to the castle.

I slept on the bus until just before 3 p.m., when the bus radio came on and rudely woke me. I had a moment of joy, though, when the radio announcer said, sounding tearful but heart-strung, "Today, 22 December 1989, will forever be a historic day. And now, we finally have the strike of three o'clock. The tens of thousands of people here are cheering wildly because the Brandenburg Gate has just now been reopened after nearly three decades. The jubilant West German chancellor, Helmut Kohl, is now walking through the gate and is being greeted by the jubilant East

German prime minister, Hans Modrow. There are no words for it, so I shall be silent and let the cheering people enjoy the moment."

The gate! Victoria's perch, finished around 1790 by the militaristic Prussian king to celebrate the restoration of peace during the Bavarian Revolution. The place where in 1963 President John Kennedy gave his "Ich bin ein Berliner" (I am a Berliner) speech. And where in 1987 President Ronald Reagan gave his speech demanding that the Communist Soviet leader "tear down this wall!" And where so many poor East Germans were, but will no longer be, shot dead. I stood up with the other bus riders and applauded Kohl's and Modrow's handshake and the opening of the gate. A few minutes later, I forced myself to end my joy. I needed to put my nose back to the grindstone of planning.

Hours later, when I disembarked the bus in Linz, I took a cab to the cozy Inn of the Woods, only a few miles from the castle. I checked in, had dinner, and went back up to my room shortly after 9 p.m. Alone, I turned off the lights, pulled down the blinds, and shut my eyes. I struggled to blot 1989 out of my mind and to see into the wordless place of Anna's mind. I tried to walk inside her so deeply that I could see only out of her eyes.

Finally, I vanished inside her. I had become her and was now in her world on August 25, 1940.

***

I am at my first destination, the handsome, sootless sandstone chancellery superstructure at Tiergartenstrasse 4 in Berlin. The late-summer breeze whips my flowery dress as I glare at it from the sidewalk. Other people pass me, most of them not even glancing at it. Their eyes instead are trained skyward, seized by the heartfelt voices of a massive sect of Luftwaffe commander Hermann Göring's Messerschmitt fighter planes, impeccably spaced in long diagonal rows—machines of war existing in violation of the Versailles Treaty. The ears of many other people are oblivious to the transcendent roar in the sky, because their eyes are buried in daily newspapers as they sit on Tiergarten Park benches, feasting on news reports of the German military victories in Europe.

The news reports have been pre-checked and double-checked for accuracy by Joseph Goebbels's Ministry of Public Enlightenment and Propaganda, a.k.a. Ministry of Truth. The ministry wants to make certain that the real truth known to outside influences like the Western democracies, and to inside influences like the Jewish community, has not been leaked. The fictional truth dripping with Goebbels's translucent varnish cleans most German eyes through the newspapers and their ears through the radio. There is nothing in the papers or over the airwaves about any of the six mercy-murder sites in the Reich; that, after all, would be the unvarnished truth. It would not qualify as news.

Yes, there is a heavy diet of military pomp to see and hear in the streets, the sky, and the news, far too much for anyone to scratch his head over the everyday goings-on in front of Tiergartenstrasse 4. On this sunny morning of August 25, 1940, even if you are an average Berliner looking over at the secret death-plan building that you know nothing about, you aren't paying attention to a short young man in a common business suit named Rudy Gendler whom you know nothing about. Why would you care anything about this average-looking young man? Why would you take notice that he's handing a People's Car ignition key to another average-looking, taller young man, also dressed in a common business suit, named Bernhard Himmel—my brother—whom you also know nothing about? And even if you are close enough to hear the shorter man say to the taller one, "Good luck in Alkoven," why would you think about it, even once?

In fact, if your spouse should come up to you right now and say, "Darling, look at that young man over there, the taller one. He is about to go live in a real, Middle Age castle and drive innocent children there to be gassed to death and burned up," you'd think that he or she had just downed a mind-altering drug with a bottle of schnapps.

But *I*, for one, hiding behind a tree, have my eyes on the two chatting young men. I can see that my brother thinks he is suddenly somebody, one of the more important somebodies nobody has ever heard of, nobody everywhere in Germany. I am impelled to follow my brother as he gets in his brand-new People's Car and heads south for Alkoven, a down-going. As of this minute, my career is focused on nonmusical humanity alone. I buy a bus ticket to Linz and board the bus. It thunders off. I am going down too. It is now past 9 a.m., and since the bus trip is an eight-hour trip, I use the time to sleep and refresh my mind. I will need to be clear headed and brave when I get to the castle.

After treating myself to a long sleep, I am rudely awakened at 3 p.m. by the static of a voice brusque enough to knock down a peace-loving soul. My eyes fly open when the announcer on the bus radio reports, "Earlier today, 25 August 1940, a group of brave men acting under the auspices of the Nazi-Vichy French government shot and killed a group of thugs in the French Resistance . . ." The other riders, all citizens of the Reich, are standing, cheering, ecstatic with the news that the Resistance scoundrels are dead. The passengers must feel fraternal in their common cheering.

We are now headed due south on our bus, straight to Linz, close to a hell—the Führer's boyhood house, now a sort of mecca. And we are also faced in the direction of another hell—the Hartheim Castle. The others, as bus riders, know they are headed south of course, but as citizens of the Reich, they are oblivious to their direction.

The thought of their blissful ignorance lights me wide awake on the bus. So I read a book I brought with me, *Wings in the Night*, stories about the mythical Conan the Barbarian. The stories are geared for teenaged boys but are troubling because of all the barbarous violence depicted. I am sickened by *Wings* but inexplicably cannot unglue my eyes from it as I am taken farther south, and also further south. Both farther and further south. I finish the book. Good Jesus!

It is now 7:30 p.m. and the bus is just pulling into the station in Linz. It is 8 p.m. when I get from there to a charming little inn, the Inn of the Woods. Being surrounded by tall pines, supposedly the sun doesn't shine on it even at high noon. When I step up to the front door, I see a brass plaque bolted next to the doorframe:

Friedrich von Schiller dined and slept here the night of 21 June 1802.

"Only through Beauty's morning-gate, does thou penetrate the land of knowledge."
—*From his poem "The Artists"*

This passage from the poem disturbs me, comes close to drawing a little blood, because I imagine that the bar in this inn is the place where doctors, nurses, and civil servants who are cogs in the killing machine at the castle hold their daily "happy hours." Maybe they need a friendly, inviting place outside the castle to get drunk. Sure, that's just what they need in order to forget what they did that day and to maintain their morale.

Spooked now, I check in, put my violin up in my room, and go down to the restaurant because I am starved and it has been a long, grueling, nerve-wracking day.

The inn is quite busy tonight, so I imagine I will need to share my table. Yes, a nice-looking man in his thirties is led by the hostess to my table. "This is fine," he says to her after glancing at my pretty face. This tall, well-tanned fellow, wearing a gray pin-striped suit, sits down smiling at me. Not one speck of danger appears to touch him. He must be a businessman passing through town. I feel constrained to ask him his name.

"Martin Bergman," he says to me while looking at the menu. Then he looks up, holds out his hand to me, and asks my name.

I figure I had better go cloak-and-dagger. I say, "I am Johanna. Pleased to meet you, Herr Bergman."

Quickly he looks back down at his menu, but then just as quickly looks back up and does a double-take of my blue eyes. He seems shy and says nothing for the next five uncomfortable minutes. The waiter comes for our orders. I have enough stolen money left to order the veal chop. Herr Bergman orders the braised duck. During the early part of dinner, with both of us loosened nicely by red wine, we talk about the azaleas and mountain laurel on the inn grounds.

"The wind whispers through the tall pines, no?" he says, and given the tone of his voice, I am only too happy to agree.

Midway through dinner, Herr Bergman finally asks a question that lightly brushes my heart: "So, what brings such a pretty young lady out here in the middle of nowhere?" He just glanced at my left hand, on which I am wearing no wedding ring, of course.

I have my secret plans but never planned how I would answer such a question from a stranger. "I am here to—to purchase wood from one of the area lumber outfits," I say, thinking it up on the spot.

"Oh? What in the world for?"

I slip up and say too much here. "Oh, my family is in the violin-making business, you see." I kick myself under the table for allowing Herr Bergman's disarming demeanor to disarm me.

"Interesting," Bergman says, his small smile growing. "What is the name of your family's firm, if I might ask?"

There is something about his friendly, supple voice that makes me feel safe now. I suppose that when a person is wondering about Hell the way I have, expecting the person to run away from a serendipitous moment of relief is asking too much. But still, I must be very careful with this question of his.

"Well, it is not really a big firm," I say, continuing the fib. "There are only my father, me, and a few others. We call our company Menken Violins, named for our family."

He says with a friendly laugh, "I almost thought you were going to say that your last name is Stradivari. But I suppose you look far too wonderfully German to be Italian."

I feel myself blushing. And the man obviously knows a little about the finest violins. "You know Stradivarius violins?" I say.

"My gosh. Who has not heard of that great instrument? The world's greatest, no? Guarneri and Rugeri violins are not far behind, of course. There is also the lesser but wonderful Himmel violin too, found almost everywhere. No offense to you or your father, but I have never heard of a Menken violin."

Nervously, I keep up the falsehoods. Will he discover I am lying? "We are a small company. Very small. Everything is custom crafted by hand. We put out only maybe forty or fifty violins a year."

"Custom crafted? Tell me how a violin is made by hand. I have really never handmade anything—well, except for the ships my grandfather taught me how to build inside a bottle."

"You made ships in a bottle?"

"Still do. My grandfather taught me when I was a boy. I really loved that man."

I give Martin a smile and a little tip of my head.

"So, tell me, Johanna—oh, sorry, may I call you by your first name?"

"Please do."

"Wonderful. So tell me, Johanna, how do you custom-make a Menken violin? I would really like to hear."

After we order dessert, I am only too willing to tell him. "Well, the wood is the most important thing. Which is why I like traveling down this way to search it out. So, the top is the soundboard, which is probably the most important part of a great violin, although I must say that every part is important, just like every organ in the human body is important. The soundboard is like the human vocal chords."

"I love what you just said, that the making of a fine violin is almost as magnificent as the making of a human life. And no two human beings are totally alike, either, just as no two Menkens are alike? Am I correct?"

"Correct—*if* you use only spruce for the soundboard. A Menken has only the finest spruce."

"We do not see too much spruce around southern Germany and northern Austria. What wood supplier around here sells fine spruce?"

"Well now, Herr Bergman, maybe you just have not looked hard enough. Some of the best spruce in Europe is found in Lower Saxony and Upper Austria. It is a fact." I am lying through my teeth, of course.

Herr Bergman wraps his smooth knuckles on the pine table. "Pine is the only thing in abundance around here. But spruce? You are putting me on, yes?"

Does he see through me now? "Oh no, Herr Bergman! You wanted to know how to make a fine violin, and I am telling you. So let us start at the beginning and go all the way to the end. First, the wood. Proper seasoning of the spruce wood for the top, or the soundboard, is key, and it is very time consuming. You cut and sand the wood and then air-dry it for a long period. Then you put it in a climate-controlled kiln to stabilize it and give it a very specific moisture content. Some violins are made better for singing than others. If a violin cannot sing, then it is not a violin as far as I am concerned." It is remarkable to me that I know such details.

"Sounds reasonable."

"The varnish you use is critical too. It is—"

He says, before I can finish, "I would imagine that the dried varnish finish, like the wood, gets better with age. Just like the fine red wine we are drinking."

"Very true, Herr Bergman."

"Do call me Martin please, Johanna."

"Certainly, Martin."

"But now, Johanna, how can the soundboard 'sing,' as you say? How can wood make sound? I would think it would be the strings that make the sound."

"The strings only make the vibrations," I say, now touched by his apparent eagerness to learn the finer details. "The soundboard is what transforms the vibrations into beautiful sound." I hold up my hand and mime bowing the air, then add, "You do think, do you not, Martin, that something should be done the right way or not done at all?"

"Oh, certainly."

"And the crafting of the neck cannot be hurried, either. And the fingerboard that goes on the neck must be made of ebony, and—"

"Ebony, absolutely, I would think."

"Yes, Martin, and the fingerboard must be crafted with precision, and . . ." In midsentence, both of us now get the same idea at the same time. We share a bite of each other's German forest cake—two silver forks passing each other slowly at the intimate, candlelit table.

"Yes, Johanna, because if not with precision, would the violin not have a mushy voice?"

"That is exactly right." I am getting excited now. "You, Martin, seem so interested in my work."

"And you, Johanna, seem so passionate about your work. I love people with passion."

"I really am," I say, trying not to blush again. It is as if this Martin Bergman is able to look directly into my heart. "And what is your passion, Martin?"

"The Reich, and Austrian and German philosophy, in that order. And I suppose I would like to get married and have children someday."

"Austrian and German philosophy?"

"Yes. I graduated from Humboldt University in Berlin and have my degree in philosophy. I have studied all the great Austrian and German philosophers: Fichte, Hegel, Schopenhauer, Frege, Wittgenstein, et cetera. My senior thesis was on Ludwig Wittgenstein's *Tractatus Logico-Philosophicus*. His final conclusion in that great work is 'Whereof we cannot speak, thereof we must remain silent.' Meaning, really, in my opinion, the highest truths are beyond language. Do you not think that Austro-German art and the humanities, and Austro-German culture in general, is the highest in all of Western civilization, maybe in the world—with all respect to our oriental friends?"

"Now that you say it, I guess I do."

"I have read a lot of German literature, too. Ever read Goethe's *The Sorrows of Young Werther*? The devastation to a promising young life that romantic love can cause! And what a breakthrough in the novel form."

"I have read a little German philosophy and literature, but music is what I mostly read about. German and Austrian music especially."

"You are kidding me! I am partial to the great German and Austrian composers myself. Can you imagine what Mozart might have accomplished if he had not died at thirty-five? Or how great Haydn's symphonies would be if instead of composing more than a hundred, he had spent all that time writing only ten or twenty? But the Russians I can certainly live without. Tchaikovsky, for example." He adds, now chuckling, "But then again, maybe I have taken my niece to his *The Nutcracker* one too many times."

"Your niece?"

"Yes, Elsbeth. She is ten, and I am like her second father. And she is smart too. I love smart children. But of course, I would love her no matter what, because she is family." He removes the little girl's picture from his wallet, smiles at it wistfully, shows me, then continues, "She has been so sad this past year. Her poor little brother, Otto, who I loved just as much, died of mongoloid complications last year." He pauses, staring into his plate without the smile. "Do you know the great Austrian Jewish composer Gustav Mahler? Do you know his *Kindertotenlieder* song cycle, 'Songs on the Death of Children'?"

"Yes, the songs are so sad."

"I quite honestly would not say sad. I would say that yes, death is powerful, but love is stronger. I would say that *that* is what Mahler is trying to convey in those songs."

I am fascinated, captivated, now. I walk around to him and take his hands, studying them on both sides. "Your hands, Martin, are so perfectly made for playing the violin. Maybe I could give you a lesson sometime." He blushes. I blush for the third time. No man has ever made me blush. I add, "Of course, it is the soul, not the hands, that really makes the music."

"Yes, the soul is what distinguishes man from animals, I suppose," he says. "It is what gives you and I the capacity to think."

I am deep in the dark woods, but the word *animal* just rolled off his lips in an endearing way, not the ghastly way it rolled through my mind this morning when considering the "animal garden" in Berlin. "Culture is food for the soul. Yes, Martin?"

"I most certainly think *not*, Fraulein. With all due respect, of course. If culture were food for the soul, then that would mean that the soul sort of eats it and then it gets eliminated and sort of flushed down the toilet. I prefer to think of culture as something that touches the soul, strokes it gently, makes it grow while staying intact. Culture is to the soul what sunshine is to the plant. The sun strikes the plant, the plant grows, and the sunshine keeps coming. The light is indestructible. The sun is a sort of food for plants, I suppose, but I prefer to call it a 'forever light.' Is that not a better way to think about it, Johanna?"

I am beyond captivated now. I am mesmerized, bewitched. I can hardly speak. "Yes," I manage. All day, being swept farther and farther into the woods, right up to the moment this man began wondering about fine violins and talking about culture, all I wanted to do was pray for my brother and Rosalie Blume. But then along comes this dark, handsome prince who adds a small measure of normalcy to the end of my day. Finally, I begin to feel a little happiness. I know I must slide back down into the woods in the morning and confront Bernhard in the castle, but for now, I want to enjoy the face and smile of this man of the arts and refined taste. I am almost twenty-one but have never felt this way about a man.

I now think I will be honest and tell Martin exactly why I am in Alkoven. He and I could be a team. Yes, I will show him the mimeograph of the instructions to Bernhard on Nazi letterhead. When he sees that human lives could be at stake, he will drop his plans and help me.

"There is something in my room I would like to show you," I say. "I would prefer that it not leave the safety of my room. Can you come up for a moment?"

"Yes indeed."

When he walks in, he sees the violin case. "Oh, your Menken," he says, smiling warmly. "You said you would teach me sometime. How about now?"

Before I can answer, he takes it out of the case, sits on the bed, and marvels at it. Showing him the Nazi document can wait just a minute. Sitting next to him, I take the gentlemanly fingers of his left hand and place them on the neck in the positions to start playing the first piece my father taught me, Mozart's "Twinkle, Twinkle, Little Star." I also show him which strings to bow with his right hand. He tries, again and again. It sounds just awful, but his intense effort endears him to me further. He stops after eight attempts, leans over, and touches his lips to my cheek.

Wine is now alive in every one of my veins. He places the violin facedown on the bed and has love in his eyes.

But then he happens to glance at the logo on the back of the violin neck: A *f* H

What he was ten seconds ago flips on its head with an unbearable suddenness. His eyes shoot up and flash at me. Love instantly becomes hate. "The famous Himmel logo," he says with a coldness I have not heard since my brother visited me in the mental hospital. "My mother had a Himmel when I was a child. A violin maker who uses her own name, Menken, in her company's name would hardly own a Himmel. You must be Bernhard Himmel's sister. He works for me. He told me all about you. You hate the Nazis, and I am an important one." He pauses and stares at me as if he is fighting with himself: *Do I kill her or force her to make love to me?*

"You, Fraulein Himmel, must be down here to try to stop your brother." He pulls a Luger from his inside breast pocket. "I could put this barrel into a pillow and quietly shoot you in the head right now. Or I could fuck you first and then kill you. Which do you choose?"

I am trembling, unable to answer. All the other hundred Nazis I know are uncouth, have no clue who Wittgenstein is, do not love mongoloids, do not listen to Jewish composers like Mahler. I am now at risk of painfully losing my innocence, or worse—of dying and becoming nonexistent, of being nothing.

Bergman stands there eyeing me, waiting for my answer.

1 1

"You do not want to give me an answer, Fraulein? Then fine. I will say it anyway. This turns out to be your lucky day." A small part of Bergman that sneaked out during dinner now momentarily reemerges. "I joined the Nazis because they promised me a castle and also the sun and the moon, but secretly I kept my stars. You are lucky that I am a Nazi who does not rape women or enjoy cleaning up blood. You are luckier still that, unlike most of my colleagues, I love German culture. I am going back to the castle now, but if my man downstairs does not see you board the bus back to Berlin in the morning, you will be shot. *Achtung*, Anna."

He bolts out of the room.

I am shaken. I am lucky to be alive. But do I abandon Alkoven and go back to the mental hospital, protecting my life? Am I concerned about the Nazi underling downstairs? Is the pope a good Catholic in my opinion? Of course not, of course not, and of course not. The audacity of me, defying the orders of SS colonel Martin Bergman! Am I crazy? If I am, I am. I must go forward as I am.

So in the middle of the night, when I believe everyone in the castle is fast asleep, I leave the inn and walk straight into the woods, straight toward the castle, straight for my brother. I sense that no one in the Reich is aware of my destination because everyone is not yet burdened with hopelessness. My violin is at my side because it is part of what I am. When I get to the castle and play for them—if I don't squeak, that is—maybe they will rise to their human senses and to civilization again. Then they could kidnap Hitler and haul him to a gas shower and then to an oven. Finally, Germany could be Germany again.

But I am getting far too ahead of myself. First things first. To the castle.

I set out in pitch black to a place that is two densely wooded miles away, crunching over dead pine needles, each one pricking its neighbor. These woods mindlessly leer. Dead witchgrass claws out of the earth. Dead tree branches whip my hands. Dead burrs prick through my leggings. The hot wind whirls dead leaves around in little tornados as sweat rivers down my shivering back. A legion of blackbirds cry in the evergreens, sounding chaotic and confused, probably wondering why they are not sleeping. This is not just any woods. It is an alien place where fright breeds in the dark and can swallow you whole if you let it. I plead with myself to fear only that which any other young woman would fear on her way to a death house. My axis used to turn at the very center of order, but I am now walking through anarchy itself.

But *never* do I lose touch with the mother thought: I am in the woods with a purpose as distant from that of any blissfully ignorant German citizen as the distance between the beginning and the end of the universe. My purpose is infinite. It is to save one little girl whom I have never met, and if successful with that, to save more children, maybe as many as 5,000 or 10,000 more, and then maybe save everyone. My end goal is to save Germany itself.

Finally, I faintly see the Hartheim Castle a quarter mile away, trying its best to present a good image. To see it in person is to be in awe of it. Categorically. My jaw hangs open in astonishment as the castle's undertow yanks me closer. Gray clouds pass across the face of a moon that is snailing across the sky, but they do not kill the moonlight; a bright-gray luminescence daggers down on the castle—Schloss Hartheim, now called an "idiot's institute" by the German government.

I see the four grandly large floors and four grandly tall spires at each corner, as if adorning a holy place. The lightning rod atop the fifth, tallest tower is impaling the moon, piercing the face of the man in the moon. Now, *there* is one fable I hope is not being read to the children inside at bedtime! I wait for the man to creep free of the rod in order to reduce my sudden superstition to a manageable simmer. I refuse to allow the eeriness of the place to become a harbinger.

I'm staring at the castle. It's staring back. I keep wanting to feel my father, smell his musk cologne, hear him saying a prayer to Bernhard and me after giving us piggyback rides to our beds. It's not too late to turn back, but I know that childish cowardice and surrender are not options. So I cat-step through the beautiful, spooky grounds on as straight a line to the castle as I can manage, then inch in the direction of the entrance that patients must use—the castle's starving backroom mouth, otherwise known as the "welcome door." Welcome to Hartheim Castle. Other than stopping Bernhard, I'm still not exactly sure what I'm going to do here, but going through the door is the only way to begin doing it.

So I tiptoe to the door. The black latch creaks. Thankfully it is unlocked. Who, after all, would want to burglarize *this* place? Who would want to kidnap a disabled person? Once inside, the castle immediately initiates me into its new rhythm, its sullen mood. The castle itself is a person, a blameless woman. She learned to laugh and be merry centuries ago but only recently learned to weep.

Bernhard must have been smitten with her when he first drove up and felt the pinnacles of their twin new existences. He must have thought, *You, Fraulein Castle, shall finally graduate me from childhood!* even though probably none of the socks in his suitcase matched. She has all the regal trappings he could ever want, and he must have imagined that those chivalrous Germanic knights he heard about in Hitler Youth had ridden black horses out of here to the Middle East to practice their religion of slaughtering Muslims. Bernhard is an adult but, with a different brain now, must think that he is a prince and that this is a place where he can chastise, hate, and thus be happy.

I creep feathery light to the huge, moonlit foyer, and I thank the moon that I see no one there. I hear only the pulse-throbs of blood in my ears. Bergman is like a queen ant, and Bernhard and the staff of sixty others are like soldier ants, apparently all soundly sleeping. So this is the perfect time to check the layout of the place. I should get on the move; the sun will be rising soon, and the grueling workday for the worker ants will be starting. Early to bed, early to rise, deals so much better with human cries, I suppose.

Although I have a certain uneasy feeling about the rear precinct of this dark castle, it's the truth I seek, so I tiptoe there. Guided only by moonlight creeping in through the windows, I come first to a colossal playroom. It is spic-and-span; no tumbleweeds of hair and dirt in the corners, as I had imagined. I see fine artwork on the walls, Renaissance-era furniture, jump ropes, footballs, dolls, stuffed animals, toy soldiers, toy trucks, fairy-tale books, four rocking horses. The room smells faintly of cocoa. For a second, my eyes water over because I feel a longing for my childhood yet again. I want to show my little brother how to start a rocking horse rocking. But then instantly I remember that this is no place for children. It is no place for *any* innocent thing. Those poor horses, being at such a place as this!

Worse, I hear a noise in the corner, frightening me. When I spin around to look, I see a person sitting in a high-backed wooden chair into which the face of a gargoyle beast has been carved. "Who are you?" I say, terrified.

"Who are *you*?" a man's voice shoots back.

"Anna Himmel."

"I am Frieden Bauer. A harmless schoolteacher is all. You look harmless too."

"I am. Nothing to worry about with me."

"Nor you with me. Whew!"

He stands and approaches me, and we shake hands. He is maybe thirty, has a boyish face, looks like a grown-up altar boy. He is impeccably dressed in white, the creases of his slacks pressed to perfection, as sharp as knives. "What are you doing here?" he asks.

"Oh, I have some important work to do," I say with vagueness, not yet fully trusting him. "And you say you are a schoolteacher?"

"Well, I should have said that I *was* a teacher until I quit a few days ago. You are looking at Stuttgart's teacher of the year for 1938. I love working with children and wanted to get here good and early to get started." He smiles wider and says, "Early to bed, early to rise, makes a man healthy, wealthy, and wise, you know!"

We share a good soft chuckle. I am more at ease now. Maybe I have found someone to be a friend here. Maybe after I explain things to him, he will help me save people.

"This castle is just magnificent, yes?" he says.

My word, is *he* ever in for a shock when he learns what the doctors do here! Shall I tell him? I edge in by saying, "You said you will be working with doctors now. I was going to say you look like you're in the medical profession, wearing that white robe. That's the caduceus embroidered in scarlet on your chest pocket, right? The symbol of medicine and healing?"

"Exactly right. They gave me this robe because I will be a healer of things. My new mission, they say, will be to improve the health of the Reich."

I'm comfortable with him now. I go out on a limb and finally admit to him what my real purpose is here.

"But I thought you worked here!" he shouts. "I figured you were here to euthanize people!"

Suddenly I realize what he is. I was hoodwinked by Bergman and now again by him. Has my eternal trust in good-appearing people become eternal naivete? Maybe I am not Germany after all. I am certainly not a poet and maybe not a thinker now. But I struggle to think. I try. I shoot straight for his head with my words. "Every life is priceless! It is absolutely abhorrent for anyone to say that a life is worth sixty thousand Reichsmarks, you murderer!" I fire him a sneer so vicious that a normal person would turn and run.

"Whoa, whoa, whoa!" he says, gesturing like a traffic cop to halt. "I am no murderer. I love children and all of mankind. When I walked out in the middle of my indoctrination session last week, thoroughly disgusted by the whole thing, the leaders explained that I will not need to hurt anyone. My job will merely require me to cremate bodies after the people have already passed, just like thousands of morticians across the Reich do every day. If not me, the leaders said, then there are hordes of other men who are dying to get this job. And the money. My word! This new job will pay more than double what I made as a teacher. I have a wife and children who want to rise higher than the middle class. And now I will finally, finally, be able to buy myself a fishing boat. Maybe it is sad, but money really does make the world go round. For everyone but saints."

Given what he will do here, I am not at all impressed by his dream of upward mobility. And the matter-of-fact way that he said it! I shoot again: "Money shmoney. Why do doctors murder people here? Why on God's earth? It is a simple question!"

Correcting words must still be part of his job. "You are using the wrong words, Anna. They do not murder here. Not at all. And by the way, you will do well not to use exclamation points in this conversation. You talk as if the doctors here will shoot people in the head or something. They are strictly against the use of guns. They do not practice violence here. Only medicine."

"You are playing with serious words and ideas. Bottom line, this is a covert death machine."

His nostrils flare. He says, now sounding irritated, "To call this place a 'death machine' is something like being against a surgeon's amputation of a brave soldier's gangrenous leg to save his life. When I talked to the leaders and then walked back in for the rest of the indoctrination, a renowned physician reminded us at the podium that the doctors' mission in their professional lives here is to alleviate human pain and suffering, as the ancient Greek healer Hippocrates taught. He added that they and the other professionals here painlessly, with gas, alleviate the pain of misfits who suffer knowing they have no future. In doing so, those pros make it impossible for the misfits to bear children who would also feel pain and suffering.

"You see? Ultimately, we as a group will minimize, and eventually erase, the fatherland's pain and suffering by, like, cutting off the head of a snake. Millions of our normal, heathy citizens suffer pain seeing the plight of people with bad genes. With all due respect, is that so hard to understand?"

"I think it is murder!"

He is getting very frustrated now. "You have a grave problem, Anna, the same one I had before my indoctrination: You think too much. You analyze, deduce, work things out in your head. If you do not stop it, you are going to make yourself go berserk."

This former teacher of the year with a hopeful family is so dangerous precisely because he looks so harmless. He gazes at a person the way an unwanted suitor does: with love the person doesn't want. He adds, "What they do here is killing, I will grant you, but not murder. Murder is the unjustified killing of a human being by another human being. You are begging the question of what is unjustified. If you ask anyone, they will say that it is unjustified to allow a person to suffer year after year and then produce a child who suffers year after year. Stopping that endless chain of suffering through the generations is a noble mission."

"Do those doctors have no hearts?"

Finally he loses control. "Here you go again with all that pudding-headed malarkey! Someone as intelligent as you should know that doctors are not supposed to become emotionally involved with their patients. You just fail to understand. Are you an idiot?"

I stand there with my jaw hanging wide open. Words will not come. After a minute, I manage to close my jaw and can only say, "Herr Bauer, you are an animal come to the underground. You should take off your shoes and see if your feet have turned into cloven hooves."

As he looks at me and swallows hard, suddenly thinking, I run off to find Bernhard. I have a hunch, though, that Bauer will stop thinking

again. I imagine he will pop up in front of me again. He has become
born again. I think that a man like him does not leave you alone until he
has converted you.

I must hurry to find Bernhard since Bauer might sound an alarm
and thus destroy my mission. Over by an outside door, there's a wooden
plaque with an empty hook for car keys with the name *Herr Bernhard
Christian Himmel* under it. Next to his name is a schedule: *6 a.m. — Leave
to pick up Rosalie Blume, 27 Apple Tree Way, Dolmer, Germany.*

That's in only ten minutes!

*I need to find and stop you right now, little brother! Then I'm going to steal your
car, pick up the little girl, and take her to safety. You, Bernhard, must be halted in
your tracks. Not even a photograph of you at age nine could make me feel sentimental
remembrance of the chocolate ice cream you used to love, or the model sail boats you
used to sail in the river cove, or the Himmel violin you used to kiss after practicing.*

I run upstairs as quietly as I can to hunt for Bernhard through the
dark rooms. In the first room, there is circumstantial evidence of human
life: heavy breathing. I tiptoe forward and see in the moonlight an old
man strapped down to a bed. I whisper in his ear, "I will return and get
you out of here." I run through the second and third rooms, the fourth
and fifth . . . and finally into the last. Bernhard is not here because when
I glance out the window, there he is, down there, about to get in the car
five minutes early. He just can't wait to hit the road for Dolmer!

I rush outside and run up to the young man I still call my brother to
stop him any way I can. Being an even quicker doer now that he has spent
eight weeks at the altar in Tiergartenstrasse 4, he instantly pulls a pistol
and pushes the barrel into my cheek; apparently he has no immediate
plans to turn human again. His breath smells like mint, though. Earlier
this morning he must have done a human thing—brush his teeth. It's a
long shot, but maybe I can reach him. "Bernhard, it is me, Anna, your
sister. Remember me?"

"I know who you are. Colonel Bergman told me all about you last
night. Now get in the car. We are going to pick up a little girl." The stench
of his words wraps my nose, overpowering the mint, but I cooperate and

get in the car because I feel desperate to save at least that one girl. That
he has a gun pointed at me makes no difference. Nothing can kill me.

Bernhard jumps in the driver's seat of his people's car, starts the
engine, and straightens the lapels of his civilian business suit. "You think
I dropped that document in your hospital room by accident? Think I went
there to chitchat and tell you how much I love you? Well, think again."
This kind of thing is what I expected from him.

"Then why *did* you drop it?"

He laughs. "Because I knew you would read it and then come down
here, down into the woods. No one but Anna Himmel would believe
such a fantastic document. How could it possibly seem true to a common
German? You, Anna, are right where I want you now. Your soul is in me,
and now I want mine in you. And once you see the fine work we are doing,
you will want to break your violin over your knee and join us. We would
be honored to have the one and only you."

"Not a chance!" I scream as the car pulls away. I fear that my scream
will make him slap me. But what I am seems to have acted on him in some
way. He flips in a nanosecond—black to white. He doesn't slap me but
instead reaches over and feels my hand. "You feel chilled on this warm
August morning," he says in a tone of honest concern. "Even though it
is still summer, let me turn on the heat. When it starts to warm up, just
let me know if you need it higher. I so much want you to be comfortable
on our drive to Dolmer. It will take about an hour."

I am dumbfounded by this kindness, this genuine human conduct.
Is Bernhard, deep down, really still the caring person he was as a boy?
Suddenly I feel entangled in both love and hate, unable to untwist the two.

We are now a few miles down the road, and because of the concern
he has shown for me, I'm still thinking the impossible is possible, that
somehow, someway, he'll recognize the inhumanity of his infantile
thoughts and the moral bankruptcy of his job. I'm hoping that he is just
caught up in a childish whim, that his ideas are simply those of a lost soul
caught up in something he doesn't understand. I'm praying for him and all
of the Reich that this is just a fad—though certainly it is an unspeakable

one! Fads are so successful precisely because those who succumb to them are ordinary people, easily hooked.

So I try to unhook him with simple reason directed at his heart: "Do you know what they really do in that castle? Do you? They murder." He slows down the car. The appearance of a glimmer across his face suggests that he's thinking.

After a few seconds of thought, he speeds up and says, "Shut up."

Are we now on the road of no return?

He looks around at the bucolic wooded countryside and proclaims, "I just love Germany, don't you, Anna?"

"We are in Austria, Bernhard."

"Austria is really part of Germany now. Don't you just love Germany like I do, Anna?"

Did he really utter for the second time that he "loves" Germany? It sounded so sincere. Is he flipping yet again? When you yourself love something passionately and then another person says he loves the same thing, you believe that his reasons are identical to yours. It makes you think that if the other person loses his soul, he can find it and stuff it back inside by being made to examine himself.

So I ask, "Tell me why you love Germany? I want to hear it in your own words." I have my fingers crossed that he's going to say something like "I love Germany because of its culture." I want him to think through his reasons, to lead his own self back to civilization. Maybe an epiphany will rise up and whack him in the head.

He says, "I love Germany because here you can get an excellent-paying job and live in a real castle without even finishing high school."

I guess it was too much to ask. "Bernhard, let's drive to Linz and get you a bus north. Father is at our house in Edelberg, so maybe you can live with the Merkels in Berlin. I will drive back to Alkoven, sneak in the castle after midnight to pick up your things, and then drive to the Merkels' and care for you until you're well." I don't tell him, of course, that I will remain down here in the woods and try to save people in the castle in the dead of night. A white lie.

"You are so funny, Anna," he says, laughing. "It is too late to leave the woods now. I am already committed. The books and the training in Berlin were unbelievable. I have received too much education to waste now. I actually got to shake the hand of our supreme leader, Heinrich Himmler, who knows Hitler *personally*." He chuckles, "I did not wash my right hand for days."

I have been thwarted again but must not give up on Bernhard. I must continue to maintain high hopes that Germany doesn't have a highly hopeless son here. Trying to reason with him yet again, this time using child psychology, I say, "All your favorite old things, things you cherish whether you realize it or not, are in your bedroom back home. I could go get them and take them to you at the Merkels' house in Berlin. You could start playing a violin again. You were getting so good!"

He guffaws like a boy and says, "Oh, stop it, Anna. You are making me blush, but I have to say 'Fuck you' to your idea about the Merkels because a castle in the woods is where I belong now."

Damn. But at least he seems comfortable with me now, because he just put the pistol up on the dashboard, close enough for me to reach. He must trust me. All day and night, until this moment, I've maintained the same straight-ahead tack into the woods—blunderingly detoured for an hour by Bergman's enchanting persona—but I always wondered how I was going to stop Bernhard after I found him. I never once imagined I might have a gun within reach.

I refuse to take the gun for the time being to try reasoning with him a third time, but now strictly as an adult. "You should go stay with the Merkels and finish your high school degree, then go on to university so that you can get a real career. The longer you wait, the longer you will get out of the habit of thinking, and the harder it will be. *Think*, Bernhard, *think*."

He laughs and laughs and laughs. Did I just tell an excellent joke? "Anna, dear, my problem all my life is that I have been thinking *too* much. Have you not heard? Germany is no longer the land of poets and thinkers. It is the land of doers. Like our dear father, I am strictly a doer now, not a thinker, and I'm making good money doing it. More than I could make with a university degree. I tell you again, Anna, you should join us. You would even get a new car and new clothing out of the deal."

I have used every argument I can imagine, but nothing has worked. Suddenly I think the answer is staring me right in the face. I can't believe it has taken me this long to think of it. The car radio. Music. I switch it on, hoping to find something upbeat and soft in a major key. Maybe a string quartet. I dial past a heavy piece with blaring trumpets, trombones, and tubas. Suddenly Bernhard slaps away my hand, tuning back to the loud brass.

"My favorite!" he cries while turning up the volume.

It is the opera *Parsifal* by the nineteenth-century German composer Richard Wagner. Bernhard shouts merrily, "It is probably the Berlin Philharmonic. The orchestra no longer wastes its time performing dirty smelly Jewish music, like the works of Mendelssohn and Mahler."

"Your boss, Bergman, adores Mahler."

"He might *like* Mahler, but we Nazis do not 'adore.' Besides, Herr Bergman will be out of a job someday when I triumph and get to manage the castle." Bernhard shakes his hands around like an ecstatic boy about to pee his pants. He can hardly wait to continue. "Thanks for turning on the radio, sister."

I am suddenly "sister" instead of "Anna."

"My training is all coming back to me. I remember now that they played *Parsifal* for us in training. Rudy Gendler. What a teacher! He said, 'No university for you, my good man. No pointy-headed intellectuals for you.' I know all I need to know from him. Except for Father, he is by far the smartest person I have ever met. He is a Wagner man."

"Rudy Gendler is a dull chip off his father's dull block. They are both animals. Where did your heart go?"

"Oh, I have a heart, sister. Do you think I will enjoy this new job? Do you think I enjoy brushing my teeth? No and no. But both must be done. Although I am glad for the euthanasia program and am excited to go on my virgin run to pick up a child, I think I will actually find this job distasteful."

Okay, we are making progress here. "So you *do* have a conscience, Bernhard. You *do* know right from wrong."

"Of course. I know it is wrong to kill innocent people. These patients at the castle are idiots, but *that* should not be a crime. Being born with a genetic impossibility of ever being an astrophysics professor or an Olympic athlete should not be an offense warranting the death penalty."

"*Exactly*. Now let's protect Rosalie somehow, and then you can take a bus to Berlin."

"But don't you see, Anna? Thanks to your continuing prompts, I remember now that eliminating idiots is so right that the bright sun of it will burn up the wrong of it to nothing. It is only natural. They told us in our training that Icarus of ancient Greece was a real person who idiotically flew too close to the sun, and then the natural thing happened—his wax wings melted, causing him to fall and crash on the earth. See the parallel, sister? The sun? Eliminating idiots will help make Germany great again naturally. A short-term pain for a long-term gain. I am only doing my part to make the world a better place for mankind. And Anna—I mean, sister—are you warm enough now? Because I can turn the heat up or down as you wish."

"You and your colleagues are killing your fellow man, not saving mankind!"

He laughs at me the way a mother laughs at her child who does a cute dumb thing, then turns up *Parsifal* even louder.

"As they taught us, the only mark against Wagner is that he was baptized into the faith. The fact that it happened in the Lutheran church where Bach was choirmaster does not redeem Richard's parents. Certainly we can forgive him since he was a baby with no choice. You *do* believe in forgiveness, do you not, sister?"

"You are sadly mixed up about this opera, Bernhard. *Parsifal* is about the Holy Grail, or have you conveniently forgotten?"

This angers Bernhard. "No, I remember! I went through Lutheran confirmation classes the same as you, bitch. The Grail is the fictional cup that filled up with the fictional blood of a real criminal named Jesus from a fictional spear wound while he was dying nailed to a real cross. Richard would agree that the word *grail* has a small *g* and that the whole opera story is a brilliant work of fiction, sister. As Rudy says, all that matters is that after the son of a bitch King Ludwig forced Richard to agree to let a Jew conduct *Parsifal* in public, Richard wrote to the king and voiced understandable displeasure. We gladly had to memorize the most important part of the letter. It said that the Jewish race is the 'born enemy of pure humanity and everything noble about it.' That is why Richard is your führer's favorite composer of all time."

"Hitler is not my führer!"

"Oh, but he is, sister, and you know it deep down inside—whether you know it consciously or not. And Richard is your favorite composer. Listen to that brass! The music says Germany all over itself, no?"

"You are a patsy for the Nazis! Those poor people in France, Belgium, Holland—"

He cuts me off. "I am sure glad that you mentioned France. Because you jog my memory of my training. Did you know that Richard was close friends with the famous French thinker Arthur de Gobineau—Arthur as in King Arthur?"

"I have no idea who de Gobineau is, but—"

"No? Well, you should. He puts Einstein and his wacky Jewish theory of relativity out to the pigs. De Gobineau was one of the first scientists to recognize the biological existence of the Aryan master race."

Oh no. I must be a fool. First, I turned on the radio. Then I mentioned France. Does what I am render me powerless to do anything right? Or is what I think I am now really what I *was*, gone forever? I am getting concerned, but I must forge ahead as though I am still something.

"That is an insane philosophy!" I shout. "Insane!"

"But it is no philosophy or religion, sister. Rudy says it is science. A person should deny the existence of God, since it is just plain silly to think that some invisible force could manufacture a woman from the rib of a man, but no person in his right mind can deny the existence of the Aryan race. To deny it would like denying that two plus two equals four.

We are merely talking about the biological makeup of sperm and ovarian eggs. You cannot deny what you see under a microscope. All that matters is science, not art. Microscopes, not violins."

"A few months ago you hardly knew what the words *philosophy* and *opera* and *ovarian* meant!"

"Now, now, sister, no reason to get all in a hissy. I shall pretend you did not say that. You are only trying to get off topic. Biology is what we are talking about, and if you would just not have a fit for a minute, I will be happy to explain."

"Say your piece and then I will say mine."

"Good. You know the great German professor Hans Günther, no? His book is right there in the bookcase of our parents' living room. It has been there ever since it was issued to me in Hitler Youth. I had never read it before, but its lessons were presented to my brain for the first time during my training—and boy oh boy, I never knew what I was missing! Günther is affectionately called Germany's 'race pope' because his teachings are divine and beyond debate. He has proven that each person in Europe falls somewhere on a vertical race scale. The highest is the Nordic race." Bernhard adds, as if this were an empirical fact and piece of wisdom, "We Nordic people have the highest character, spirit, bodily structure, and physical beauty, and we come primarily from northern Germany, Scandinavia, and the Netherlands originally. And—"

I can't help but interrupt. I am livid. "You had best speed it up and get to the end, or I am apt to pick up that pistol and shoot you!"

"Ha! You do not have it in you to kill a person, which is why I do not care that the pistol is there within your reach. Now let me finish." Bernhard continues calmly and matter-of-factly, as if he's trying to simply teach me a foreign language. "More than half of all Germans are pure Nordic. Look at you and me. We come quite close to pure Nordic." He glances into the rearview mirror and seems to admire his face—and the car veers into the other lane.

"Bernhard, keep your eyes on the road!"

"So sorry, sister. But just look at the two of us. Both of us are fairly lean and have narrow faces, blond hair, blue eyes, fair skin, prominent chins, and narrow, straight noses with low bridges. We two are probably pure Nordics, or pretty damn close. And get this: The Führer actually does not care that a person has slanty eyes. The Japanese and Chinese are called the 'Aryans of the East' and generally are admired by him. They are honorary Aryans under our laws. Remember when our father, bless his heart, thought we were yin and yang? Too bad he could never figure out who was who. Myself, I think each of us is both."

"You are making me sick. I possess absolutely nothing of you."

"Oh, don't say that," he responds, his memory of his new knowledge cracking open wider, "because you are beginning to sound like you are a member of the Western race, which is the next one down the scale from the Nordics. It is also called the Mediterranean race. Spaniards, Italians, Albanians, and Greeks are good examples. Then down, like mercury falling in a thermometer, getting colder, weaker, comes the so-called Dinaric race, also called the Adriatics. The people of the Balkan countries—Serbia and so forth—are good examples.

"Tumbling to the very bottom, you have the East Baltic race. They are mostly your Slavs, Jews, and Romani, or what we call gypsies. The East Baltic people—and I use that word *people* advisedly—tend to have bad personal hygiene, are corrupt, and are prone to criminal activity. It is an empirical fact, or so I am told. This is one of the reasons why scientists like Günther classify East Baltics as biologically subhuman.

"But guess what? Things get far simpler when it comes to physical and mental misfits, since even a child can make the determination with nothing but his eyes. To find a physical misfit, you just look at the person's body. To find a mental misfit, you just look at a person's test answers. Either category of misfit can come from *any* of the races. It is almost, but not quite, a shame when you see one these days, because you know that he or she will need to put to death. In a perfect world, not even an alligator would be killed. They cannot help that they are vicious. They are vicious merely because biology intended it.

"Have I told you that I will specialize in mentally misfit children—

idiot children, to use one less word and be more efficient? They cannot think and, just like alligators, they should not have to die because of it. But unfortunately, when you put a grown-up naked male idiot in bed with a grown-up naked female idiot, then you're going to get a baby idiot every time. So we terminate idiots when they are children for the good of the human race, not to mention to save money.

"Believe me, sister, I will probably shed a tear after my first passenger is terminated, but in twenty years when I look back, I will feel proud that I really accomplished something in my life. The illegal interbreeding of the races will have reached an all-time low by then, and the generation of pure Nordics will be well underway for the first time in the history of man. Happiness in man will increase. Just imagine where our Reich will be in a *thousand* years if we just stick to the plan."

Bernhard seems enamored of himself for knowing so much about so little. He has expert knowledge of one of a hundred subjects: the theory of Aryanism. From the moment we got in the car until now, he has talked in a circle, ending where he began. It is as if all of his brainwashing and all of the books he has read recently have narrowed down his knowledge to that single topic. Such talk from him—not merely the words, but the mental gymnastics too—would have been impossible before my father drove him to and enshrined him at Tiergartenstrasse 4, but it is pouring from him now. Does he really understand his new vocabulary? It's extremely dangerous to use words while having no comprehension of what they mean, because if a person keeps repeating those words over and over again, he starts to believe them in his mind, then in his heart, then in his soul. And then, he's apt to stop trying to understand the words and to just act them out like an unthinking animal.

I say with utter despair and resignation, "It pains me to say this. You are no longer my brother."

"No? I am sorry to hear it. But speaking of France and pain, sister, have you ever heard of the great French philosopher René Descartes?"

"Please spare me your SS doctoral education."

"Of course you have never heard of him, because you are an artist.

Descartes observed that animals do not talk, and therefore, he concluded, they do not think. And—"

"Stop! And what does that have to do with pain?"

"Shush. And because animals do not think, they do not feel pain, and therefore—"

"That is ridiculous!"

"And therefore when we kill animals, they do not feel pain—animals like the idiot *Homo sapiens* we will bring to the castle. And I say that with all due respect to them. You cannot teach an animal, and therefore an idiot, to feel pain. It would be like trying to teach a pig to sing. You will waste many days of your life and will just end up with an extremely pissed-off pig! I like pigs, but they are so dangerous when they get angry, no?"

This leaves me speechless. My hand flies across and pinches his wrist before I can think. "Ouch!" he cries.

"There. That proves it. You are an animal, yet you just felt pain."

A growl stuck in Bernhard's throat lets loose. "I am a human!" He nurses the pinch mark on his wrist by licking it. "Since I still love you, you bitch, I will pretend you did not do that. Instead, I will stay calm and teach you more of what I was taught.

"Western civilization goes in cycles. Think of the Roman Empire. Birth, growth, maturity, and death. Before the next birth, there is a necessary period of low living. Very low, much lower than the Dark Ages. So low that Herr Spengler calls it barbarism in his great book. Remember the book that has a bad binding because you threw it down the stairs? Spengler showed he has a second-rate political mind for voting for Hindenburg over Hitler back in '32, but he is a first-rate history thinker. Germany, you would have to say, and I think he would agree, is now straddling a period of barbarism on the edge of rebirth. Barbarism is a necessary precondition to our rebirth. You see?"

"Stop it now!"

"In fact, I now have my own barbaric nickname for myself. I will share it with you. My undername is Conan, as in Conan the Barbarian. I am the reincarnated Conan. You believe in the Hindu concept of reincarnation, no? You should because the swastika on our national flag is an old Hindu symbol."

"There is no logic to that!"

"Oh, but the world has a new logic now. One that you cannot possibly comprehend because of what you stubbornly still are. You can read all about me, Conan, in a book titled *Wings in the Night*, and then maybe you will evolve to something better. Our father has read it. After my training, I took it from his bookcase with his blessing. And you have heard of Friedrich Nietzsche, no? Now *there* is a Conan disciple and *real* man, a brilliant academic philosopher, a good German through and through! I am a good example of what Nietzsche called the 'superman.' I am an *übermensch*, a superman, a higher man that will help make a higher mankind. The ape is to the man of the former mankind as the former man is to the superman. See, sister?"

I am even more speechless now, hardly knowing what to say. The only words I can think of are "The idea is barbaric!"

"Precisely! *Great* use of that word. I guess that what you are might change for the better. I have memorized my favorite passage from the Conan book: 'The ancient empires fall, the dark-skinned peoples fade and even the demons of antiquity gasp their last, but over all stands the Aryan barbarian, white-skinned, cold-eyed, dominant, the supreme fighting man of the earth.' What do you think, sis?"

This professor of Aryan theory with no high school degree turns up the radio. Wagner's *Parsifal* now enters more flamboyant moments. Bernhard hums, "Dah dah dum, dah dee dum," then continues, "And war is a necessary element of the period of barbarism. War cleans. Barbarism can be a beautiful thing when it has the correct set of aims. Like the cleansing of germs. The raising of mankind and—"

"I heard all about it from that so-called man Frieden Bauer, and am sickened by it. Do you hear me?"

"Please be patient, sister. I am just now getting to the best part of my teachings."

All I want to do is pick up the pistol and shoot him right now, but I

don't—because he's my own brother! Bernhard continues to use words I
don't think he knows the meaning of:

"As I was saying, the eradication of disease ultimately raises mankind
into a higher state of being. The so-called human beings we collect at
the castle have a need. They need to be put out to pasture, so to speak.
Descartes said in the Latin, '*Cogito, ergo sum.*' 'I think, therefore I exist.'
The eating bodies we are bringing to the castle do not talk. They make
noise, but they have no rational language. Therefore they do not think. It
follows that they technically do not exist. Their ultimate duty to mankind
is to become actually, not merely technically, nonexistent. Utter not-ness.

"You see? Rome was not built in a day. Therefore, what we will
accomplish at the castle and all over Europe, and indeed the world, will
not be finished in a day or a year. It will take us years, maybe even decades.
But when we get there, it will last forever."

Bernhard turns up the Wagner even louder and now is in such a state
of mania that his face is turning red.

"You are a madman!" I scream. If only for just one minute I could
be like Hektor Himmel, uncivilized, the lowest of the low, a barbarian.
If only I could descend into Bernhard's kind of anarchy, his kind of
upside-down heaven, and hate him long enough to shoot him dead! Does
Bernhard think that killing is foreign to me, that I don't even know where
the trigger to the gun is? Is *that* why he lets it sit within my reach?

I have no rational argument left. The bottom of my barrel is empty.
As a last resort to reach him instead of the gun, I say, "Do you remember
the prince in 'Snow White'?"

He flinches. Without answering me, he turns off the radio and slows
the car to a normal speed. All is quiet. There is relative normalcy.

After a few minutes of peace, I can tell from the dark dots on his suit
lapel that some tears have dropped from his eyes. Apparently he cannot
see straight through his watering eyes; he steers the car onto the shoulder
and stops. Suddenly he seems not to know where he is.

What's this? On the back seat he's got the Grimms' fairy tale book
he couldn't live without as a toddler, probably for children to entertain

themselves and leave him alone on the drive from their homes to the castle. He came prepared. Reaching back and fondling it, he suddenly has a rational look in his eyes like he did all his life before the training. Does he suffer from a split personality? Is he able to flip from one to the other at the drop of a Reichsthaler five coin?

Looking straight ahead, apparently afraid I will see the tears in his eyes, he manages to string together words from the scrapheap of his childhood consciousness:

"Anna, Grandpa Himmel came to talk with me when I was a boy, you know, just weeks before he died. He promised me—me, Bernhard—that I would grow up and become the next generation of Himmel vio-violin makers. That was the happiest day of my life. My future was so certain that I could see and touch and smell it on the factory floor."

Then Bernhard looks at me with rational but sullen eyes. "But now, Anna, as you know, the factory is used to store bombs. A person could not make a single violin there now if his life depended on it. The bombs are stacked everywhere, from floor to ceiling to the windows painted over black. The craftsmen have been fired. SS men with attack dogs roam the floors twenty-four hours a day."

Bernhard takes his lucky charm out of his pocket—the Reichsthaler five that my father gave him, with the Potsdam Military Church on one side and the eagle and two swastikas on the other. A sun of brilliant normalcy now shines in his eyes as he avoids looking at it. He rolls down his window and throws the coin out, then brushes his palms together in an appearance of finality.

12

"Keep thinking that thought, Bernhard!" I yell. "Take off your SS pin and throw it out the window too!"

Preparing to throw out the pin—two silver bolts of lightning—he removes it from his lapel and licks away a tear. He feels it, smells it, looks disgusted by it, and then his lips curl into a smile and his eyes glimmer into wide circles, as if he has just rediscovered something. But then he switches back on the radio—the conclusion of *Parsifal*—and his smile deforms. Suddenly his eyes snap back to attention as though nothing has happened. He refastens the pin, rushes out of the car to pick up the coin, wrings the sunshine out of it, and jumps back in the driver's seat, stomping the accelerator to the floor. The car jolts off, both it and he reabsorbed in their identical futures. He says in an iron voice, "We should be at Rosalie's house any minute now, bitch."

The sun inside me tumbles below my horizon, and I fill with a grotesque chill, now feeling my love for him start to ice.

"Here, take it," Bernhard says, grabbing the pistol on the dashboard and handing it to me. "Put it in your coat pocket. You might need it later if Rosalie Blume gets too far out of line." So Bernhard has just lurched back down into stark madness as suddenly as he hurdled up out of it. He suddenly seems to believe that since the reversal of his future as a violin maker is obviously not something that can be killed with a gun, his body cannot be killed with a gun. He can't comprehend that I know better, because he can't comprehend that what *he* is now is the perfect opposite of what *I* am. Now hopeless, I pocket the pistol in order to be finally done with the matter.

The Nazi convert pulls into the Blumes' driveway. Straight ahead is the house where I imagine little Rosalie cheerfully raises her baby doll in the sun, listens to her parents reading her nursery rhymes at night, and dances in the moonlight. He shuts off the engine and removes his SS pin again, hiding it in his pocket—circumstantial evidence that he still has at least a small conscience. He orders, "Wait here, Anna, and do not be naughty."

The pistol is in my coat pocket, all right, but it may just as well not be because despite his insanity, I am still consumed with one thought: *How can I shoot this poor lost boy, my own flesh and blood?*

When Rosalie's mother answers the door, the little girl is holding her hand. I am concerned for the mother as a mother, but my main attention is on Rosalie as a human being. I roll down the window frantically and yell out, "*Achtung*, Rosalie!"

Bernhard is crazy, but crazy like a fox. He laughs off my words, telling Frau Blume, "Oh do not mind that overgrown child in the car. She is just another mentally retarded patient I am taking in for medical care." So what can I do but sit there like a nothing and watch the young mother smile as Bernhard sparkles with laughter? I am about as useful to Rosalie as the millions of good Nazi-blinded people all across the Reich.

Frau Blume puts her little girl's hand into one of Bernhard's, and with his other, he takes her small suitcase. Rosalie makes a sour face when he tries to take hold of her doll, then smiles and kisses her mother on the lips. Frau Blume gets down on her knees and hugs and kisses her daughter for a third time. "Goodbye for now, darling," she says to Rosalie. "Your father and I will come pick you up and bring you home in a few weeks."

These parents, born trustful like all other people in the world, believe Rosalie's trustworthy pediatrician, who read about a medical breakthrough by a Nazi doctor who wrote that "mental retardation is now treatable by an astounding new therapy."

When Rosalie arrives at the car, Bernhard allows me to move to the back seat where I can entertain the little girl during the drive to the castle. Rosalie lives in her own world. This sweet girl with round cheeks, small red lips, and blond hair is her doll's mother. When I ask her about the little thing, she points her face at mine, smiles, and says, "Sweet baby. Came out my belly."

Bernhard appears nervous. Why else would he be shivering in the late-summer heat? He utters not one word for a long time on the drive back to the castle.

A half hour after we leave the Blumes' home, we momentarily drive out of a wooded area into sunshine. Bernhard appears nervous and squints at the bright light. Seeming surprised by the light, he pulls the cars onto the shoulder, wipes the perspiration from his forehead, slips on sunglasses, and stares ahead in silence for minutes. Does he want to move out of the bright sunshine and into a brighter light? Is he delaying getting back to the castle? Has he decided to take Rosalie back home and then drive to the bus station? Finally he turns around to face Rosalie.

"Do you know how to rock your baby?" he says to her. Immediately she does a human thing—rocks her doll in her arms. Rosalie comprehended. She thought. Therefore, even according to Descartes, she exists and is human.

Bernhard seems to warm up to Rosalie and then spots the Grimms book next to her. It also spots him. It is the first material object he can remember coming into his life. He slips into the back seat next to Rosalie and me, calls on a ghost, and reads her "Snow White" with the utmost seriousness. Is he giving himself one final chance to come home to himself? Perhaps, because just as our father did with us as small children, Bernhard repeats to Rosalie the last few paragraphs of the story three times, laying great emphasis on the words announcing the planned wedding of "great splendor and majesty" to take place at the prince's father's castle. He puts his arms around Rosalie, looks her straight in the eyes with a smile, and adds his own personalized ending: "And the prince and Snow White lived happily ever after in the castle."

Rosalie is now smiling as broadly as I've ever seen a human being smile. She returns to rocking her baby, the two little princesses now in a higher peace. I imagine Rosalie wanting her baby to grow up and become a woman, because then when Rosalie gets old, her daughter could reciprocate and take care of her. Rosalie seems to understand the familial facts of human life.

In short, Rosalie looks like a human being to me. I saw deadly germs, vermin, under a microscope in high school biology class, and Rosalie looks nothing like one.

I am ready to slide around into the driver's seat and take Rosalie back to the safety of her home while Bernhard casually repeats the word *castle* from the fairy tale. The word seems to act on him in some strange way. "Castle," he says again. Then again. Suddenly the river of his youth evaporates, and his body absorbs all darkness in the Reich. He glares at Rosalie and says with a crooked smile, "It is to the *Hartheim* Castle that we must go now, little one."

So it turns out that my imagined homecoming for him was itself a fairy tale. The true tale of what the Nazis steeled into him at Tiergartenstrasse 4 must have been like the ring of a bell—something that not even God can undo. Bernhard tosses the book aside, jumps back up front to the driver's seat, and now away we go for the last stretch of this, his maiden voyage through the woods.

After some minutes, I see familiar landscape whispering to me out of Bernhard's earshot that we are only a few miles from the castle. The impossible decision of whether to take out the gun and kill my brother can no longer wait.

This is my judgment moment, one that must be carefully considered, leaving no stone unturned. I think, *If I do not kill Bernhard, there is a good chance that Rosalie will die. If I do kill him, I can reach over, stop the car, throw the body out, and drive the girl to safety.*

I look at her. She is smiling. What a smile! It seems genuine; I'm almost certain that she lacks the brain power to form the intention to fake a smile. Her happiness right now might be felt only at some primordial level, unlike the kind you get from winning a Nobel Prize. But nobody, especially not the doctors in the castle, who obviously were trained in Western science, can claim that the musculature creating the smile on Rosalie's face created it from nothing. Surely those doctors know that every effect has a cause.

I close my eyes and imagine Heaven. If I do kill Bernhard now and try to get in when I die, Rosalie's parents will not need to guard the gate in tears and hear me sob, "I am profoundly sorry, Frau and Herr Blume, but I had to spend all my energy on not killing my own flesh and blood." Therefore they will be spared from having to respond, "Anna, you are a selfish, evil woman! You are such an omnipotent force all across the fatherland that you could have accomplished a feat that normally would take a billion good citizens to accomplish. You allowed yourself to be your brother's keeper and let our Rosalie die. We will not let you pass through the gate!"

And now that I have put it to myself *that* way, the question of whether or not to kill Bernhard becomes purely rhetorical; merely posing the question underscores the only correct answer. So no, I will not need to play God. I will not need to make myself a judge who must ponder and weigh whether Bernhard should live or die. *I've been way overthinking this whole thing. It's so simple! Bernhard wants to kill; therefore he should be killed. Period. End of analysis.* At last, I feel that my constitution—that which makes me me—enables me to kill my only brother. It has been such a long climb in my mind, but at last I am to the top. I have taken the final step from shock to acknowledgment. The connection between my brother and me is now fully dissolved. I want my flesh and blood dead. The end.

Oh no! I have wasted far too much time chattering in my mind and thinking! The car is parked, and Bernhard and Rosalie are out and skipping hand in hand to the welcome door. I jump out of the car and sprint toward them with the pistol, screaming, "*Achtung,* Rosalie!"

"Hear those noisy footsteps behind us, Rosalie?" Bernhard says to her even though he knows she doesn't understand. "Do not be frightened, little one. It is only Anna Himmel with a gun. Artists do not know how to kill. I promise you."

"Yes I do!" I cry, running toward them as another young, whiskerless male driver speeds away in a car—he too consumed by an occult spell. I want to stop that young man, but at this moment I have the power to save only Rosalie. Today I cannot save every person in the castle, much less save the entire nation. They are now only ten feet from the welcome door, so if I'm going to shoot, it's got to be *now*. I need to get close enough to miss Rosalie. I halt three feet from them, take aim, and fire.

The bullet whizzes past Bernhard's head, the echo spiraling through the pines. He coughs out devilish clouds of smoke, "See, little girl? I promised you that Anna Himmel is not the type who knows how to kill. I never break my promise."

I am an utter failure as a killer of human beings, as bad a killer as I am a violinist. I see Martin Bergman, the most senior prince at the castle, looking at me from his suite and laughing. He motions two burly Nazi guards to seize me and bring me inside. Bernhard and Rosalie are now through the welcome door. It swings shut with a thwack loud enough to be heard all over the Reich, but no one outside the woods is listening.

I will need to wait for a second chance to kill my brother because the two Nazi brutes now have me by the hair and are hauling me in to face the Wittgenstein scholar. Once I am inside Bergman's suite, he slams the door shut. The thick Chinese rug in which cloven footprints are embedded inhales the soles of my shoes as I stand afraid and still. On the monogrammed china plate on his dinner table is a stripped rack of lamb. A devoured lamb.

As Bergman removes the toothpick from his mouth, he says, "I am disappointed in you, Anna. Very disappointed. I told you last night to return north, yet you are still down here in the woods, still insisting on murdering your own brother. Do you honestly think I ever would have let you fire at him if I thought you had any chance of hitting him? You, Anna, do not have what it takes to kill *any* human being."

"Yes I do, and I will!"

Bergman wags his finger at me as if I've been a naughty little girl. "Your brother is well liked at this castle. Some nurses even love him. What he has become gives him such joy compared to anything else he has ever known. He can hardly stand it."

"I know that deep down you want to order Bernhard to drive that little girl back home. You cannot tell me that you did not feel something warm and kind in your heart last night at dinner. I could see it in your eyes."

Bergman laughs now—and what a demonic laugh it is! "Yes, Fraulein. I did feel something wonderful, but you had to ruin a perfectly lovely evening. I thank my lucky stars that your own violin blew your cover."

"If I ever get out of here, I will call the—"

"Call exactly who?" Bergman interrupts again. "The authorities? *What* authorities? The Gestapo? The SS? We *are* the SS. Your brother has finally broken out of you, Fraulein. He is anything but music or art."

"You are a monster!"

"Guess what? Last night I told you I would let you live because you are far too much of a national treasure to die. But today I am going to put a little twist on that. Today I feel you should live because you will be useful to the Reich in a few years."

"The day I fall so low as to do something useful to the Nazis will be the day I kill myself!"

"Anna, you have no right to feel that way. No right at all. You are German culture, as I understand it, and you could never kill yourself even if you wanted to. Until this very moment, I thought of German culture as something that will become, in five years or so, like the phoenix of ancient mythology. You know the old story, yes? A phoenix is a large, colorful bird that rises from the ashes of its predecessor phoenix, and I had thought that German culture was something that would rise again after we do our genetic housecleaning throughout Europe. But if we keep

you alive, dear Fraulein, we will already have our grand old culture, and
nothing will need to rise again! You see?"

"You are mad."

"Yes, I think I will put you somewhere where you can stay alive
during the war but get skinny and weak, someplace in Germany where
you will be no threat to our gene cleansing." He looks up at the ceiling,
as if thinking. *Will he think, like he did during dinner last night?* After many
seconds he looks back down at me and says with an unthinking smile,
"Yes, I will put you in a concentration camp for the remainder of the war,
with strict instructions to keep you alive. A place where temporarily you
will be nothing, ha-ha!"

What happens next has always remained unimaginable to me. He is
so angry that I wanted to kill my brother, his prodigal son, his image, that
he steps down lower than he did in my room last night. He now looks
like a man without a mind, lower than the lowest animal. Like an amoeba
that eats its prey by surrounding it and subsuming it into its body. He
rips off my dress, leggings, panties, everything. I try to think of some
musical phrase to lose my mind in, but even a single one is ungraspable.
This chief prince of mayhem rips off his trousers and thrusts evil into
me while humming a tune of beauty. He rapes goodness and erases it
from the Reich.

"Darling," Bergman says afterward, cleaning himself up, "open the
door and see what is coming. In fact, walk through the door and follow the
gurney all the way down to the shower and see what will happen there." So
I run out to the hallway and look, squeezing my violin so tightly against my
side that it falls from my hands. It is as if time were split in two, because
the alchemized grease on the gurney wheels allows it to fly clattering to
the end of the hallway while the alchemized lead boots on my feet leave
me trudging in trailing clangor. The distance between me and the man
pushing the gurney, between good and evil, widens.

When I am finally able to inch 200 feet down to the shower, I am the
first moral citizen in the Third Reich to see what millions and millions
of my good Reich fellows don't see through the shower-door window:

Rosalie, standing as dry and naked as a bone, holding her little doll and smiling, singing, and kissing it. I try to rip open the door to grab her out, but it's locked. Then I see an unspeakable impossibility made possible by the horror invading all my senses: a hole the size of a dime in the side of Rosalie's head out of which brain tissue is oozing. An ice pick is stuck in her eye socket. Blood is dripping down her cheek. My knees buckle and I scream and vomit.

Bauer walks up, looks in the shower, and sees all. He says like a child whose little chemistry experiment went awry, "Unfortunately the medical procedure did not work. The castle doctor called it a lobotomy, said he read about it from the Italian doctor who is pioneering it. Look at the girl's head and eye. It is a little gross, no?"

I want to strangle him for having just committed the understatement of the century, but I cannot take my eyes off helpless Rosalie. A hissing comes through the showerhead. She isn't getting wet. It's a dry, gas shower! Is she to be executed without even being given a court trial first? Even Jesus, the single most dangerous man ever known to the Roman Empire, was given a trial before His execution.

And Rosalie's family is not allowed to be here and witness the gassing through the glass. Even Jesus's mother was allowed to attend His execution. Rosalie, all alone except for her daughter the doll, collapses to the shower floor like a flower being pelted with sleet. As her expression turns to a physiognomy of agony, she thinks to pull her daughter to her chest. She just thought; therefore she felt pain. Her little chest heaves. It heaves again, then again. The heaving stops. She goes limp. The little daughter tumbles out of her arms. Their four unblinking eyes stare at me. Rosalie is suddenly as alive as the doll.

Rosalie Blume is dead.

My God. She is gone. I could not save even a single life. Oh, what I can no longer do when given a task! How foolish I have been! Un-Anna-Himmel-like, to say the least. And how quickly I just sped from the killer's guilt to my own. I am profoundly guilty. Everything I have ever been no longer exists. I am nothing.

And what about that hissing brick oven over there and the pile of coke fuel next to it, begging for their secret photograph to be taken together for the Führer? They can't be what I think they are! The ash stench hammers my soul into the ground. The coke looks like brimstone. I inch toward them. The oven chamber's brick archway, a half halo, is agonizingly stylish, the work of a master mason. It is unheard of for a German master craftsman to fail to put his signature on his commodity. Hanging next to the oven is an iron stick used for stoking. Standing a bad vigil at the open oven, is the twisted Bauer. There is something about him that craves fire, yet he is vanquished of all light. He is to perform his first rite of cremation, to cut his black teeth, to bathe in ash.

Bauer howls to me, the stone floor trembling, "They gave me a quarter liter of liquor this afternoon because of the strenuous and nerve-shattering nature of my job. I will get the same amount every day, they said. I asked for a two-day advance of liquor. They gave it to me, since today marks the loss of my cremation virginity, if you will. Maggots sure will never eat little Rosalie, I am happy to say!

"Oh, did I mention that I will make damned better money in this new job? My base pay is more than two thousand Reichsmarks a year, if you can believe it. And that is just my *base*. I will get fifty more Reichsmarks for a special family-separation allowance, thirty-five more for being a stoker, and thirty-five more for keeping this all a secret. Not to mention the liquor. I sure will be able to buy a new fishing boat now."

So, burning human bodies is now a boon making Bauer's and his family's lives better. It is therefore his new justice. He adds, "Thank God I am just a burner-upper after—to use the words of the leaders— these useless eaters of food and wasters of money have already been redeemed. And here, feel my iron tongs." He touches those two gears in the extermination engine to my arm.

"Get them away from me, you sick son of a bitch."

"Do not be afraid of the tongs, Anna. They are used merely to remove the larger pieces of bone and skull that do not get fully burned to ashes. We cannot keep the oven going forever. Coke costs money. We take the larger chunks of bone over there to the crusher where they get ground up for garden fertilizer. I learned that what we do here is part of the circle of life. Oh, and since we cannot possibly know whose ash is whose—it all looks the same—we at least put *someone's* ash in an urn for delivery to the next of kin. A necessary error, but harmless. How could the families possibly know the difference?"

I shut down my capacity to hear him, but he forces me to keep my eyes open by propping my lids with broken toothpicks. He even strongarms God to watch. The deceased Rosalie is outside the oven, lying on a gurney with wide-open eyes, bleeding fear of the horror of what is about to happen to her body. After snatching a gold-filled tooth with a pair of pliers, Bauer follows his instructions and gives Rosalie no choice whether to have her body burned or buried. Even Jesus, a deceased convict, was allowed to remain a body of flesh and blood and be placed with dignity in a tomb.

Bauer grabs Rosalie's hair with one hand and her feet with the other, rears back as if about to throw a bale of hay into the back of a truck, and hurls her into the oven. He watches with eagle eyes as the body collides with the orange embers, making a burst of flames. I fall on my knees in terror when I realize for the first time in my life that what I am witnessing is not only possible but in fact the truth.

Yet regret suddenly bursts over Bauer's face when he sees that rush of flames. His feet are liberated and he takes a step back. I am amazed that he has any ability to reverse left in him. He whispers a pithy speech, ostensibly to me but really to himself, I imagine. Using an introspective "I," he says, "I pray that this job gets less stressful with time. I cannot leave now, can I? I have already quit my job as a teacher. I have already burned that bridge. I cannot possibly turn back in any event, because what would my good wife and children say? I must steel myself, must accept that I am what I am becoming. I cannot watch Rosalie burn, just cannot watch. Instead, I must go get ready to haul in another body."

Reversing that step back, he walks ahead and unavoidably glances at the burning body, then runs off to the gas shower to see what's waiting there.

I could not take my eyes off the burning from the first moment. I cannot move, as if my feet are sunken in dried cement. I try to hide my eyes, ears, nose, and mouth, but I have only two hands. The spectacle I see leaches into all of my other senses. That which I see I cannot not smell, cannot not taste, cannot not hear, and cannot not feel in my own flesh and bones. I cannot find the words: *gruesome, ghastly, grisly, grotesque,* and *glowing flesh* cannot possibly describe a horror that is infinitely horrible. Soon those words do not exist because I have just retched them into the flames of the oven. There is nothing more I can utter that would make any sense because my entire lexicon has been reduced to nothing.

My final resistance is to pass out on the floor.

An hour later, I awake gasping for air, weeping, ungraced, broken, transmuted, and struggling to untangle the truths I have witnessed. Language has returned, but the traumatism strikes me that Rosalie was at least a hundred human nouns: a girl, a daughter, a sister, a niece, a granddaughter, a friend, a playmate . . . And she was at least a thousand human adjectives: smiling, loving, lovely, cuddly, important . . . All the nouns and adjectives one could think to describe her were stolen from her, burned to nothing. She is now reduced to three things: a small pyramid of ashes, a surely unwanted savings of money to her parents, and a memory.

But I am not finished at the castle because I need to find the letter to her parents. So I ascend toward the light and, stopping halfway up, go into the records office, where thankfully the staffers are gone for the day. I look and look until finally finding a file that says, *BLUME, ROSALIE HELGA, born 21 June 1933: ARYAN.* Inside the file is a pre-signed letter, dated what? What? September 30, 1940, a month *after* the cremation today! It oozes deceit:

30 September 1940

HAND DELIVERED

Frau and Herr Robert Blume
27 Apple Tree Way
Dolmer, Germany

My dear Frau and Herr Blume:

Please accept my sincerest condolences on the passing this day of your dear daughter, Rosalie. Pulmonary tuberculosis usually takes years to develop into a fatal illness, if it is fatal at all, yet somehow it developed in Rosalie and took her life with a suddenness rarely seen.
She was making such good progress with her mental retardation cure, and you can rest assured that my medical staff and I made Herculean efforts to save her from a tuberculosis death. I can assure you that she never suffered. I am afraid that a rush cremation was necessary to prevent tuberculosis germs from becoming airborne and spreading to other patients.
Rosalie's "big brother" and driver, Herr Bernhard Himmel, shall tender to you an urn containing her remains. He is also returning to you Rosalie's little doll, which I can assure you has been sanitized.
I remain your humble servant.

Warmest regards,

Hans Strasser
Hans Strasser
Chief Internist
Schloss Hartheim

Strasser lied about both the cause and the date of death. At least we have something to measure a lie about a date—a calendar. The lie about the cause of death cannot be measured at all because the distance between body and mind is immeasurable. Tuberculosis is a disease of the body. Murder is a disease of the mind.

A heap of broken soul, I lie in the records room, staring at the ceiling, waiting for the sun to set so I won't be seen trying to leave. Finally, in the dark, I hobble to the castle's front door and struggle to open it to get outside. But it seems the castle is not ready to spit me out yet, because there at the door, in the castle's closed mouth, I reread the spitting plaque and faint with that pyramid of ash imprisoned in my mind.

13

In the morning, I was shaken awake in my room at the Inn of the Woods by what I thought was the goddess of death draped in a maid's uniform, trying to fool me, her dark eyes licking my face less than a foot away. She told me that she rushed in the room after hearing shrieks, but I was certain that she had snuck in to kiss me on the lips. She insisted on knowing my name.

"Anna Himmel," I breathed frightfully. She regarded my mussed clothing and my two-day beard and my crooked face as if I were certifiably insane. Trembling, I jumped up and rushed to the door to escape. "But, sir, I only wanted to—" she said as I slammed the door shut and darted toward the stairs.

I ran out of the inn and took a cab to the castle, a few miles away. Inside the front door, there was no plaque about the castle's ghastly mission. "Deceit!" I screamed.

A middle-aged woman rushed to me, glancing at my scraggly beard and dirty clothes. "Do not be afraid," she said. "I am a castle employee and have been working here for twenty years." I hadn't had coffee yet, and in my hazy mind I wondered whether she was a nun who had stayed on as a nurse after the Nazis confiscated the castle. Why would a nun blaspheme her own soul like that? She wore a flowery dress exposing half her calves and had no crucifix around her neck. Where was her habit? I was as befuddled as I was frightened.

As soon as she saw the fear on my face, she said, "Please do not be afraid. I am harmless and have been greeting castle visitors ever since the memorial opened here in 1969. Let's get you some help now. Maybe you would like to go to a homeless shelter with a psychiatrist on staff?"

A memorial? Twenty years? 1969? I did the simple math. I pinched myself just to make sure. It hurt. So yes, I was back in 1989. Did I have a terrible nightmare? If so, it seemed as real as my throbbing arthritis. In documentaries on public television, I had seen gassings and burnings of bodies in concentration camps well after 1940. But it seemed as if I had witnessed, with all five of my senses, a little girl's flesh roasting, her blood bubbling, and her hair flaming in 1940, shortly after the war started. Finally, I reoriented myself and realized I was Henry Schultz and had taken a bus to visit the castle. I lied to the woman and said I had Alzheimer's.

The ghoulish ordeal was behind me, but the kind woman took me by the hand and insisted on walking me through the castle. "After all, that is why you came, no?" she said.

Obviously she didn't know I had already seen more than enough of its hell. I let her drag me through the public section, hating every step as she spoke about what had gone down there during the war. She was kind, but I was so put off by her words that I tried not to hear. My ears, though, couldn't avoid eating every rancid word. I thought it was scandalous that it had taken so long—until 1969—to create a memorial there. A full quarter of a century had passed since the last "unworthy" person had been "redeemed" at the castle as part of the "disinfection" of the Third Reich.

I burned inside. Intellectually, intuitively, viscerally—even metaphysically, if there is a meta-sphere in which the human mind can travel—I was profoundly angry, even ashamed as a human that people

like those doctors and nurses and civil servants and stokers, but mostly
Bernhard, had once walked among humankind. If they had been there, I
would have become a serial killer myself and strangled them all to death
with my bare hands, then willingly marched to the gas shower for my
own execution.

Foolhardy, I insisted on seeing an oven. The guide, pleased to take
me to one, mentioned that the stokers had received free liquor because
of the "stressful" nature of their work. I was stunned by the word, which
was exactly what I had imagined Frieden Bauer telling me. My imagination
suddenly came alive and stepped into reality. The truth burned on top
of my skin, simmered just under it, and was no longer buried in cold
darkness.

I had never been able in the present to see the truth of the past. It
took me more than fifty years to finally descend and find it, and now I'll
forget my own name before I forget the past. Touching that oven was a
rebaptism of sorts. I remembered a simple truth I had learned as a boy
in church school: you can't blame evil events on God's inaction. On the
night the Wall was assaulted, I had been unfair to God when I cried inside
that God never stopped the Nazi machine. The creak of the oven's rusty
steel door was a voice reminding me more of what I had learned in church
school: Once God gave man free will in the Garden of Eden, whether to
eat the fruit of the tree of knowledge of good and evil was, by His design,
no longer in His hands. He left the decision to humans alone.

Sometimes in bad moments I have questioned the existence of God,
but even if He does not exist and the Garden of Eden never existed and
both are pure fantasies invented by the human mind for whatever reason,
it proves that humans are responsible for inventing evil. Because who
else? But now that I have survived Alkoven, do you notice me concluding
that the earth is an evil place? No, because I have chosen to be positive.
Positivity and negativity are within my control, and I choose to believe
that the earth has a good record for remaining void of human evil and
waiting for the advent of human goodness.

If the span of the earth's existence is compared to twenty-four hours beginning at midnight, human evil didn't appear until after 11:59:59 p.m. Most astrophysicists believe that the earth formed roughly 4.6 billion years ago and that organic molecules making human life possible already existed at that primeval time. Microbial life first appeared about 3.8 billion years ago when certain organic compounds fortuitously copulated in the oceans. Pre-mammal life didn't venture up on land until roughly 2.8 billion years ago, and pre-human mammals didn't walk upright on two feet until about 2 million years ago. *Homo sapiens* didn't spring up into apelike people until roughly 300,000 years ago. It was probably then or a short few tens of thousands of years later, a microsecond before midnight, that human evil was first invented; for the first time in the history of the earth, a caveman might have used an implement—perhaps a large arm or leg bone—to kill or maim another caveman who was poaching his food. A microsecond is not perceivable or even conceivable by the human mind. So I repeat: the world has a decent track record of avoiding evil and waiting patiently, something not far short of forever, for wholesome goodness to emerge. It's only my opinion, but there you have it.

The guide told me in her practiced voice that when US general George Patton's army liberated the castle in April 1945, soldiers found a box of documents and photographs revealing the atrocities. Maybe the approach of the US troops was so sudden that the evildoers had no time to destroy the evidence, but in my mind they were psychotic and left it all there by design, wanting the world to be aware of their accomplishments.

"One of the documents," the woman said, "lays out the monetary savings estimated by the Reich over time for not having to feed, clothe, and house the tens of thousands of 'planned economic transfers' who were 'processed' at the six euthanasia sites: 885,000,000 Reichsmarks." That's $2 to $3 billion in 1989 US dollars. It seemed a staggering number at first, calculated by men who had walked away from humanity and had no love except self-love. But within two seconds the figure seemed infinite, literally, since a single life is priceless.

That's when the bile in my stomach roiled. It flamed up my throat and spilled out, burning the rest of me and a little getting on the poor woman's shoe. That's why I'd make a terrible World War II historian even if I had the brains for it. It was not only the thought of the T4 Program's witchcrafted gene theory and its monetization of death that riled me, but also the sketch Anna made of Rosalie Blume, indelibly fixed in my mind's eye. Still today, almost a year later, I am haunted by the image of that little girl going forward with me yet walking backward only a foot away with her face to mine. I see her face even more clearly when my eyes are closed.

After that hobble-through at the castle, I was done at that place, that repository of historical stink that probably had been filled with the scent of flowers before the Nazis. I took a cab to the bus station in Linz, the city near Hitler's birthplace, the innocent city that, inspired by his megalomania, was to have been his rearchitected cultural capital of the universe. Not even Rosalie's spirit could push Adolf's spirit down to the ground. I was almost glad that the next bus to Berlin was not for another five hours because it gave me an excuse to rent a car and flee Linz straightaway. I didn't want to be with other people anyway.

Before taking the road, I tried to phone Anna in Edelberg. I needed to hear her voice, having the outrageous thought that she might not have survived *my* ordeal. I needed her to know who I had become. But what if she picked up the phone and said, "Hello?" What could I say that would change history? With a bad case of nerves, I dialed her number having no idea what to say and was almost relieved that she didn't pick up.

I needed something like a long car ride to get my head screwed on straight. Once I was inside the car and the doors were locked, I finally claimed full ownership of myself. During the first fifty miles, I repeatedly found myself driving in excess of the already generous speed limit, as if trying to outrun the reaching claws of the castle. I imagined Anna there in the car with me, reaching out the window to bat back those claws.

Still overwhelmed by the question of whether Rosalie had survived Hartheim, I felt compelled on the drive north to stop by her hometown of Dolmer, East Germany. If she was still alive, there was a chance she still lived there. It was only sixty miles out of the way, so how could I fight the impulse to go there?

I stopped in Dolmer and first drove to a store to find a phone book. There was no one with the name Blume listed, but since it's a small town, I checked the one cemetery. Finally I found her in a corner below a pear tree that still had a few leaves. Her crooked little slate headstone was sprinkled with moss and moon dust, and I sank when I read the simple words chiseled into it:

ROSALIE HELGA BLUME
GEBOREN DES ENGEL:
21 JUNE 1933
STARB AN TUBERKULOSE:
30 SEPTEMBER 1940

Born of the angels on June 21, 1933, and died of tuberculosis on September 30, 1940. I sank not so much because Rosalie was dead but because some of the information on the headstone perfectly matched information I found in that imagined file at the castle. The file said she was born on June 21, 1933, which matched the date on the headstone. And Dr. Strasser's imagined letter to the parents fraudulently implied, by its date, that she died on September 30, 1940, which also matched the headstone. This was bizarre, almost eerie. I imagined an urn buried beneath the headstone and had an alarming sense that Rosalie was not content lying beneath such a deceit.

I picked a dead hydrangea flower, the best I could do for December, and placed it on her grave. I stood there until a strange hymn stopped singing in my head and then got the hell out of there. I drove into town and tried calling Anna. Her phone rang off the hook. Not only Rosalie but Anna too was beyond my reach.

The somber mood stuck after I got back on the road. At my late-morning coffee break, I was compelled to throw out *Wings in the Night*— the collection of Conan stories. I'd have gone to the extreme of burning it if I'd been alone. *Wings* deserved to be burned even though the author had probably intended it to be fun reading for boys when he wrote the stories in the '30s. On that particular day, I could not bear to have it hidden even in the trunk. It was Anna's book. She must have valued it for some unfathomable reason. If she wanted it replaced, I would have to hold my nose and buy her another.

At my lunch break, I sat next to a talkative German man.

"Since you are on vacation and driving to Berlin," he said, "you should stop for a few hours in Dresden. A cultural gem, an arts city, a small piece of heaven."

I said, "Thanks," but I thought, *No thanks.* If it was a small piece of heaven now, it was a much larger piece before Valentine's Day night 1945, when it was decimated by Allied bombs for no tactical reason. To put myself there would have been another self-punishment.

I did, however, think about stopping in Leipzig and seeing its storied St. Thomas Lutheran Church, with Bach's indoor tomb and the sanctuary in which Alfred Himmel had his life moment. But all I could imagine as I approached the Leipzig highway exit was Richard Wagner's infant head being anointed at his baptism at that church. Some say the jury's still out on whether he was an anti-Semite. When I got past that thought, the car was past the exit.

It was close to midnight by the time I finally arrived back at the hotel. When I collapsed on the bed in my room, I felt that something had at last set me back up on firm ground and given me permission to sleep. I could practically taste slumber, couldn't keep my eyes open. Otherwise, I would have driven to Anna's flat and waited for as long as it might have taken her to open the door.

The next day was Christmas, and for the first time in my life, it didn't feel like my favorite holiday. It felt only like the day after I had endured the castle. Of course, I tried calling Anna about a hundred times, but she never answered. I returned the rental car but afterward felt crazy enough about her, and paranoid enough that she was rejecting me, that I jumped on the next bus to Edelberg and banged on her door for minutes. I needed to breathe in the same room as her. And I was altered. Before Alkoven, I had felt tenderness and affection for her; afterward, I adored her, maybe even loved her in a strange way. It wasn't a simple romantic feeling but instead was now deeper and more complex. For instance, the idea of her and the idea of the sex act now came to me from two different worlds. I started having a moonstruck idea of holding her the way I remembered she would hold her Himmel as a little girl—like a newborn bird, unable to fly, the most unprotected and breakable thing in the world.

I willed her apartment door to open, but my will failed.

I returned to the hotel and went to the lobby but felt detached from the holiday festivities. Given my state of mind, not to mention all those forty-two magical Christmases with Helen, there was no magic in Christmas in Germany that year. Heaping plates of German pastries— marzipan cookies, cinnamon sweet rolls, glazed butter biscuits—were everywhere in the lobby. Big deal. A fire was crackling in the large stone fireplace next to a fifteen-foot-tall Christmas tree decorated with white candles and handblown glass ornaments. A smaller big deal, but getting warmer.

I finally got into a better mood when I imagined my mother and father smiling as I ripped the Kris Kringle wrapping paper off the chocolate Luger present she had labeled from Kris when I was a boy. All cynicism finally vanished when I saw hanging above the fireplace mantle a large, traditional German Christmas wreath made of fir-tree branches and holding twenty-four decorated boxes, each one containing a gift. This became an entirely different kind of big deal because a smaller version hung above the fireplace mantle in my boyhood home. My appetite returned, and I ate lunch at the hotel, a sliced goose breast sandwich on sourdough bread, as a children's choir sang old German holiday favorites. Sunlight flooded through the tall lobby windows, forcing me to shut my eyes and see Anna singing in the church choir at our Lutheran confirmation.

After this, as is the German tradition, a teenaged girl wearing a floor-length, white-and-gold dress, angel wings, and a gold crown came in, took down the gift boxes from the wreath, and handed them out to children. She became the girl next door to my childhood home. I couldn't get away from Anna and didn't want to. Except for her physical absence, everything in Germany was perfect for that moment.

With Anna on my mind, I shot up and tried calling her to invite her to attend that evening's special concert with me. Her apartment was only slightly larger than a jail cell, yet I must have let the phone ring a hundred times. I went up to my room and had a long nap to forget her for a while and give my heart a rest. When I awoke, it was time to go to the concert, but Anna's phone was still ringing off the hook. Too bad for her. Worse for me.

The concert was held at the Schauspielhaus in East Berlin, the old music and theater hall just a few hundred yards from the Brandenburg Gate. To me the place is a gift from the gods because it's the venue where Anna made her national solo violin debut in 1931 at age twelve. The tickets to the inside hall were sold out, so I stood outside in the cold with 20,000 other people. From huge screens outside, we all witnessed Leonard Bernstein, the maestro of the New York Philharmonic, conduct an orchestra composed of musicians from the two Germanys and the four post-war occupation powers in a performance of Beethoven's celestial *Symphony No. 9*. The chorus of 200 came from multiple choirs, including the large children's choir of the Dresden Philharmonic. Some think the Ninth is overly performed by orchestras and overly listened to by people on their stereos. They say that classical-music afficionados aren't much interested in it in this modern age. Maybe they're right. I don't know. But that night, at that place, standing with all those thousands of elated Germans—my word.

Beethoven's choral lyrics in the fourth and final movement are taken from Friedrich von Schiller's 1785 poem, "Ode to Joy," except that in this special performance, the word *freude* ("joy") was substituted with the word *freiheit* ("freedom") to celebrate the fall of the Berlin Wall; von Schiller, standing at the front of the Schauspielhaus in the form of a shimmering bronze statue, didn't seem to care. I'm afraid that I had memorized the German words of the finale too well as a boy. Probably much to the annoyance of everyone around me, I sang out with the choir—insanely off-key, I'm sure:

O freunde, nicht diese Töne!

(O friend, no more of these sounds!)

Sondern laßt uns angenahmere anstimmen

(Let us sing more cheerful songs)

Und freiheitnvollere

(More songs full of freedom)

Freiheit!

(Freedom!)

Freiheit!

(Freedom!)

. . . .

Deine Zauber binden wiede

(Thy magic power reunites)

Was die Mode streng geteilt

(All that custom has divided)

Alle Menschen werden Brüder

(All men become brothers)

Wo dein sanfter Flügel weilt.

(Under the sway of thy gentle wings.)

. . . .

Keisen Kuß der ganzen Welt!

(This kiss is for all the world!)

Brüder, über'm Sternenzelt

(Brothers, above the starry canopy)

Muß ein lieber Vater wohnen.

(There must dwell a loving Father.)

A great-uncle of mine once claimed that his soul could touch those of departed loved ones. I hadn't believed in that sort of thing, but I'll say that on that one night, as the huge chorus and I reached the height of song in the last movement, I felt the presence of Rosalie Blume. It was a strange feeling in my arms, legs, and chest, a sensation I had never felt before and haven't felt since. I looked up into the black sky as I sang and swear her face was a constellation, having no idea how it had become such a perfect grouping of stars. It hung over me.

When the final note of music was struck, there was only silence for a moment. Who would want to be the first to break the hushed spell? When cheers finally screamed through the air, the young man standing next to me had tears in his eyes. When I looked at him, he turned his face away. I doubt it was from my lousy singing.

The manic joy in me lingered, but only for ten minutes. Walking to pick up a cab, I passed a house in the dark. The December air was cold, yet a window was wide open. Strange. As I got closer, I heard a song and saw two stereo speakers on the windowsill, as if the resident wanted people outside to hear. I stopped and listened, recognizing the music as Gustav Mahler's sorrowful song "I Am Lost to the World." A woman soprano sang:

> *Ich bin gestorben dem Weltgetümmel*
> *(I am dead to the world's turmoil)*
> *Und ruh' in einem stillen Gebiet!*
> *(And I rest in a quiet realm!)*
> *Ich leb' allein in meinem Himmel*
> *(I live alone in my heaven)*
> *In meinem Lieben, in meinem Lied!*
> *(In my love, in my song!)*

Can a song be a prelude to a mass human tragedy? To me, at that moment, Mahler's mournful music was the embodiment of the fifty or sixty million good people who perished in the war. For strength, I looked for Rosalie's living face in the stars. It was gone. I went back to the hotel. I couldn't sleep. I drank all the miniature bottles of booze in the refrigerator.

Such was my night. It would be time to fly back to America the next day. Like a broken record disc, I tried unsuccessfully to call Anna the next morning. I became afraid now. What if she had fallen in her flat and couldn't get to the phone? What if this or that? I had been there the day before and pounded on the door, so I decided not to go back and miss my flight. If I could have just heard her voice, I gladly would have paid Lufthansa good money to reschedule the flight for a few days later.

So I packed up and said goodbye to the concierge. Outside, before climbing into the airport cab, I said goodbye to some people and things and good riddance to others. Good riddance to the Hartheim Castle, the two skinheads at the Edelberg bus station, and the town's Frankensteinian electro-hum, and then a second time to the castle even though it, as a thing in itself, was innocent. Goodbye to the Spree River and to the memorial cemetery in Edelberg and to Anna's and my lost bedrooms on Linden Street. I said goodbye to Rosalie last. I refused to say goodbye to Anna because I had a strange inkling I would see her again someday.

Before the plane took off, my fear over Anna got the better of me. I started thinking the worst again: she was dead. For a crazy minute or two, I even wondered whether she had ever existed, thinking that the woman who long ago had claimed to be Germany was a figment of my imagination, a phantasm, only a concept. I buckled myself extra tight in my seat and wondered again.

14

The morning after I returned to Iowa, I jumped out of bed at dawn to the revelry of a rooster in a dream. My foremost business, even before making coffee, was to try to control my nervous fingers and dial Anna's telephone number. The phone rang and rang, rang until I lost track of the minutes and finally hung up. There was no apartment super to check with. I had never met any of her friends. So I spent that first morning finding and calling all the hospitals in the Berlin area. There was no one by the name of Anna Himmel. The person was nowhere. Only the concept was somewhere.

So I compartmentalized and moved on to my second business— answering the question I had been unable to face head-on forever.

On the eve of my trip to Germany, the doorbell had rung after dark. I was forced to answer it since I knew it was probably my sixteen-year-old grandson, Billy Schultz, the only person in the world after Helen's passing who would give grumpy me the time of day. Before he returned home that night, we discussed the Berlin Wall. Then, from left field, he asked a seemingly simple but impossible question: "Why did so many Germans just sit back on their asses and let Hitler do all that horrible stuff?"

"It's unexplainable," I replied. I added, wanting to change the subject, "But how about those Chicago Bears?"

But the honors student persisted. "Come off it, Grandpa. You grew up in Germany. You should know. You're fairly smart. Everything has an explanation."

I felt desperate to say something that sounded intelligent, didn't want him to know how ignorant his grandfather is. After thinking for an eternal minute, the best I could come up was "German culture was maybe the highest in the history of humankind, and then one man masterminded the worst evil in the history of humankind. The millions of good German people back then never dreamed that such ungodly evil was possible. By the time they realized a nightmare was coming true, it was too late to stop it."

But Billy wouldn't let it rest on that either. "You can do better," he pressed. Having been a math major in college, I had never been one for philosophy or the other humanities. For me, there had always been a single correct answer to any query. "Billy, I'm afraid that's the only answer there is. I know only that the Nazis started the war, that forty or more million Europeans died in it, and that God didn't stop it."

"You can do better than even that."

I stared him down, exasperated. "Even if there's an answer, I refuse to comprehend it because of what it might be."

"Okay, okay, I'll stop badgering you." There was a long silence while Billy seemed to chew on a thought. Finally he took it upon himself to say, "I knew about poison gas showers and cremation ovens. But all those tens of millions of people dead? Unbelievable." He hesitated, and then it was as if he thought he had just been visited by the gods of reason. He said, sounding certain, "One thing's for sure, though. It's so incredible that it could never happen again. Not in this modern age."

"Billy, you've hit the mark."

That was then. I wondered on the plane back from Germany, *Oh really? Never happen again?* I began to suspect that now, after having suffered a once-in-a-lifetime nightmare—or whatever it was—maybe I could answer Billy's question. I was now anxious to solve the riddle, finish the equation, figure out the mindset of the German people of the war era. I thought that Billy might have been wrong, that the gods of reason might have no familiarity with the unthinkable.

Not that I needed some intellectual to tell me what to think, but I wanted to do some reading and then wrap up a final answer in a bow. I didn't need to leave the house to get reading material, needing only to go to the cellar. I climbed down there and tried to remember where I had put the books so many years before. They weren't over there, or over there, or inside there either. Finally, I crunched over dead insects and pushed aside cobwebs to get to a dusty, old, forgotten box in a far corner. The three books on the Nazi era were something like ghouls in that box, buried deep under this and that. I had received them as gifts years before but never touched them after that.

It struck me as interesting that I had saved them; like my childhood memories, the books had been stored in a dank place that gets no light, yet I hadn't parted with them. My memory and the books were all mildewed cousins. I took the books up to my den, wiped them off, and dug into them for the first time.

I found too much info on why the Germans of the '30s and '40s had tolerated and, in many cases, actually indulged the Nazis. Some of the writings were contradictory or just plain impossible to comprehend. One theory easy to understand, too easy, held that the Nazis had a secret base in Antarctica and another in the center of the earth that allowed them to exercise exceptional powers. Another said they had been trained by aliens from another galaxy. For a minute, I laughed at these quack theories, but then shuddered when it dawned on me that they were almost as plausible as the fantastical but true Nazi nightmares.

The first serious idea I read about was the so-called *Sonderweg* or "special path" thesis. "Historical determinism" was what one of the authors called it. This theory holds that Nazism was no fluke or aberration but rather the natural and inevitable result of German nationalism, authoritarianism, and militarism dating back to the Middle Ages. It made me ponder the Himmel warriors going centuries back to the first Erich Himmel, so this doctrine had a certain appeal to me at first.

But when I thought about it with more scrutiny, the authors seemed to be really saying, in so many words, that the people of Nazi Germany had no minds of their own, that history moves independently of human influences. I, for one, think that every person has free will. After all, didn't Hektor Himmel have a choice when he raped that girl? Didn't Alfred Himmel have a choice in St. Thomas Lutheran Church and later when he quit the army and conceived the violin company? And didn't Alfred almost certainly teach his children how to make decisions? Didn't his descendants learn how to do that right down the family line? Didn't everyone in the world? I believe that the Germans of the '30s and '40s were no different from other people and therefore had a choice, so ultimately I washed my hands of the determinist theorists.

My eyes glazed over while reading the other theories. There's one called the dispassionate objectivity doctrine and another called the revisionist history doctrine. There's the internationalist theory, the functionalist argument, the structuralist idea, and the blah blah blah. I tried to synthesize *Sonderweg* and the other serious theories by putting them into something like an electric blender and turning it on high, thinking it might be good to taste an indivisible mixture. But the end product tasted awful. I knew too many diverse Germans to pin any one academic theory on them all.

Thousands of people were probably born evil, like the Nazi bigwig Rudolph Gendler. Anna's father was probably born good but turned evil for financial reasons. I knew good people like her mother, who stayed good but was a puppet with Herr Himmel holding the strings. And then you had Herr Vogel, a good and highly intelligent man who just went with the flow, and you had my good grandpa Lutl, who loved Nazi Germany primarily because he revered kings and despised democracy.

Then there was my good father, who cracked up from the evil, and my wonderful mother, who fled and wasn't there to do anything to stop it. And good people like Fraulein and Herr Blume, who were snookered by their trust in their fellow man. And cultured people like Bergman, who got intoxicated by power and prestige. And there was my best friend. He was born good and stayed good until his natural human weaknesses allowed the Nazis to murder the mind he was born with. He turned out worse than the other evil persons combined.

Bottom line: In the books there was only a loud silence explaining nothing to me. The only book that made any sense was one in my den I hadn't cracked open since my boyhood. In it were the words of Johann von Goethe, the German poet and novelist who died 100 years before the birth of the Third Reich: "I have often felt a bitter sorrow at the thought of the German people, which is so estimable in the individual and so wretched in the generality." Perhaps Germany was doomed from the start.

I made a fire in the fireplace, threw in the mildewed books, sat back and watched them burn, and thought. I was still baffled after fifteen minutes, so much so that I both had no answer at all and was furious with my brain. I called Billy over to the house to try to explain the non-answer in person. When he made a face like he had just tasted something bad, I felt I had to manufacture something, anything not completely covered in bosh. After chanting the endless purities of Anna for longer than Billy could stand, I felt forced to end and say, "Nazism was evil times a billion, and there was only one Anna Himmel, not a billion of her." It was as good as nothing. Billy gave me more credit, saying the answer was only next to nothing.

After a minute of silence, Billy curled his lips, and his eyes glimmered as if he had just made the first wheel. And this time he wasn't visited by any false gods of reason. He touted the diametric opposite of what he had said with certainty on the eve of my trip to Germany a few weeks earlier. "When you said you were going to vacation in Germany come hell or high water, I did something I rarely do: I thought. Then I got on a roll and thought some more. I took a long walk and kept on thinking. In a nutshell, I now believe that Nazis could happen again. Definitely, no question."

That, of course, was no shocking revelation and certainly no answer to his original question; it's what millions of people have thought for decades. But I do think it marked a teenager who had become an adult thinker.

That observation of his was surpassed by what he said a few weeks ago at his neighbor Ahmed Hussein's funeral. I knew Ahmed through his grandfather. People of the Islamic faith bury their deceased within twenty-four hours of death, so Billy and I had to get to the mosque before we had much time to really think what to say to the family.

The mosque was packed with a few hundred students and adults. At the end, maybe not quite following Islamic orthodoxy, the father asked whether anyone had anything to say. Billy stood nervously, walked to the front, and spoke a few words to the crowd, his voice shaking: "The gang that beat my friend Ahmed to a pulp and killed him just for being a Muslim are the real losers." Billy stopped, appearing not to know what else to say. But he knew now because he had thought. "As long as there are people who think that their manhood lies in clenched fists and other things of war, evil will always exist, even if we will never understand why." For the next half minute, you could have heard a pin drop.

I couldn't believe he was my grandson. Then I could. Then it struck me that he is much more than my grandson. He is the great-grandson of my mother.

15

For seven straight days I tried phoning Anna time and time again without success, allowing into the house the chill of a phantasm. I considered buying a plane ticket to go to Edelberg and sleuth around, but finally on January 20, I saw the reality of a letter from her in my mailbox. She was real. Instantly I recouped my wits, though it took a moment of nervous fumbling to rip open the letter:

15 January 1990

Dear Heinrich,

I must say at the outset that I feel bad for not saying goodbye. After you left my flat that morning, I woke up and did not feel so well. I have been on medication since that day and now I only want to sleep. Until a few days ago I did not feel like getting out of bed or doing much else.
I did not mean to talk your head off that night or get you so upset. You must think I am strange. I have not been this mad at my deceased father

and Bernhard in fifty years because I have never wanted to think about what they did.

It was so very nice to see you after all these years. If you ever get over here again, please look me up. And of course, I am hoping that the two Germanys will reunite, sooner rather than later. Before I die, I am praying.

Best wishes,

Anna

"Mad" at her brother and father? I guess Anna Himmel did not understand how to hate. I had drawn her into that conversation that night, and by the end of it, my intentions had been not only to heal her but to have her let go and feel something worse than "mad" about her father and brother. In any event, the letter gave me what I wanted—an invitation to visit her again. I just needed to muster the courage to go. For me, building bravery—I think of being on the Navy ship to Okinawa in May 1945—is a process.

In April, I felt the urge to write to Anna to pick a date for a visit. She wrote back and said only "a visit sounds good, later this year." I didn't rush her. By the end of May, we were writing to each other once every other week. I presumed we were "dating" by mail and was disheartened that she called us pen pals in one of her letters. I wanted to be more than her pal but was afraid to tell her the truth.

Probably never in her life had she felt romantic anyway. She now seemed preoccupied by German politics. She wrote in June, with more life in her voice, "There is still no official reunification—maybe someday soon—but we do now have a treaty between the two countries for economic union. Thrilling." Between the lines, I faintly heard the dusty violin in the corner of her flat.

She wrote in July, "That ghastly wall is finally being torn down by the government!" She had never used exclamation points in her letters. I was inspired enough to write back and tell her, for the first time, that I had

gone to see the castle, although I spared her, and myself, the gory details
of my nightmare—or whatever it was. I was afraid to write more than a
single, unemotional sentence about stopping at Rosalie's grave.

In late August, I finally had the audacity to take the reins and start to
write a letter inviting myself for a visit. What happed next was uncanny.
As I was writing, it was as if I were inside her mind because the postman
dropped this grace into my mailbox:

22 August 1990

Dear Heinrich,

*This will be short, as I am not feeling 100% today. I am sure you have
been watching the news lately, so you already know that we East and West
Germans have reached a point no one ever thought would come.*
*People are calling it the "Turning Point." Official reunification of East
and West Germany, and therefore East and West Berlin, is scheduled for
3 October. I have not been this happy since I was a child. There will be a
national celebration in Berlin that night. My long-lost cousins in Bonn that I
never met are coming. I would like it if you could come too. I will understand
if you have no interest.*
*But more, I want you to know that I was very moved by your letter about
visiting the castle and then stopping at Rosalie's grave. I had no idea you
went. I was most happy about that. So now, there is a final part of my story
I feel I can tell you. But only in person, eye to eye, not in a letter.*
Please will you come, yes?

With the warmest regards,

Anna

It seemed to me that after fifty years, her healing had begun. There
was something almost comedic about her letter, though, because if she

had been able to glimpse inside me, she would have known that she did not need to practically beg me to come.

And more than just my heart was involved. The phrase "final part of the story" got to me. I had to go for that reason alone.

Margaret Thatcher, the prime minister of Great Britain, whom I had always respected, suddenly seemed somewhat arrogant to me. She had recently said publicly, when asked about reunification, "We beat the Germans twice and now they're back."

I arrived on the morning of October 2, the day before the scheduled reunification and the gala in Berlin. My chest was thumping before the plane touched down. I had gotten very little sleep as a result, but I couldn't resist rushing straightaway to Anna's flat before checking into the Edelberg Inn. My hands were sweaty when I rang the buzzer. But when she opened the door, she blessed me with the largest smile I had ever seen from her, which put me at ease—although again, she didn't take my outstretched hand.

I handed over the scrapbook on the castle and the T4 Program, which I had taken from her flat that December night. I quickly confessed that I had trashed her book *Wings in the Night*. She laughed and said, "Good." I had flip-flopped over what to bring her as a gift. Chocolates even from Switzerland had seemed too common a thing. Perfume even from Paris seemed too intimate. I settled on buying her a gold rococo-style frame and put in a black-and-white photograph of her house from 1935.

She claimed that she had never had anyone to do the city with, so I took her to Berlin on the bus. We strolled a few blocks to the Pergamon Museum and consumed hours absorbing the art and artifacts of the ancient Greek and Roman periods. By then it was late afternoon, and I offered to take her to dinner to a restaurant of her choice.

"No," she said. "I have planned a special dinner at my flat, and you are the guinea pig. Braised duck breast with a raspberry sauce, julienned vegetables, Rhine wine, German forest cake." It was choice, all of it.

After dinner we talked for a few hours about nothing important, and around 10 p.m., I crammed enough courage in myself to spill the question, "Are you ready to finish the story?"

She was not. "Tomorrow, when it is light out," she said. I thought she must be joking.

"Does the night make you superstitious?" I asked, tossing back a jest.

She didn't answer. There was only silence and her deadpan face. That night, there were no stars, no moon, and no jokes. I mumbled a goodnight and went to the inn.

The next morning I bought some fancy sandwiches and fruit and a bottle of expensive wine, thinking we could have a picnic somewhere to open her up. We moseyed along the river for a while, then spread out a blanket at the cove and had the picnic. Anna suddenly seemed impatient to hear about Rosalie's grave.

"Does her headstone still say she died of tuberculosis?" she asked, as if the stone could have been re-chiseled into the truth. "And does it still say she died on 30 September 1940?"

"Yes and yes," I had no choice but to say.

"Oh," she said, seeming disappointed with the only answer she could have expected.

Probably procrastinating, she said she wanted to see the overgrown lots where our childhood homes had stood side by side, which she claimed, somewhat dubiously, she had never once visited after the war. So we picked up and walked there. I breathed in the coo of a nearby dove. Freedom and reunification were in the air everywhere in town, and after inhaling some of it herself, she unveiled the words, "It would be amazing to build a house on this empty double lot, no?"

"Sure," I agreed with my mind only on the mystery of the end of the story. "But what about the rest of the story?"

She was ready to talk now. The peace she had sought at the double lot had found her, as if the mood at that particular spot had lifted her free of something.

"The rest of the story is not pretty, if you want to hear it," she forewarned.

"Of course I do."

This time, unlike the night in her flat last December, she drained the mercy-killing swamp in the castle in short order, using measured phrases and without shedding tears. I listened quietly. She said only, "I took the bus to Linz and went to the Nazi castle in Alkoven where my brother was working, but I could not stop him." Then she dove straight to Rosalie, passing over the girl's murder and burning in seven useless and sterilized words: "You should know what happened to her." She didn't know how right she was.

She couldn't get to the following day fast enough:

"Bernhard and Rudy Gendler handcuffed me and put me in the car the day after Rosy died. Rudy grabbed my violin, jerked it out of the case, and was about to either take a chunk out of it with his teeth or break it over his knee. Bernhard flew into a rage, grabbed it back, and punched Rudy in the face. With Rudy looking bewildered, they scuffled. Then Bernhard wiped Rudy's hand smudges off the violin, put it back in its case, laid the case down softly next to me in the car, and sped me to Dachau, saying not one word along the way. It boggled my mind. For those few minutes ending with the scuffle, he had been his old self."

"I suspect there was a small part of the old Bernhard left somewhere deep inside."

"Perhaps, but only for that short minute. He dropped me off with a guard inside the front gate at Dachau, ripped up a note that said to keep me alive, and sped off without saying farewell." After shaking down her mind for a rational explanation, she said ruefully, "I guess Dachau was not a place where even my brother said 'farewell' to arriving inmates."

"Oh Dachau!" she blurted with a pained expression. *Dachau.* Shocked that she had ended up there, I stared at her forearm, wondering why she had no number tattooed to the underside. She must have seen my gaze. "Numbers were needled into your arm only at Auschwitz." Well, there was another putrid morsel of war history I had known zero about. "At Dachau, they let you keep your name and then worked you to death."

Oh Dachau! I shouted silently to myself, trying to hide my own pained expression. That quaint town, settled in the ninth century. It was flowing with landscape artists and intellectuals before the war. Then came the modern-day Huns.

"The more pig dogs we strike down," a Nazi official said in a speech on the day the camp opened in 1933, "the fewer we need to feed." Just Anna's mentioning the name of the town brought back a rhyming jingle after more than fifty years—the rhyme I first heard around '35 when I was fifteen, four years before the war started: "Liber Herr Gott, mach mich stumm, das ich nicht Dachau komm" (Dear God, make me dumb [ignorant of the evil of the Nazis], that I may not to Dachau come). By the end of the war, there were only a few precincts in hell more hellish than Dachau. Auschwitz, where more than a million souls were murdered, was one of them. Dachau, by comparison, was a country club. "Only" a little more than 30,000 people were murdered there.

When Anna mentioned Dachau, every feature in her face transformed. It was the shutting off of a light switch. Instantly she became caught in the same web of despair and self-worthlessness she had spun when we talked in her flat in December. Her memory seemed to contain no end of Dachau atrocities: "The day I arrived, I had never seen so many dazed, hungry, tired people. Most inmates were alive. Many were half alive. Some were dead. My job was to move corpses to the pits. The first time I did it, I was sure I would never see the outside world again."

After she had been there a year, she could only keep her eyes open for an hour or two at a time. The swales under them were constantly black and blue from the beatings. Only once every five or six days did this skinny woman have the bodily urge to shuffle to the outdoor human-waste buckets. She hardly knew her name. As she poured it all out to me, I saw and heard and smelled everything. Buckets of shit and piss. Puddles of slime. Meal bowls of boiled fish heads. The wail of a siren. The loud clack of a gun. The scream of a human voice. A dead body with a bullet hole in the temple.

After being there fifteen months, Anna was a scrawny seventy pounds and couldn't do her assigned job—she could no longer lift a dead skeletal body. So they whipped her. She showed me, lifting her coat and blouse to the small of her back to reveal the snaking scars.

"But in late '41, I struck it rich—or so I thought at first. An officer from the castle, an animal named Bergman, become assistant commandant at Dachau and sought me out, brought me into his house inside the camp, watched me gulp mug after mug of water, and then had his way with me. And then again. And again and again. For years.

"He did not marry. Why would he, when he had me to be his personal maid and cook—and to do the shameful thing to me in his bed? At first, he wanted me to give him a violin recital every night. I tried, but my hands did not work. I could not get the bow to the strings. There was no music in me, but only shame. So he just shamed me even more for not playing. A vicious circle. In the bed in the dark, every twitch of the mattress was his naked body slugging closer to me. Sometimes he invited his friends over. He was a good sharer."

It was unbelievable to me that her Himmel violin had survived and made it to Dachau. Perhaps it was a miracle.

Not long after a single person—the Führer, in 1941—answered the so-called "Jewish question" for all of the continent and decided that all eleven million European Jews must die, Anna began waging an impossible battle to blot out of her mind the clouds of human ash blotting out the sun over Dachau. Even in the relative safety of the assistant commandant's house, I think she dangled between the luxury of being dead and the horror of being alive. She thought about breaking from the house and running, which she said would have been suicide, but she couldn't break from life. "The greater life that death would bring could wait. I was just not ready for the afterlife." I think her grace refused to die.

"Didn't your parents wonder where you were?" I asked.

"Ha! The assistant commandant wrote them a letter saying I had visited Bernhard at the castle back in 1940 and then run off to America. It must have seemed true to them, because they never searched for me. I was not allowed to use the phone or mails to contact them."

She managed to get through every day by rising early enough to see the sunrise, though each morning she must have wondered whether she would see another.

"The sun shone on that spring day in 1945. First I heard the usual—a whistle from an incoming train, the hiss of steam, boxcar doors rattling open, terrified people shouting, German shepherds barking, separated children crying. An hour later, I heard the unusual—a faint roar in the distance. Then squeaks, like steel against steel, then loud steel squeals."

Anna's eyes closed; her shoulders shrank.

"The squeals kept getting louder. An awful noise, the sound of fright. Definitely tanks. Panzers? I said to myself, 'The Nazis know they will lose the war. They must be coming to kill us. There is no time to gas us and burn us in the ovens, so they will just machine-gun us down.' *Go ahead and murder us*, I thought, because I was already dead. I felt nothing when I saw the first tank puffing out smoke on the horizon. The next thing I remember is a US Army soldier waking me up in the dirt. The assistant commandant had escaped in his car without time to pack his champagne or anything else. The inmate water and food was rotten. I used his champagne to soothe the dry throats of other inmates and his caviar to fill their empty bellies. They cried and smiled large, and then I knew the sun would rise the next day. When I walked to freedom through that black wrought-iron front gate that read, *Work Shall Set You Free*, there was nothing left to ask God for."

I was breathless. Anna herself had to come up for air at that point. It was shortly after 3 p.m. After minutes of silence—what could I possibly say?—she asked, "How about you, Heinrich? Where were you at the end of the war?" She needed a breather, and I was only too willing to step out of that long, crawling river of sorrow into a shorter but raging one and to talk for a while.

"On the day Germany signed surrender papers in May of '45, I was aboard a US Navy ship bound for Okinawa, Japan. That island was a relative heaven compared to your hell at Dachau. Only thousands died at Okinawa. I'll admit that as terrible as I feel for those innocent Japanese civilians who burned to a crisp or died later from radiation poisoning, I selfishly applauded those nuclear bombs dropped on Hiroshima and

Nagasaki in August. They meant that tens of thousands of US soldiers, including me, wouldn't need to invade the Japanese mainland. Those two bombs probably allowed me to stay alive and come back to Donsville to do what God intended, namely, to find and marry Helen, start a family, buy my hardware store, and hire my damaged father at the store. My children and grandchildren, and my whole adult life, might well be the fruit of those nuclear bombs.

"But staying alive and coming home to the States also meant that I could start loving my mother again. I was all done hating her. Of course, I also loved my father, who died of a broken heart in 1970, but it was Mother, who had died of cancer a week earlier, who I came to put on a pedestal. She was never unprepared for the unexpected, even if it was unthinkable to the average person. That one day in Germany in 1936, after talking with you, she grabbed the unexpected right by the short hairs when her broken-down husband and little Nazi teenage son needed it the most. I started loving her again when I got back from the war, but when I got home from Germany last December, I added her as a saint to my book of life."

"You are right; she was a saint," Anna said. From that mention of my mother, she seemed eager to lead the conversation again. "I told her that day in '36 to take you all to Iowa, but as for me, something inside me told me to stay. I still knew what music was then, but after Dachau, I did not know what it was, hardly knew what the word meant. Yet, for a reason beyond me, I could not part with my dusty violin with the rusty strings. It was part of what I was. You understand?

"So I took it to Berlin, packed it away, and became a German-language teacher at the American school. When the school closed in '47, I had no idea that Germany would be sliced in two in '49, did not know that Edelberg would become Communist. As of '47, Edelberg was the only place I had ever known, and I needed a job, so I went back there instead of running away to the western part of the country. I found work in Edelberg where most of the other migrant residents worked—the new hydroelectric plant."

"I can understand what you felt for Germany. But a person takes their heart wherever they go. Even to Timbuktu. Why did you stay in Germany? It was a broken country. There wasn't a single person or thing to come home to. Not your family. Not one friend. Not your childhood home. Not even most of your town. Why didn't you go someplace else, like maybe England, where you could have a fresh new start on life?"

"It would have been impossible for me to leave Germany after the war for the same reason it was impossible before the war. You cannot move North America to South America, because if you did, it would not be North America anymore, yes?"

How could I possibly disagree with *that* reasoning? "Then why didn't you at least continue playing violin?"

"Arthritis."

I looked at her with even more disbelief than I had last December when she made the same outrageous claim.

"You do not believe me?" she asked.

"I know you have bad arthritis *now* because I saw the pill bottle on your bureau. But arthritis forty years ago? I can't buy it."

She knew her jig was up. Her eyes fell to the ground. "The honest answer to your question is not very complicated, Heinrich. Right after the war, Germany literally got broken in two. Therefore I could not avoid getting broken in two. A person's hands and arms die when her heart is cut in half."

That answer would have to do—at least for the time being. "And what was your job at the new plant?" I asked.

"Telephone operator. At least I could wear earphones and not hear the electric zaps outside. My job was to say hello and push jacks into holes. Except when I was pulling them out. Finally, near the end of 1957, I invited six people from the plant over to my flat for a conference. I was so filled with hope that I was shaking."

Six unwed people came to her flat one night in November 1957 as the Cold War continued getting hotter—the East German Big Brother's launch of the Sputnik satellite the month before had made the Communists the first into outer space. Anna must have dreamt of having enough meat to make her content, or of being able to criticize her government without risk of being shot, or any of a number of other gifts I was taking for granted then.

With her imagined future pointing the way, she unfurled a speech to those friends crammed into her flat. "I said to them, 'There will never be a day when freedom comes knocking at our doors. We will meet here next Tuesday at 8 p.m., regardless of the weather. Pray that it is snowing heavily to make us not visible. Our escape is not real yet, but next week it will be when we get to Julia's brother's house in West Germany."

The border between the two Germanys, about a hundred miles west of the enclave of West Berlin, had been fortified in 1952 but was porous in many places. When Tuesday night arrived, they trudged together through the woods, and after hiking for three days, they finally reached the border and snuck through. They were free. For three minutes.

I can see it, hear it. A hundred yards into West Germany, an East German police truck whined up from behind. A man said, "You think the State is just going to let you fly the coop?" But they weren't shot. Instead, the kind policemen redeposited them in the hydroelectric plant—their purgatory—and then they suffered the constant watch of Communist eagle eyes.

"Heinrich, who gave the government permission to force me back down to a job that was one of the lowest-paying at the plant? One step out of that telephone operator's chair and I would be suspected of being a spy. I refused to accept a vocabulary that included words Communists spoke, so I said nothing, was afraid to speak to anyone. I lost most of my friends. They said I had been trying to escape *them*. By the time I worked up the courage to think about escaping the country again, it was 1962, the Wall was up, and I could get shot trying to climb over it."

After she decided not to try a second escape, she fought to upgrade her sadness to indifference. She was successful. Indifference now lay at her center, the empty center where her self resided.

"But I didn't want to feel wholly indifferent about life. I wanted to do the things I imagined people in West Germany were doing. You know, the kinds of things your mother and mine did before the war. So I joined a garden club, went to the movies, took Sunday drives in the countryside, went out to dinner—all in my mind. I put myself where I would be safe."

Though she was born to be with people, she made a solitary life for herself in her imagination, where nothing could hurt her, including the past. I think the prospect of a normal life existed only in theory. Whatever was happening outside her mind was not for her. Her world now began and ended with her idea of what it should be. Except for love. I think she had a human need to love a man, but those gentle waves never came. In her self-imposed isolation, she had never even dipped her toes in the water.

"I did not know how to love any longer. I forgot what love is." Three decades, from the early '60s through the day she retired last year, can be written in a single sentence: she sat in a wooden telephone operator's chair ten hours a day on weekdays, took long walks along the Spree River on Saturdays and Sundays, and talked to neighbors over tea most evenings. "My favorite part of the day was the night because then I could sleep. The part of the day I hated the most was the morning because then I had to wake up."

I bet she never sang in the shower—and it was not because the hot water only lasted a few minutes. Her one refuge must have been under the blanket of her bed. What do you say to someone like that? But though she had had an impossibly tough life, I wondered whether she could have done more to normalize it in the later years. All I could think to say was "So you didn't play your violin in real life, but why didn't you at least play it in your imagination?"

"Because I could not imagine the two pieces of my heart coming together. That was the one place where my imagination did not work." She paused for an eon, then finally said, "Heinrich, I am sorry, but I do not think I can go to Berlin tonight for the celebration. You can go with my cousins without me." Given her state, I could say nothing in response. Suddenly it was clear to me that enough years had passed without music that her entire life had calcified to a brass hardness, perhaps at a slow rate like a heart involuntarily does. But calcification is calcification.

So I left it at that. I didn't think there was more for either of us to say. "I'm sorry you feel that way about tonight, but thanks for sharing the rest of your story." I stood to leave and resume my life. I gave her my hand. Oddly, she resisted.

"And now I want to hear the rest of *your* story," she said, still sitting without budging.

"Excuse me?"

"Your trip to Alkoven."

"No. Would serve no purpose."

"Maybe it would. Come on, I want to hear about Alkoven. The castle."

Reluctantly I slunk back down, squeamish and wanting to say as little as I could get away with. "What's to tell? I took a bus down there, stayed overnight, went to the castle the next day, saw a cremation oven, and stopped by Rosalie's grave on the way back to West Berlin."

"When I first saw you yesterday, you were different. Something had changed."

How could I disagree? So I had to go a step farther. "I imagined the end of the story you never finished."

"And?"

"And it still haunts me."

"Haunts you? And?"

I was becoming annoyed. "Christ, it doesn't matter, since it was all in my imagination."

"Go ahead and talk about it. The best thing to do for a terrible anxiety is to talk it through. Why do you think I was willing to talk about my years at Dachau and after? Think I only wanted sympathy? Think again."

I was afraid she had a point. Suddenly I felt selfish for withholding my hellish imagination after she had shared her real hell at Dachau. So I talked about my imagined ending of her story, calling it a nightmare.

16

For my own sake, my own protection, I wanted to recall as close to nothing about the nightmare as I could. Who wants to hear terrible events that happen only in someone's fanciful imagination? And who wants to repeat something so ghastly? What good would it do? It was no less fictional than Star Wars. What Anna was asking me to do seemed not only ridiculous but also anathema to this day of celebration.

But then the imagined roar of the bus to Linz cracked the dam, finally making it burst. How could the details not flood back? I couldn't forgive my memory for being so perfectly perfect, so damn unfractured and clear.

"I imagined hopping on a bus south. In midafternoon, the radio on the bus came on and I think I heard—I mean, I imagined hearing—news of men in the French Resistance being shot and killed. Then I had a strange feeling, somewhat stronger than mere fancy, that I had to find and stop a friend or something. I rode the bus all the way to Linz. And then I saw that I was checking into the Inn of the Woods a few miles from nearby Alkoven. Near the castle, right? There was this man at my dinner table in this inn. A cultured man. He said his name was Martin Bergman."

Anna looked like she had just seen a ghost. Maybe she had, because her eyes widened and swallowed me. I told the rest of the sickening story, despising every second of it and watching her eyes grow as I went on. I told her every imaginary detail—the high-lit lowlights of walking through the woods to the castle in the dead of the night, meeting a former schoolteacher named Frieden Bauer, riding in a car with Bernhard to pick up Rosalie and hearing his poison, trying to shoot Bernhard in the head but missing, suffering though the gassing of Rosalie in the shower, being forced to watch her body burn in the oven, finding the fraudulent letter from a Dr. Strasser to Rosalie's parents, and the rest. The whole sick chronicle creeped and crawled for more than thirty minutes. By the end, Anna's mouth was wide open and her fingernails were pressed into her cheeks.

"That's all of it," I said. "I imagined being you, but I'm sure you didn't go through anything so utterly terrible as what I imagined."

She stared at me incredulously. Unable to talk at first, she finally said, "Unbelievable, absurd. That is exactly what happened with *me* at the Inn of the Woods and the castle." If it was possible for her eyes to grow larger, they did. "Maybe it was the Devil. Maybe he strongarmed the truth into you."

I was as incredulous as she, but for a different reason. After taking a deep beath, I dismissed out of hand the talk of the Devil. But I couldn't dismiss her completely because she seemed absolutely certain that I had imagined the innermost details of her experience at the castle in 1940. I was not quite ready to admit such a gruesome scenario. First I wanted to gently shake her down to see what she might say. "Anna, you can't be serious that you actually experienced all of that. Besides, the events are simply unbelievable. None of that really happened to defenseless children as early as 1940, right?"

"Yes it did! You said you imagined that Rosalie was gassed to death in a shower room in the castle in 1940, that her body was tossed in an oven like garbage, and that as her body burned, it smelled like meat roasting. That is exactly what *I* experienced in the castle, all of it, in 1940."

It jolted me into mazement a second time.

"Shall I go on with the details? You mentioned them, every one."

"Please no."

She jumped up and gestured with her hands like a person discovering for the first time that an atom can be split. Did she feel a divination? If she did, then I think she felt it for *me*. She said, "Was it telepathy? Did you have extrasensory perception? It does not matter. All that—"

"Doesn't matter? As if the explanation means nothing?"

"It does not matter in the least. All that matters is that *now*, finally, after fifty years, you understand all of what *I* understand. You swam in the same dark deeps that I did, and when we could swim no more, we both sank to the very bottom. You may as well have been me. No one except Bernhard as a boy has ever tried to be me."

I waited for my mind to conceive a response, but none came. The ghastly truth began to prickle over me. I had hoped none of it had been fact, especially not in a magical place and as early as 1940, roughly the year we unsuspecting Americans came out of the Depression and the happy days promised by President Roosevelt were here again. Anna added, "In 1940, you were in America the beautiful. Purple mountains. Sweet land of liberty."

I didn't care that she was being snide again because suddenly I felt pathetically small. I realized that the truth that had unfolded at a faraway foreign castle was only a handful of sand in a desert of all the abominations of the war. I held a silent requiem with myself, picturing things I had seen on television documentaries in my living room: German shepherds mauling starving Jews in the Warsaw ghetto, naked skeletal bodies stacked in pile after pile in concentration camps later . . .

I was ready to end the conversation and go massage my mind with a bottle of wine, but she had more to say. She sat back down. "And now you should understand, *firsthand*, why I have not played my violin for the past fifty years. I may just as well have killed Rosalie with my own hands. For a half century—winter, spring, summer, fall, and at home, at work, during the day, and in my dreams at night—I have sat in Bernhard's car, feeling his pistol in my coat pocket. I could have pulled it out and put a bullet in Bernhard's head. I could have steered the car over, pushed on the brake, pulled the body out by the collar, and left it in the ditch. Then I could have driven to pick up Rosalie and her mother, then her father at his work. Then could have found a back road leading into the free sector of France, sold my Himmel for lots of money, and bought them ship tickets to the United States or Canada.

"But none of that is what I did. After the war, I refused to play my violin because I did not deserve to have it, especially not a Himmel. My violin should have saved Rosalie's life. It did not. I had to live with that every day. I could not play any more than I could raise from the dead a human being I killed. Okay, as you Americans say?"

Her eyes broadcast deep contrition. Then she buried her head in the blanket, every muscle in her body quivering, a disturbance convulsing under her skin. Though she still wouldn't let me touch her to comfort her, at least I was there a few feet away. "Anna, I don't mean to preach, but you've got to stop blaming yourself about that girl. You've buried yourself in regret for fifty years. Enough. Reunite with who you once were."

Her figure flickered annoyance. "You sound like someone's father," she grumbled. "You of all people should not talk about reuniting. You have pushed most of your family away and have done nothing to change it." Though her words were smothered in the blanket, I heard them loud and clear. They hurt. I left her alone to be cruel to herself so that I could be cruel to myself and think about my family when Helen was alive.

Anna rocked herself into a disturbed sleep. But sunlight through the trees smiled at her. So did the chirping robins, getting ready to fly south for the winter. From her uneasy movements, it was plain she was dreaming. When she awoke endless minutes later, something happened, a slow-motion chain reaction taking an indeterminant time. How long does it take for a rosebud to open when light comes? I'm not certain, but I strongly suspected that when Anna Himmel was at her weakest, she rose to her strongest. She seemed to feel something in the long-ignored center of herself. I could see something coming; then it came, taking all the time in the world.

Eventually she released her face from the darkness of the blanket, and a small smile began pulling at the corners of her lips. The twitches crept away. She buried despair alive and replaced it with a growing radiance. Cold self-loathing, which she had felt for so long that she had forgotten it, began to disappear, and the void started to fill with warm understanding. At last, all was done. It was behind her.

She jumped up in defiance of her age, as if fifty years had just been compressed into those indeterminate minutes. She said, "Heinrich, you are right. I have been a fool. Let's go to my flat and get supper and then get ready for Berlin tonight. Amen."

What wonder was this? What miracle? She looked around squinting, as though she had been blindfolded for half a century. We started walking back to her flat, and thirty yards ahead we came across a sea of little suns fanning white petals in the breeze—a large patch of wild daisies in autumn bloom. She smiled and picked far too many for the empty vase on her table, hilariously embarrassed to be that girlish again.

Back at her flat, it was lentil soup again, but this time with bologna sandwiches. Anna searched for dead insects in the bag of lentils and, finding none, cheerfully poured them in boiling broth before making the sandwiches. Just as we were finishing supper, there was a knock on the apartment door. For a second I wondered where the security guard at the front door was, but then remembered that Anna's building had no security. Anna opened the door and found the cousins she had never met before: Roberta and Peter Himmel and five well-groomed children, having driven east all the way from Bonn. That first tiny family union was marked by awkward hugs and few words, but the nine of us, crowded inside the tiny apartment, drank hot chocolate and got acquainted.

The oldest child, Greta, age sixteen, asked about the violin in the corner, missing a string. She spoke in German rapidly, so I struggled to understand. "I play violin myself in the school orchestra," I think she said to Anna. "I heard all about you when you were a girl. Will you play something for me?"

"Oh, I have not played since the war," Anna said.

"Oh? A war?"

"World War Two."

You would have thought Anna had said she hadn't played since the Crusades. Greta's eyes shot wide open. "You are joking with me!" she said.

"No. Arthritis."

"I can vouch that she has bad arthritis," I said in German.

Greta gave up. And that was that.

At 9 p.m., we all climbed into the family's nine-seater expensive custom van and went to Berlin to be part of the reunification celebration. We parked and walked a few blocks to the area of the parliament building—the Reichstag—and the Brandenburg Gate. Tens of thousands of East and West Germans—at exactly midnight to be simply "Germans"—were packed together in a scene that reminded me of Times Square in New York City on New Year's Eve. There were plenty of oompah-pah brass bands and food-cart vendors, even an ancient man with a cart of roasted chestnuts. Though a few minor skirmishes by so-called anarchists and skinheads broke out, they were quickly quashed by the police, and we felt safe.

Firecrackers were going off everywhere, and we watched the sky light up with fireworks. A few minutes before midnight, an exact replica of the Liberty Bell in Philadelphia rang out. The dark past was tolled away, and then the breath of the future rose into the night.

Something happened at midnight that surprised me—shocked me, really. It was not the clarion pealing of the bells or the cheers or the fireworks or the overflowing beer steins or the 100,000 exultant people crowded together as one. It was not the reunification that became official at that moment or, with it, the rolling facedown of Arthur de Gobineau in his grave, the landing of a phoenix in Victoria's chariot, or the hoisting on the Brandenburg Gate of the black, red, and orange flag of one Germany. All of those fabulous events happened, but I had anticipated them. What was so stunning at the stroke of midnight was the touch of Anna's four fingertips to my cheek. She had always refused my hand and hadn't even touched a man since being cradled in the arms of a US soldier at Dachau in April 1945. I was thrilled all the way to the tips of my eyelashes. I didn't say that I loved her because you don't risk ruining a miracle.

By quarter after twelve, the Himmel children were yawning, so the nine of us walked back to the van with Anna's hand slipped into mine, a union for all of united Berlin to see. After loading in, I asked Peter to drop me at the Edelberg Inn, but Anna jumped in and said, "No, wait, come back to my flat with me, Heinrich." She leaned over and whispered in my ear, "There still is one little part of the story to finish." Thomas, the thirteen-year-old, snickered through his nose, probably thinking Anna had just whispered to me to come back to her flat to get intimate.

The cousins dropped us off at Anna's apartment and went on to the Edelberg Inn.

Apparently there was no final part of the story to tell. I had never felt so gorgeously duped. Anna said I could take the foldout sofa and she would take the foldout chair. I thought myself chivalrous by insisting on the opposite.

The next thing I remember was waking up eight hours later with Anna curled up next to me on the sofa. Her knees were on my thigh and our shoes were off. Her head was resting on my chest, and warmth rose off her skin. A lake of yellow autumn sunlight coming in through the window covered her. She seemed to make the sun pause for a moment.

"I hope you like scrambled ostrich eggs and fried potatoes," she said once she had blinked herself awake.

Ostrich eggs? "I'm not all that hungry," I said, feeling starved. "I think I'll just have plenty of potatoes."

She smiled. "I am teasing."

We had a healthy laugh. She turned the scrambling of communist chicken eggs and the braising of communist potatoes into an art form. After we started eating, she said, from the blue, "Heinrich, there is something I must tell you."

It turned out that there was, in fact, one final part of the story.

There was a long silence. Finally she said, "I will just say it. I have cancer. Lung cancer."

God no. I tried to put the words back into her mouth, but they were already gone, leaving a trail of havoc. I could only reach out and take her hand as if trying to comfort an injured child. She added, "They think it is from when they ripped out all the asbestos in the plant in the '70s. For two weeks it was like a snowstorm in there."

She looked like she wanted to say more but was too boiling hot to speak, an infectious boiling that also infected me. She simmered until she was cooled enough to talk. "The management finally gave us face masks two days before the job was finished."

She was falling, and I had no words to make a net. There was no textbook. *God-damned Communist plant* is what I thought. "My God, how long do you have?" is what I said.

"They do not know. Maybe a year. Maybe more. Maybe less. But that is only what *they* say. I say differently."

Our conversation was interrupted by the door buzzer. It was the Peter Himmel family stopping by to say farewell before going to Berlin to sightsee. Greta rushed in, out of breathe, and said to Anna, "An old man, probably in his eighties, is outside. He says he is feeling celebratory and has never met you but heard of you before the war. He is practically begging for you to come out and play something on your violin."

Anna turned crimson and went into her shell. "Oh no," she said. I could tell from her eyes that this really meant the opposite. She played hard to get by saying, "I told you about my arthritis. Besides, I have barely played since before the war."

Greta, the brave, budding violinist, took the liberty of grabbing the violin. Had the missing string been replaced by Anna overnight or instead by someone, or something, else? Maybe magic? I would never know. Greta took the violin and Anna by the arm out of the apartment, scurrying back only long enough to grab Anna's coat. If I had not spent three hours with Greta and her family the night before, I'd have thought, from my first impression, that she was a spoiled, pushy West German teenager. She had come dressed like a showcase for the casual section of a fashion magazine, had talked about having her own bedroom, had mentioned the soft leather seats in the family van.

But I had been wrong about her, as I had been so many other times in Anna's flat. The previous night in Berlin, Greta had talked about the history of the flag. She knew that the national anthem melody was based on Haydn's Emperor Quartet, that Beethoven had been Haydn's student, that the woman on top of the Brandenburg Gate was an ancient Greek goddess named Victoria. She had been curious about how the Himmel factory had been destroyed, and when I made the mistake of telling her that the building had been used by the Nazis to store bombs, her eyes welled up. To me, the most amazing thing about her was her face. It resembled Anna's more than a little.

The rest of us followed Anna and Greta outside. Anna greeted the old man, who said he lived across town. She hadn't practiced in half a century and seemed not to know anything to play. "I have forgotten everything," she said to him. Her face turned red.

"Then just play the national anthem," he said. "It is a slow, simple melody that stays within one octave."

"I know," she said. She stood silently for a minute, flexing her fingers and wincing.

"Go ahead, Fraulein Himmel, play it," he insisted. Anna continued to stand there, holding the antique Himmel as delicately as if it were a Dead Sea Scroll.

A person came out of the apartment building to listen. Apparently not wanting to disappoint two people now, Anna placed the violin under her chin elegantly, drew the bow to the strings like a hand touching a butterfly, and played the anthem—the easy first-violin part to the Haydn quartet. Her playing had a few minor squeaks, but anyone with half an ear could tell that here was a player who once had been great.

She seemed embarrassed, even a little disoriented, by the slight squeaks. Probably to get herself back on track, she played the simple C scale: Do, Re, Mi, Fa, So, La, Ti, Do. She held the high "Do" until it diminished into the elegance of nothing, the way her breath rose and vanished into the breathless cold air.

Then she played the opening melody of the anthem again, this time gliding the bow through the air with a greater grace and playing with only a few small squeaks. I almost felt that I, a musical imbecile compared to her, didn't have the right to hear it. By the time she was finished, four more people had come out of the apartment building to listen, so she smiled and moved on to Haydn's first variation of the anthem melody, playing better and better with each passing musical phrase.

Then more people gathered in the small crowd, their mere presence seeming to help her rediscover something like an ancient language having no words. Time was winding backward. I know I'm biased, but now her playing was so gorgeous that I swear her eyes brightened from grayish blue to dark blue. After the first twelve bars of the second variation, she must have thought she was fourteen again, because it seemed that her eyes turned lighter blue. I saw her in her home bedroom across the way—I see her again tonight in my den—wearing her white dress with pink lilacs and packing her brown leather suitcase for a national concert tour. I hear the suitcase latches clicking shut, then hear her at my front door, telling me, "Heinrich, don't you know? Good Jews and good gypsies are just like other good people."

Five more people came out of the apartment building to hear.

Now she is past the twenty-fourth bar of the second variation, and I watch her eyes turning even lighter blue because she is becoming twelve again and making her debut at the old Schauspielhaus in Berlin. I am right there in the city, hearing her play a Brahms concerto. But back in front of her apartment building I hear the thirty-second bar of the anthem variation, and just as suddenly, she is ten again, with light-blue eyes and performing at the little Edelberg Theater. I am right there, watching her from the front row, crunching on a candy bar and hearing the Schubert Ave Maria for solo violin. It is so close to my seventy-one-year-old ears I can feel the breath of the Schubert.

So there had not been a slow death over fifty years after all. There had merely been a long, long hibernation, and the reason for it no longer existed. The colossal force that had almost vanquished her no longer existed. She had willed it away at midnight the night before. Standing before the small crowd of twenty in front of her apartment building, she was restored enough to begin playing the third variation on the anthem melody.

Time is rewinding faster now. I see her playing at age four at the church preschool. I used to think that a memory necessarily contains the past, but this one contains only the future because I now see her in the womb and am watching her being reborn. What one woman can do!

But alas, eyes are not hands. Anna's hands stopped about twelve bars into the third variation. They just couldn't go on. The fingers of both hands had flickered low, then out. Grimacing, obviously in discomfort, she drawled softly to the crowd, "That is—is all I can do."

Then she did something I never would have dreamed of. She walked out into the small crowd and handed the violin to Greta. "Here," Anna said to her. "This is for you. May you play it often and keep it in the family."

At that moment, you would have thought that Greta was a little girl on Christmas morning. Her mouth and eyes formed perfect circles. "But this is an original Himmel," Greta said incredulously, "one with a spruce soundboard and ivory string screws."

"Well, I will die someday, no?" Anna said, smiling now. "Consider it an early inheritance."

Running her fingertips along the spruce soundboard, Greta smiled too, transfixed.

"Don't you have something to say?" Greta's mother said to her.

"Oh," Greta said. "Thank you!" She was so beside herself that she had forgotten to say it.

"No, I mean the other thing," Greta's mother said. "What you have wanted to say to your lost cousin Anna since you were a little girl and started taking violin lessons."

Greta looked at her mother, then at Anna, and said firmly with no further hesitation, "I want to grow up and rebuild the Himmel factory. I hope I can find the money."

Anna blinked her eyes dry.

Greta and her family gave Anna hugs, said tearful goodbyes, and went on to Berlin to sightsee. Anna and I went inside and had tea. Prickles of boiling water hissed out a radiator pipe, and I blew into my cupped hands to warm them. Over the next few minutes, the tide in me rose, and I finally overflowed. I said, "Will you m——" The rest of the question jammed up inside me. It fluttered, then flew away. I could say only that I wanted to finish the conversation about cancer. "I'll take care of you," I said.

She was in that lake of morning sunlight again but then did what a morning glory does at night: close up tight.

"I said I'll take care of you," I repeated.

She opened up long enough to say, "Nonsense. I am fine. I will beat the cancer. I really believe it will disappear." She put the palm of my hand to her chest. I thought she was trying to make me feel where her lungs were, where the cancer was, where life was finally walking away from her. "Feel it thumping?" she asked. "A good, strong heartbeat. I am fine."

So I planned to leave alone on my scheduled flight the next day. "Why not stay a few more days?" she said. "We could go to Berlin again and have some fun."

"As much as I would like to, I can't. Leanne, one of the granddaughters who doesn't think too highly of me right now, has an important part in her high school play, and it opens in two nights. I committed to being there." Anna and I spent the rest of the day strolling along the river and then cooking together.

The next morning, while I was waiting in her flat for the airport cab, I went to her bookshelf and pulled out the sketch of Rosalie she had made after the war. "Why did you draw only Rosalie?" I asked. "Why didn't you sketch *all* the children at the castle as a group, or all the patients, for that matter? Or for *that* matter, all of Germany, as ridiculous as that may sound. You wanted to save every person and every thing."

She cracked an odd smile and smuggled out a small laugh, then said, "Do you think I am magic or something? When I was a girl, I was crazy enough to think I was Germany. I was foolish, a dreamer with her head up in the clouds. But at the castle, I was just one person trying to save one little girl."

Then the damn cab drove up. I lingered in front of her, not wanting to leave, heartbroken that she would be all alone with her cancer. I thought of asking her to come with me to the States for cancer treatments, but I didn't. How could I ask her to leave? Even though she had long ago stopped believing she was Germany, to me she was.

The driver finally started honking, so she walked me out to the cab. We stood there silently with our eyes locked on each other until the cabby snorted impatience. I couldn't take my eyes off her as the car pulled away. After she disappeared from sight, I saw a new man reflected in the car window. The first thing I would do after getting back to Iowa would be to call my four children and seven grandchildren and tell them what a fool I'd been for allowing the loss of Helen to turn me into a curmudgeon. I had forgotten the correct order of things. I would cater a reunion at my house, and then we could be a family again. My daughter Amanda had asked for a small family reunion shortly after Helen passed. It never happened. Because of me.

After Anna vanished from sight, I didn't spasm with anxiety over her the way I had on the morning I left her flat and went to the castle. She was no longer a bird with broken wings but a woman with her feet on the ground, reunited with what she was before the war. During the flight home, when I least expected it, her parting words popped into my head: "Come back to Germany soon, maybe next time for longer. Or longer than that. Or even longer than *that.*"

It's a month later now, and I'm in fact going back to Germany. Tomorrow morning, except not for forever. I'm not going back to ask Anna to marry me and to build a house for us on the double lot where we lived as children. I'm going back for Anna's funeral.

When her friend called and told me she had passed, I was devastated, was left cold by a light snuffed out. She had refused treatments for the cancer, having had a lead-solid belief that it would vanish on its own while the truth of her belief was about as solid as a vapor. Anna must have thought that cancer is human. I think the one time in her life she did not think was when she thought that cancer thinks.

I also believe that Anna was wrong about something else. If you ask me, she was more than what she thought she was. To some who never met her in the flesh, maybe she is more like an idea than a person. I, for one, know she was a real person and not mere theory; she touched my cheek in the end, and I felt her human warmth.

I also think that German history is filled with her. My opinion is that she already existed in something like a cocoon when Germanic culture was still just a glimmer in ancient people's eyes. She broke out, and her wings took more complex colors into the First Reich and then into the Second. When the Third Reich forced her back into the cocoon at a mental hospital in Berlin, she had the audacity to break out again with a plan to save the entire nation. She had to start small, with Bernhard and Rosalie.

And how could she *not* find her own brother? They really weren't two separate people. She was *in* him, and after he reinvented himself, he wanted her out in the most profound way. He reached in himself and threw that part away, leaving her at a place of death, Dachau. After that, she rose up the ladder by going to a place that was only half dead, Edelberg. But finally, after half a century, she did what only she could have done: she climbed out of that black hole, that collapsed star, and returned to what she had been before the war. Nothing, much less terminal cancer, could change what she was millennia before her 1919 birth certificate says she was born.

That's my own theory anyway. Some may say it's absurd, that a person is just a person, not also some concept. Others who find some truth in it may think it's too wordy. I'll admit only that it is much more elaborate and grandiose than Anna's own humble view that she was just one person trying to save one child. You'd think that Anna would have been the best authority on herself, but I'm not certain of that. Not at all.

When that friend phoned a few days ago to say Anna had passed, she mentioned a notebook she found on Anna's table. In it, she said, is Anna's unfinished story about a castle and some disabled children. It seems Anna was planning a national tour—not with a violin but with the story. Apparently she wanted to tell it far and wide in Germany, starting with those who know the least, grade-schoolers. I think that her life was not hers to live as any other person would live theirs. So it is up to me now to finish the writing. I will give the finished product to Billy so he has something of me to pass down the family tree other than my coin collection he will inherit.

But first, I will travel to lecterns across Germany in Anna's stead. I think I really was miraculously in her mind, because at this very moment I feel a slight resonance: *"Heinrich, take me with you."*

ACKNOWLEDGMENTS

I wish to thank all the fine people at Koehler books, with special thanks to my amazing editor, Hannah Woodlan, and to Danielle Koehler, Greg Fields, and John Koehler, wonderful professionals who guided me through every step of the journey to publishing. I also want to thank Anita Mumm of Mumm's the Word and Stuart Horwitz of Book Architecture, two independent professional editors par excellence who read early drafts of the manuscript and made many intelligent and important suggestions. I wish also to thank retired English professor Thomas Smith, who grew up next door to me and who taught me some of the finer points of writing long after I took my last English composition course in college. A true word-Smith, Tom made many excellent comments to an early draft.

I also thank my sisters, Kathy Sturges and Deborah Hearl, who read early drafts and gave me strength. Last and foremost, thanks go to my wife, Valerie, and two grown daughters, Caroline and Natalie, whose love and support cannot be put into words. It can only be felt.

CPSIA information can be obtained
at www.ICGtesting.com
Printed in the USA
LVHW100557141122
732905LV00006B/382